TIME WILL TELL

Cover photograph by Cheney's Studio of Hampton, Virginia
Courtesy of the Hampton History Museum

authorHOUSE™

1663 LIBERTY DRIVE, SUITE 200
BLOOMINGTON, INDIANA 47403
(800) 839-8640
WWW.AUTHORHOUSE.COM

© 2005 Ann Davis. All Rights Reserved.

No part of this book may be reproduced, stored in a retrieval system, or transmitted by any means without the written permission of the author.

First published by AuthorHouse 12/30/04

ISBN: 1-4208-0982-2 (sc)
ISBN: 1-4208-0981-4 (dj)

Library of Congress Control Number: 2004098756

Printed in the United States of America
Bloomington, Indiana

This book is printed on acid-free paper.

Eberhard Greger
Born September 15, 1915
Lieberose, Niederlausitz, Germany
Oberleutnant zer See, October 1, 1939
Command of U-85, June 7, 1941 – April 14, 1942
Photograph courtesy of Dr. Hansjürgen Fresenius

Acknowledgements

First, I want to thank my country, the United States of America, for the rights we have as citizens. It is with respect for the freedom of speech that I pursued this story. It is because I was allowed to see previously classified documents in the National Archives that I am able to tell it.

My research took me to a number of excellent libraries and archives and gave me an opportunity to correspond with and interview many people. I was able to locate Dr. Hansjürgen Fresenius of Germany, the only living relative of Eberhard Greger. I am indebted to him for the photographs and personal history of the captain. I am most grateful to Drusilla Gerlach for acting as our interpreter.

I appreciate Wolfgang Klaue, a former burger of Lieberose, Germany, Herr Doringhoff of the German Federal Military Archives, Herr Fiedler of the German Military Agency and Horst Schwenk, Director of the U-Boat Archives in Germany... for corresponding in English.

I wish to thank Sally Peters Carter who now lives in England for sharing her letters home to Hampton during the war. Sally was a Doughnut Girl in England.

My good neighbor, Mr. Herbert Goldstein, and his family. He was a delightful resource. He died before the book was complete. We miss him.

Cheyne's Studio   Cheyne's

Ann Darling Tormey and Gwen Amory Cumming, who as children collected things for the war effort and are now active in opening the Hampton History Museum, for making time to reminiscence with me. And Michael Cobb, curator of the museum for his help.

Thanks to members of the Roper crew for their correspondence. Though some of them remember the events differently than I have told here, I wish to express only gratitude to them for their service to our country.

Cora Mae Reid of the Hampton University Library for helping with the story of the institute and Mary Lou Hultgren, curator of the Hampton History Museum for helping with the story of the institute. Reuben Burrell, photographer at Hampton Institute during WWII and still, and Joseph Gilliard, who was supervisor of the navy Model Ship Shop at Hampton.

Two Tuskegee airmen, Col. Frances Horne and Chief Grant Wiiliams, were most helpful in telling me of their experiences of the war. I appreciate their time and hope their story gets told many times over.

Arthur Jacobs of Phoenix, Arizona for giving me encouragement and advice and sharing his story of his family's interment in the United States during the war.

Fred Imlay, a former NACA wizard, and his wife, Harriet, lifelong friends and to Mary Alice Hurlbut, Ethel Brittingham and her son, William, Simon Gaskill, Daisy McMenamin, Dr. Thomas Sale and Katherine Harrell, residents of Hampton. And to Bill Council, of Hampton, who served in the Army in World War II.

Thanks to my husband, Bill, and my children Bert Davis and Kym Smith for their "magnanimous" assistance and for tolerating my World War II time warp.

The author did research at each of the following:

American Red Cross Archives
Daily Press Library
Ft. Monroe Casemate Museum
Hampton Historical Association
Hampton National Cemetery
Hampton Public Library
Hampton Roads Naval Museum
Hampton Roads Transit
Hampton University Archives
Institute of World War II, FSU
Library of Virginia
Mariner's Museum Archives
National Archives
Newport News Public Library
Norfolk Naval Air Station
Norfolk Public Library
Richmond Public Library
United States Naval Institute
Virginia War Memorial Library

THIS BOOK IS DEDICATED TO THE MEMORY OF THE 46 CREWMEMBERS OF THE U-85

Heinrich Adrian, 27
Herbert Albig, 23
Gerhard Ammann, 21
Fritz Behla, 20
Wilhelm Brinkmann, 21
Erich Degenkolb, 19
Kurt Fräsdorff, 27
Albert Frey, 21
Eberhard Greger, 27
Walter Günzl, 23
Otto Hagenmaier, 21
Oskar Hansen, 25
Herbert Heller, 23
Helmut Kaiser, 24
Walter Keifer, 19
Johann Killermann, 21
Josef Kleibrink, 20
Wolfgang Komorowski, 24
Ernst Kückelhaus, 23
Helmut Lechler, 23
Johann Letzig, 21
Willy Matthies, 24
Willy Methge, 21

Herbert Peemöller, 25
Artur Piotrowski, 26
Oskar Prantl, 25
Fritz Röder, 22
Heinrich Rogge, 22
Hans Sänger, 25
Kurt Schneider, 21
Gustav Schon, 20
Erich Schorisch, 21
Karl Schultes, 22
Günter Schulz, 20
Joachim Schulze, 19
Werner Schumacher, 23
Horst Spoddig, 20
Friedrich Strobel, 29
Eugen Ungethuem, 36
Herbert Waack, 26
Gerhard Wagner, 23
Heinz Waschmann, 21
Konstantin Weidmann, 28
Heinz Wendt, 28
Martin Wittmann, 27
Hans Wobst, 20

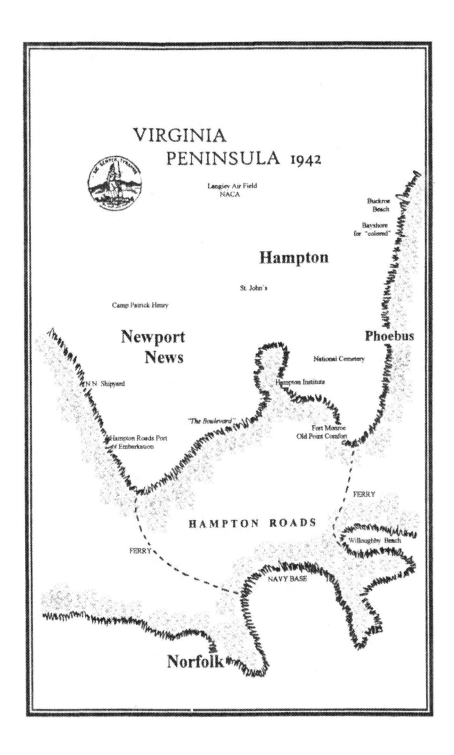

Illustrations:

Cheyne's Studio (prior to the war years)

Eberhard Greger, Captain of the U-85

The Chamberlin Hotel with Copulas

Streetcar

The Langley Theatre

Victoria Boulevard

Hunt's fishing boat

The Darling family home

Army Goods Store

Car parked in downtown Hampton

Hampton Institute

Interior, Brittingham's Furniture

"The Dips" at Buckroe

Ferry at Fort Monroe

Photo of Captain Greger

Hampton Institute's Clock Tower

Hampton High School Cheerleaders

Tuskegee flyer

Vmail

Fishing boats

Interior, St. John's Historic Church

Downtown Hampton

Lizzie's grave, beside the cemetery wall

Roper's report

Ann Davis'

TIME
WILL
TELL

Even the most civilized of peoples can be fired with passionate hatred for each other.

Carl von Clauswitz

One
Spring of 1942-

The guard walking the waterside seemed the only disturbance in the peaceful neighborhood as Julia Keegan watched him pass in front of her apartment.

He takes his paces solemnly, thought Julia,
But he looks like a man playing soldier.
What is he guarding anyway?
The naval base is on the other side of the water.
I should think he feels quite ridiculous.

At least he has orders to stand watch.
I am the ridiculous one.
Like a fool I sit here night after night
Watching for Joe to come home.
Hoping he'll be early...
Hoping he'll be happy to be here.

When Julia and Joe were first married, they moved into the third floor attic apartment of the Bryan's home. They sat at this window watching as the naval ships were deployed to the other side of the world. It was hard to believe the Japanese had attacked our ships in Hawaii. It was harder to believe German u-boats were sinking ships off our shores. The United States had been drawn into another world war and our ships and planes, our tanks and men were being sent "over there" to fight again.

Julia and Joe talked about when he'd come back from the war and they'd move into a house of their own.

*We were happy
though he was impatient to enlist
and I was troubled he was going to enlist,
The British had nearly won the war.
Joe would be back soon.*

The house faced Hampton Roads, a large body of water between Hampton and Norfolk, Virginia. Once the guard passed there wasn't much to see. Since the dimout had been ordered, it got very dark at night and hardly anyone was out on the street, or the water. The cool breeze coming in the window gave Julia goose bumps. Still she didn't want to shut the window. That would make her feel even more alone.

Julia wished the government hadn't removed the copulas from the top of the Chamberlin Hotel. It looked strange without them, but they said they made too good a target for the enemy. Of course she couldn't see the flattened top notches of the hotel at night. Unless there was a very bright moon, she couldn't see it at all.

She focused on the moonlight reflecting in the water. The streak of light wiggled with the water's ripples. For a moment Julia thought she saw something cross the line of moonlight. Was something... or someone out there?

Chamberlin Hotel   *Cheyne's*

Where is the guard? He's missing something.
   Perhaps nothing but a log,
But he'd probably get excited over a log—
         something to check out.

Julia leaned over to see if the guard might be coming this way. He was too far away to notice what Julia had seen. Julia heard a dog barking. It sounded as if it had discovered someone. She knew that would be Joe walking home from the streetcar stop. The dog always tipped her off.

Julia moved from the window and hurriedly brushed her hair so she'd look fresh for her husband. She was right. The dog was barking as Joe passed. He was home, at last – no earlier, or later than usual.

She knew not to ask her husband how his day had been. Ever since the Army classified him a 4F, Joe never had a favorable thing to say – about anything. Julia thought it was time he got over it, but he just wouldn't let it go.

"I was sitting by the window, watching for you," she said. "I can tell when you're coming because that dog always barks at you."

"Stupid mutt," Joe said.

"I was getting downright chilly at the window," she said.

"Then why didn't you close it?" he asked.

"I liked it. I was just saying that after such a warm day, it cooled off. I thought I saw something…"

"It wasn't cool back away from the water," Joe interrupted her. "Do we have something to drink?"

Julia fixed him a glass of tea.

"The guard had passed when I saw…" Julia tried again.

"Why don't you go on to bed? I'll be up awhile."

"Don't you want something to eat?"

"No. I just need some quiet so I can read this goddamned report."

   I wanted to talk to my husband.
      Does he have to bring work home?

"Okay," she said and leaned down to kiss him. He gave her a matter-of-fact kiss and that was that. It was no different from last night and the night before.

There was no view of the water from the bedroom. Julia would rather have gone back to the front window to watch the guard. But Joe had sent her to bed so he could have the room to himself. Unable to make her eyes stay shut, she stared into the darkness of the room.

If only I could sneak out
and walk along with the sentry.
He'd probably like to have someone to talk to.
I could show him where I saw something in the water.

I wanted to marry Joe since we were kids.
Now, we're married
and he's so upset about the Army,
he's making both of us miserable.
I'm not to blame he has a bad eye.
I wish I hadn't let him talk me into getting married
before he " went overseas."
I really think he brings work home so he won't
have to talk to me.
If we hadn't gotten married,
he could have gone back to Blacksburg.
He shouldn't blame me.
It was his idea to get married so quickly.
What will he say when I tell him I'm pregnant?

Kate will be home tomorrow, thank goodness.

****

That same evening on the other side of Hampton in an area called Phoebus, Rose Washington invited her husband to sit on the porch. "It's pleasant outside," she told him.

Soon, when the warm weather settled in, the Washingtons would spend most of their time at home on the porch. Neighbors all along County Street would do likewise for the summer heat made it unbearable to stay inside.

This April night, Rose and Thomas welcomed the first aromas of spring as they wiped the pollen from the porch furniture. "In another couple of weeks, the lilacs will be in bloom," Rose said. "Edna's pear tree's already bloomed. I wish we had planted a pear."

"Now don't you start thinking of plantin' anything this year. There's a war on, you know."

"If there was any forgetting, I'd have those tombstones to remind me."

The Washington's two-story shingle faced the Hampton National Cemetery. For years they had watched the rows of uniform white stones spread out over the land before them – each grave honoring an American soldier who had served his country. Many times they had stood to the outside of the cemetery's brick wall as our military dead were brought there to rest.

"Ever since the President announced we were in the war, I've been dreading those dreary processions."

"Well, none of our boys are buried there."

Rose knew what Thomas meant. Only white men had been allowed to serve in combat units in the First World War. Thomas had tried to enlist in 1917, but the recruiter said, "Go home, boy. We don't need no niggers."

"Back in my day the sight of a colored man in the uniform of the United States infuriated the whites," Thomas said. "They thought we'd get highfaluting ideas about our place in society. Wilson bought our votes with his promise of 'New Freedom' and he betrayed us. So this time we've voted for Roosevelt 'cause he said he'd end segregation in the armed forces. We'll soon see what comes of that."

"I pray to the Good Lord everyday there won't be any of ours called up to fight," Rose answered. "I didn't want you fighting in that war and I don't want our Samuel going off to fight and get killed in this one. If'n the whites don't want you, why don't you just let them do their own fighting?"

Thomas didn't argue with his wife. He knew Samuel would sign up if he had half a notion he'd get to fight like a man. He talked of little else. He wanted to fight for his country – not just wash dishes and peel potatoes – fight. He wanted to prove he was as good as the white boys – and better. Thomas certainly had no desire to see his boy buried across the street. But Samuel would make a good soldier – just as he would have. Would the government ever see a colored man as equal to a Caucasian? He doubted it.

The setting sun made the rows of white grave markers glow with splendor – like valiant soldiers standing at attention in dress uniform. To Thomas they suggested the superior whiteness of the soldiers who were buried there. "Wonder if those white boys had known they'd be laid down smack in the middle of niggatown for the rest of eternity, wonder if they'd have been such good soldiers."

"Thomas!"

Rose said no more. Thomas knew she didn't like him to use the word 'nigger.' Besides, as she had told him over and over, "We are educated. We are not niggers!"

Indeed there were an unusually high number of educated Negroes living in Phoebus. Many of them attended Hampton Institute that was one of the few schools offering higher education to colored people in America.

Thomas had told Rose that no matter how much education a man of color might get, to the white man, he'd always be inferior.

In the National Cemetery there were graves of Negro soldiers who served during the War Between the States and the Spanish-American War. Their grave markers were inscribed "U.S.C.T." (United States Colored Troops).

"Thomas, here comes another of those awful convoys. I'll be so pleased when the new military road is completed and they don't have to go by here to get to the fort."

"Do you want to go back inside?"

"Inside – outside, makes no difference. We can't hear ourselves think. Might as well sit here. You think I could forget there's a war on with the military parading by at all hours of the day and night?"

"I can't hear you!" Thomas shouted.

The roar of the heavy trucks grew louder. There was no point in trying to talk above it.

"Lord, help us, Thomas!" Rose exclaimed. "Why are they stopping?"

The line of military vehicles stopped in front of the house. Men were leaping from the cabs of the trucks.

"What on earth are they going to do?" Rose screamed. "Why are they stopping here? Where's Samuel? Oh, God, where is Samuel? Lord have mercy on us all!"

"Calm down, Rose."

The commotion brought the Washington's neighbors outside.

"What's going on?"

"God in Heaven, we're being invaded!"

There was shouting from one porch to the next.

"They're our troops," Thomas called back. "Come on, Zack, let's go find out what this is all about."

The two men went out to the street asking, "What's going on?" They were ignored, or told to get out of the way. The gates were opened. The long convoy moved into the cemetery as a crowd of citizens gathered on the street outside. A group of men in prison garb were directed to dig graves. Two long rows of graves. There was wild speculation about what was happening.

"Why are they doing this at night?"

"So many graves!"

"Are there no families of the dead?"

"Are those poor men digging their own graves?"

Thomas got one soldier's attention, "This is none of your concern.

Why don't you get your people back inside?"

"But who's being buried here?" asked Thomas.

"Just a bunch of merchant marines who washed up on our shores. Now, back up."

Thomas turned to his neighbors and repeated, " 'Just a bunch of merchant marines' he says. The Army don't bury a 'bunch of merchant marines' here." Thomas wasn't about to leave. They would have to force him.

The army men apparently weren't too concerned about Thomas and his family and friends who had gathered around the walls of the cemetery. They went on with what they were doing as if they weren't there. A third row of graves was started. Rose counted twenty-nine in all. Then wooden crates were unloaded from trucks in the convoy. Pallbearers in army uniforms carried the crates to the newly dug graves. There was a ceremony. In the dark of night two Navy chaplains read over the rows of wooden boxes and opened earth. A Navy squad fired three volleys and a bugler sounded taps.

It was all done expeditiously and with military order. The crowd of civilians gathered on the outside of the cemetery wall numbered almost as many as the military within it. And someone in that crowd overheard something not intended for public knowledge.

"Those were the bodies of German submariners!"

Thomas ran to Bailey's grocery on the corner to phone the Daily Press. "They need to get out here and find out what's going on."

Edwin Meyer, a young reporter who was working late at the newspaper office, answered the telephone.

"Did you know that the crew of a German submarine is being buried in the National Cemetery at Phoebus?"

"No. No I didn't. Who is this?"

Thomas didn't want to give his name, he just said, "I am... I live in Phoebus... near the cemetery," and hung up.

Thomas and his neighbors searched the morning newspaper. There was no mention of the mass funeral. Everyday they checked the Daily Press for some story about what had happened that night in the National Cemetery.

Two

"I'd rather a view of a lovely beach across the water than the Norfolk Naval Base," Julia said as she and her sister stood at the window. "Still I love the breeze we get and I like to just sit and look at the water. I spend a lot of time by this window. I feel like I know the guard down there. I've spent so much time watching him."

"Why on earth is he there?" Kate asked. "Have you ever seen any reason for him to have to patrol this area?"

"One night I thought I saw something... but he didn't. He was past where Congressman Bland lives when I saw something in the water close to the edge... just over there."

"What did it look like?"

"For a brief moment, it looked like a person in the water."

"You mean, like someone swimming out there?"

"It was so dark, I don't know. And then Joe came home and I forgot about it."

"I think your little love nest is wonderful," Kate said. "It's so cozy. Just perfect for the two of you."

"This wasn't the time to get married," Julia confided. "I know I should be happy Joe isn't halfway around the world, but sometimes, he might as well be."

"I thought you were pleased he got on at NACA."

"I thought it was ideal. He'd be out at the Langley Field doing his part for the war. Mrs. Keegan was thrilled which only made Joe mad. She had been so against him dropping out of VPI to join the service. When it worked out that he didn't get in, he acted like she had planned it."

"Is he still upset?" Kate asked.

"I tried to help him understand how his mother felt. Now he treats me like I was part of a conspiracy. He doesn't talk to me."

"He'll get over it. He'll be like he used to be. He just needs time."

"Kate, have you heard what people call the men who work at NACA?"

"No. What?"

"They call them 'Nak-ka Nuts.' And say they're men with thick glasses and slide rules. Men who get out of going to war because they're so smart."

"There are a bunch of intellectuals at NACA, most of them from the North," Kate said, "but that's nothing to hold against them. What do the letters stand for anyway?"

"National Advisory Committee for Aeronautics. It's a mouthful. The people who work there are not a popular group with the locals. Joe is used to being one of the boys. He wants to be in uniform. It doesn't help that he has to go to Langley everyday…or anywhere else around here. All the boys his age are in uniform – except the "Nak-ka Nuts.""

"Well, someone ought to tell these crazy people the men at NACA are just as important to the war effort as any of the soldiers. That's what I heard."

"Even if you convinced everyone else," Julia said, "you couldn't convince Joe of that now. He's bitter. At least his three years at Virginia Tech, got him a good job, whether he likes it or not."

"I know what you need," Kate said. "You need to get out of here. Come with me to Grandview tonight. They usually have a good band. Tommy Dorsey was there the last time I went."

"You forget. I'm married," Julia said. "I can't just go dancing."

"Well, I don't see why not. You still have legs, don't you?" Kate looked at her sister and sighed. "I heard a group of women are meeting at Hampton High to put together care packages for the boys. Jane says they meet every Thursday evening."

"I'd be the only married woman there whose husband isn't serving overseas."

"So. Maybe you can improve relations…" Kate shrugged.

"I won't go and that's final," Julia said. "I'm sorry, Kate. I didn't mean to tell you my troubles. Joe and I will work this out."

"I know you will," Kate said. "But, I'd like to box his ears in."

"See? I shouldn't have told you. Please don't say anything to him."

"Of course, I won't," Kate said. "Still, I don't like that he's making you so unhappy."

"All that is the matter with me is I'm bored. And I don't think I can get a job…"

"Sure you can!"
Julia shook her head.
"And why not?" Kate asked.
"Because, ... I think I'm pregnant."
"Oh, Julia! Does anyone else know? Am I the first you've told?"
"Un-huh."
"Are you all right? Have you seen a doctor? How long? When?"
"All I really know is that breakfast doesn't want to stay down. I don't have a fever. I feel fine as the day goes on, but in the morning, I'll be sick again."
"Well, this will make old sour puss happy!" Kate said.
"Do you think? I've been thinking he's sorry we got married," Julia said.
"That's not so and you know it! Joe always wanted to marry you. He's going to be so happy when you tell him. I know he will."
"Thanks, I needed you to say that," Julia said. "I will tell him this weekend – Sunday, when he's off.
"Now, tell me about your training in Washington. It seemed like you were gone forever. I shouldn't have encouraged you to join the Red Cross."
"Why do you think that?" Kate asked.
"Well, you hardly wrote while you were gone for training. I missed you."
"There were some days I wished I hadn't listened to you. How did you say it?
"I remember...
"You said, 'if I weren't married I'd join the Red Cross and travel...
" 'See the world,' you said...
" 'Don't sit here watching the action pass you by.' "
"Did I really say all that?" Julia asked.
"You did. Oh, and you said, all I wanted to do was go to the USO to dance with the GIs."
"And you said, 'What's wrong with that?' "
"And you said, 'You're going to fall in love with one of them and then he'll get shipped out' ... Now, you say, I shouldn't have joined the Red Cross," Kate said. "You didn't get letters because I had no time to write. That was the toughest course I've ever taken."
"I'm sure it's not as tough as the nurses have it."
"No, but I wasn't about to be a nurse. You're the nurse in the family. I don't want to stick people with needles, or spoon out castor oil. I'd have never joined up if you hadn't told me the Red Cross had a recreation division."

"So, tell me," Julia said, "what was so tough about it?"

"As if the classes aren't enough, they have this physical training course that they borrowed from the army. It's unbelievable what they put us through so we can serve doughnuts to GIs."

"Have you actually made doughnuts yet?" Julia asked.

"Oh, yes. But they don't spend much time with that. They say we'll get plenty of practice. They brought us down to Camp Patrick Henry for another course and an opportunity to practice what we've learned on some of their GIs," Kate continued. "They call it 'the gentle art of keeping GIs happy' and they had some mighty cute GIs for us to practice on." Kate winked at her sister and smiled.

"When will you know where you'll be going?" Julia asked.

"Didn't I tell you? We're heading to London. Yesterday we were issued our uniforms. I had to buy my shoes, luggage and underwear."

"Didn't you have underwear?" Julia asked.

"In big bold letters, it said, 'ALL COTTON.' There'll be no lacy panties for the duration." Kate stuck out her bottom lip.

"That's too bad," Julia said mocking her sister, "But I'm so excited for you. London!"

"I promise I'll write. I want you to keep me posted on how you're doing. If you have this baby before I get back, you have to tell him about me so he'll know who I am."

"You'll just have to get back," Julia said. "How can I have a baby without you here?"

****

"They're going to announce another civil defense drill's coming up," Charles Magivens told Thomas. Thomas was behind the counter in Fuller's Restaurant. Charles, a white man, was seated on a barstool having a cup of coffee.

"It's supposed to be the most extensive civilian defense drill we've had. When they sound the sirens, all lights are to be blacked out. Everyone is to get off the streets and seek shelter. Everyone. I'm supposed to stop the streetcar right where it is, and tell my passengers to run to the nearest shelter."

"Wonder if this has anything to do with our army burying those u-boat men," Thomas said.

"I didn't hear about that. U-boat men? You mean Germans?"

"Sure as shootin', Mr. Magivens. Right in our National Cemetery. I saw it myself."

"When?"

"Middle of last month. The peculiar thing was they buried them at night."

"Wonder why I didn't hear about it?"

"The government hushed it up. I'm sure of it. Now they want to have another drill, you say?"

"And they're going to announce there'll be a fine and maybe jail time for anyone who doesn't follow all the rules," Charles said.

"What kind of fine? What rules?"

"I was told two or three hundred dollars and several months in jail –if you don't get off the street and shut out all your lights."

"Why, none o-f us have that kind of money!"

"And there'll be civil defense marshals in every neighborhood to see that people cooperate."

"They 'bout scared Rose out of her skin when they came to bury those men in the cemetery. When I tell her about this, she'll want me and Samuel to stay home 'til it's all over. We may never see the light of day again."

"I was saying how I expected some of my passengers wouldn't like my telling them they had to get off the streetcar. 'Well,' they said, 'the regulations are law. If people don't cooperate, the marshal will take care of them.' You say they buried Germans right here in the soldiers' cemetery, Thomas?"

Streetcar   *Cheyne's*

"If you don't believe me, Mr. Magivens, ask any of these folks in here."

Charles had known Thomas for years. He knew Thomas would not make up such a thing. "Germans, buried with our soldiers! Can you beat that?" Shaking his head negatively, Charles paid his bill and hurried out to the streetcar right on schedule.

He was pleased the war was extending the life of the old streetcar system – and so, his job. Every available means of public transportation was needed for the ballooning wartime population. Though new buses were also running, the old streetcars continued sliding back and forth along the rails. When he got to the end of the tracks, Charles would shift the backs of the seats so the passengers would face the other direction. Then he'd remove the brake and controller handles and take them with him to the other end of the car. The two-faced car was ready to travel back the way it came. Though living on borrowed time, his streetcar was almost always filled to capacity.

From Phoebus Charles took the streetcar back over the Queen Street Bridge into Hampton. It was seldom full in the middle of the day. Residents of Phoebus with jobs in Hampton were about the only ones who regularly rode over Hampton Creek. The tracks ran to the outside of the bridge's railing and, if passengers looked down they would get the feeling the streetcar might tip over into the water below. The workers were half-asleep when they went in town to work – and so tired after long days of picking crabs, or shucking oysters, they paid no never-mind to notice the eerie ride over the bridge.

Three

Julia Keegan had ridden the streetcar to downtown Hampton in the morning. When Charles let her off at the post office she'd asked when he'd be back.

Julia had a package to mail to Kate. It was some silly stuff – a bag of Mary Jane's candies, a box of Cracker Jacks and an old photograph of the two of them playing in the sand at Buckroe Beach when they were small – in with the soap and toothpaste Kate had asked for.

From the post office steps Julia eyed the crowded street of her hometown. The new telephone exchange building faced the post office. The Woodmen of the World Building had been raised a couple of years ago to make room for the modern exchange. This strange architecture in the background of an ocean of people made her feel no familiarity with her surroundings.

She hesitated – not at ease with stepping into the swarm of people. She noticed a bunch of GIs had stationed themselves on the curb "inspecting the local merchandise."

She was about to go back inside when she met Margaret Goldstein coming out the door.

"Margaret, it's so good to see you. Are you going to your mother's shop?"

"Yes, Julia."

"Do you mind if I walk with you?"

"I'd be most grateful. I can't get used to all these people."

"Were you mailing something to your brothers? What do you hear from them?"

"The two we worry the most about are Gene and George," There were eight Goldstein boys and just two daughters. "Gene's in the Navy's medical corps and George is a pilot. I use up all my sugar stamps for cookies. I send each of them a box most every week."

"The rest of your brothers are still at home?" Julia asked.

"As much at home as a man can be in war-time. Stanley's in the Home Guard, Daniel and Herbie are in the Reserves, and Irwin is making training films for the Army. They're all in the war one way or another."

"How's your mother. It must be awful with so many men in one family."

"Mama's the Rock of Gibraltar. She takes one day at a time. Keeps busy. Papa has left the grocery business for Daniel and Herbie to manage. He spends most of his time with us at the dress shop."

"Are women still buying new clothes... with the war on?"

"That's not a problem. There're lots of functions – fund-raisers and such. Hampton women have never been such socialites. Papa's worried we soon won't be able to get the stock to keep up with demand."

"Do Gene and George write about what it's like over there?"

"George writes about flying over beautiful fields of tulips. One wouldn't know there's a war on to read his letters. Gene doesn't paint such lovely pictures. He says things like how eating food from a can is only slightly better than going hungry. I suppose he's just trying to make sure I understand he needs the packages I send him... But you haven't told me about you. You and Joe finally got married?" Margaret asked.

"Yes. We're renting an apartment at the Bryan's home on the Boulevard. Joe's with NACA."

"That's splendid. I wondered if he'd ever get you to the altar."

"We were married by a justice of the peace. Joe was planning to enlist right away. A big wedding seemed impossible."

"Have you seen this movie?" Margaret asked looking at the marquee at the Langley Theatre.

"Joe works long hours. We don't have a chance to go to movies."

"I saw their first one, *Buck Privates*," Margaret said. "This one has Abbott and Costello *In the Navy*. They are funny. What we need is laughter."

A couple of blocks from the post office, the sidewalks were not so crowded. The two young women chatted about school days when "we didn't have a care in the world."

"I'm so glad we bumped into each other, Margaret," Julia said. "I need to hurry on to the market so I can catch the streetcar."

"Tell the grocers if they take too long I said they'd give you a ride home."

Langley Theatre   Cheyne's

"I will not. I have enough time if I go on now," Julia said waving to her friend.

The senior Mr. Goldstein had built a grocery in his front yard at the corner of Queen Street and Hope. "The perfect spot for a first class grocery." The Colonial Store on Kecoughtan Road was closer to where Julia was living, but her mother had always shopped at the Sunshine Market and Julia especially liked the Goldsteins and their special market. They would help Julia figure out what she could get with her ration stamps.

Other grocers will do it too, I suppose,
but I feel more comfortable with people I know.

When she'd finished her shopping, Julia waited for the streetcar.
"There's the young lady," Charles said as he came to a stop in front of the grocery.

Seeing the car wasn't full – there was plenty of room for her and her parcels of groceries – Julia smiled. "Perhaps I've found a good time to run my errands," she said to the motorman.

"Indeed, you have, miss. Mornings and evenings this car is packed. The men think they're the ones fighting this war, but you ladies have your share of battles – coming in town to mail your man his homemade cookies and do your shopping when the place is full of men in uniform from all over the country."

"It's my sister..." Julia tried to correct him.

"Yes, sir-ree. You little women don't have it easy. And you have to be just as brave as your men."

"My husband is – "

" I served in the Big War and my wife had to do it all without me. It wasn't easy. I know."

A passenger pulled the cord to tell the motorman he wanted to get off at the next stop. More people got on the streetcar and the motorman started talking with another passenger.

The old man thinks my husband's overseas.
I guess because I had a package to mail to Kate.
  I tried to tell him he was mistaken –
  I was mailing the box to my sister
  and my husband is at NACA.
I'm not alone.   *But the man wouldn't let me talk.*
 I feel like I lied. Should I say something now?
 No, forget it Julia. He was just talking.
   He won't remember you, or care.
Besides I am alone.
 Joe's never home.
 Mother's the president of her garden club,
  the treasurer of her choral group
and a chairman of whatever else
 she can get involved in.
  She's always got on a hat.
My school friends have scattered,
 they're not married and they go to the USO.

Four

Julia had insisted Joe take a walk with her. That was the only way she could get him away from his books.

"Honey," she'd said grabbing his hand, "what would you say if I told you you're going to be a daddy?"

"I'd say, what did you say?"

"You heard me right."

"You and I are going to have a baby?"

Joe was excited for a few days. Then he was asked to teach an evening class. He had little time at home and most of that he spent working with books and papers scattered over the kitchen table. Julia wanted to get up early to see him off to work, but an unrelenting case of morning sickness, meant she'd only be a bother to him. Sometimes days would pass without their hardly talking to each other.

NACA was growing. Julia knew they had brought in people from all over the country to work there. There was a rooming house on the Boulevard, called the X-Club, where some NACA people were housed. With an ever-increasing workload, Joe looked tired. Julia envied, and even resented him, for having so much to do.

Julia had a letter from Kate. She took out paper and pen to write back.

>Dear Kate,
>Wait 'til you see me! I'm loosing my waist and I look all puffy. Mother says I'm just holding fluids

Julia tore up the page and began again...

Dear Kate,
People are beginning to notice I'm babyed. I look like a blimp.
Everyone says I shouldn't overdo, but I feel fine.
Julia tore another page and threw it in the waste can.

I've got to get out of here, she thought.
Kate will read between the lines.
I've got to change my mood before I can write to her

She scooped up the pages of Kate's letter, slipped them into the envelope and shoved them in her sweater pocket as she headed down the stairs. She had read the letter several times. She'd read it again.

"Hi, Julia." It was the landlady's child.
"Hello, Bertie. Didn't you have school today?"
"Yes, but they let us out early. We had an assembly. It was all about civil defense. They told us the Germans might have spies right here in Hampton."
"Oh, I don't think so."
"Mother doesn't think so either. But they said we must report any strangers we see."
"Have you seen anyone suspicious?" Julia asked.
"Not yet, but I'm looking."

That's a start, thought Julia as she left the house.
I can write Kate that Bertie is protecting the homeland.

She turned away from town and started up the Boulevard.

Why am I so pouty?
I have lots of good things in my life.
I have Joe... well, when the war's over,
I'll have Joe and the baby
and Kate will come back
and everything will be great.
I hate this war.

Julia had walked a couple of blocks. She remembered an old house in the neighborhood. One that Bertie said was haunted.

While Bertie watches for spies,
I'll go visit the ghosts.
I've always been fascinated by haunted houses –
I'd like to have spirits around to talk to.
Ghosts are really harmless...
and I'm quite sure they care less than I do about the war.
It's a nasty war.
It has left me out.
Everyone is in this war, but me.
It's like I'm not a part of the world I'm living in.
Like a ghost, I'm untouchable – I cannot touch.
The streetcar man assumed my husband's overseas.
If he were, maybe he'd write love letters to me.
At least war brides get love letters.

Julia marched up the broken sidewalk in front of the "haunted" house. She knocked on the door and stood there as if she expected ghosts to open the door and welcome her. She didn't actually believe in ghosts, but she wanted to.

She cupped her hand around the doorknob. It wobbled and the latch released. Julia hesitated. "I shouldn't go in," she said.

"I should go in. That's why I'm here.

"Hello," she whispered, stepping inside.

She heard something, but not an answer – perhaps a cry.

Oh, my. Is someone in here? I should leave.

But Julia didn't want to go. "Hello," she whispered again and then, louder, louder and louder, "Hello, hello, hello. You needn't bother to answer – if you don't want to. I'll just sit on the steps. Would you like me to read Kate's letter to you?" She climbed up six or seven steps so she would have light from the window. "Kate is in London serving doughnuts to our men over there. She's with the Red Cross."

Julia was quite sure someone was in the house... upstairs. If they had any business being there, they would answer her. She was going to talk and someone was going to listen.

"I love this old house. I wonder why the people moved out. My little friend, Bertie, says the house has ghosts. Do you believe in ghosts? Well, I promised I'd read Kate's letter. Here goes.

Dear Julia,
I've always wanted to come to London. Walk

down Oxford Street to Regent Street to Piccadilly Circus. I wanted to see Buckingham Palace and the Tower of London. Well, here I am. I never expected to be driving down the streets of London in a two and a half ton army truck. We've had two days of driving lessons and I've seen the sights of London from high up in the driver's seat of an ugly army truck. I stripped the gears of that truck at every crossing, but this darling sergeant was so patient with me. My arms ache from steering the thing and I've a pain in my leg from trying to press the clutch to the floor, still I'm ready to drive across Europe if necessary.

Today they had us giving out cigarettes, Lifesavers and chewing gum to the guys. The boys are all so sweet and appreciative. Tomorrow I have to get up at four a.m. I'm on the early morning doughnut-making detail.

Please write. I want to know when you first feel baby kick. I wish I could be there and here too.

Give my love to all. How's my handsome brother-in-law?

Julia mumbled a response to Kate's question, "I wouldn't know." She folded the letter and slipped it back into its envelope. Did she hear something upstairs? Boards creaking?

"Hello? ... Well, if you knew my little sister," she continued, "you'd find it unbelievable – her driving that big ol' army truck."

I know there's someone up there, she thought.

Julia stood up and put the letter back in her pocket. She came down the stairs – walked over to the fireplace – went into the dining room – and the kitchen. There wasn't much to see, but she liked the house. The floor was tracked and it looked like someone had been cracking open pecans in the kitchen, but who and when she might never know. She returned to the living room and thought she saw a figure move on the stairs.

"Hello. Is someone there?"
Silence.
"Well, I should be going," she said aloud. By this time she was a bit concerned about the little noises she heard.

It's only ghosts like Bertie says,
     she thought and laughed at herself.

She called out, "I'll be back."

When Julia opened the door, a cat came scampering down the stairs and ran out ahead of her.

"All that time I was talking to a cat," she said as she pulled the door to unlocked. "The cat's a good listener. Perhaps if I bring him a treat, he'll become my friend."

Dear Kate,

    The landlady's little girl is watching out for German spies in Hampton. You need not worry about us – the German Army couldn't get by Bertie.

    I ran into Margaret Goldstein in town today. She says Eugene and George have both enlisted. One's in the medics, the other is a flyer.

    (I'm sure you can guess which is which.) Remember them in your prayers.

    I visited a dandy deserted house in the neighborhood. It reminds me of some of the houses on Victoria Boulevard – only this one's an old farmhouse. It seems someone found it before I did. But that's okay; I'll share. He's a bewitching black cat unlike any I've ever seen. His little round face is coal black and his yellow eyes are so bright they seem to light up like fireflies on a dark night. He has just a touch of white fur that gives him a collar. The rest of his bushy fur has a reddish tint. He's really quite the dazzler. He followed me most of the way home, but as Mrs. Bryan said, no pets, I petted him and then chased him off. I do hope he'll be friendly tomorrow. Perhaps I'll take him a scrap of something to eat.

    Mother had her picture in the paper. Her garden club was promoting Victory Gardens. She's pictured with a shovel digging in the garden. She was wearing a hat and white gloves.

    You'll be pleased to know I look pregnant now, or else I'm 'wearing the bustle wrong,' as Mrs. Whittaker used to say. All of my dresses ride up in the front. My feet are swelling and I may have to start wearing my slippers to the market. Don't laugh.

    I know all the boys love you as much as you love them. Your letter was wonderful. I get tickled every time I think of you driving that horrible army truck!

    Please stay out of harms way. I'd never forgive

myself if something happened to you.
Your loving sister,
Julia.

Victoria Boulevard　　　　　　　　　　　　*Cheyne's*

Five

Rainy weather kept Julia inside for several days. She helped Bertie with her arithmetic homework, wrote a letter to Kate, listened to the radio and watched the soldier continue his lone parade along the muddy shoreline. She tried to telephone her mother several times, hoping to be invited to dinner, but Mother was never home. When the sun finally broke through the clouds, Julia searched her cupboards for some treat she might take the cat.

I hope he's still there.

The door to the apartment was at the bottom of the staircase. Julia thought she heard a knock.

"Is that you, Bertie?"

The door opened and Bertie started up the stairs talking breathlessly as she climbed. "Mom wants you to come to dinner tonight. She's invited several of the soldiers from Ft. Monroe. It's a project her Sunday school class is doing. You know, make the soldiers feel at home kind of thing."

"Please, thank your mother for me, but I won't be able to come."

"Why? Please, come. We want you to."

"I appreciate the invitation. I really do. But Joe might get home early tonight."

"Then he could come, too. Please."

"Bertie, you're so sweet. And your Mother's kind to think of me. But thank her for me, will you? Come, sit down a minute."

"I can't stay. Mother wants me to help her. But I wanted to tell you about this person I saw near my school today."

"Tell me! Did you catch a spy?"

"I don't know he was a spy, so I can't call the authorities yet, but – "

"Go on. But – '

"This person had on a raincoat..."

"It was raining, Bertie."

"Yes, but he had his collar turned up like the pictures on spy comics. And he was smoking a cigarette just like they do."

"Well, now. This could be a suspicious person."

"What should I do? Suppose he's a German spy?"

"I wouldn't say anything just yet. If he's at your school tomorrow, don't go near him. Go inside and tell your teacher. Okay?"

"I knew you'd say that. Tell my teacher. She won't do anything. I think I should follow him. He'll lead me to his hideout and I can call the FBI."

"That's not a good idea, Bertie. You can't be following strangers to goodness knows where. You could get lost. I'm sure your mother wouldn't like it... and I'm sure you know that. Right?"

"Kinder sorter. But what's the fun of spotting spies if you can't spy back?"

"Spies have to be trained. You and I aren't trained. Now, promise me you won't follow anybody."

"Okay. I wish you'd come to dinner."

"I wish I could, Bertie. Be sure to thank your mother for me."

"Oh, this letter came for you today."

Bertie handed Julia an envelope and then punished every step as she descended to the door. "Bye, Bertie. Thanks, again!" Julia called after her.

"You're welcome."

> *Now I can't go to see my four-legged friend,*
> thought Julia.
> *I might not get back before*
> *the Bryan's guests arrive.*

"And, no, my dear husband," she said looking at their wedding photo, "I won't entertain the troops while you're gone. I only wish you would come home early sometimes. I'm so lonely."

She tore open the letter. It was from Kate.

Dear Julia,

    They say absence makes the heart grow fonder. And they're so right. I do miss you. Today we made a trip in the club mobile. Thank goodness, they don't expect us to drive that thing! It's the size of a greyhound bus. I can't tell you where we went – we're not allowed to say. But we stopped along some water to picnic on the grass (K-rations) and I tried to picture you and Joe with your blanket spread on the waterside in front of your little love nest.

One of our girls got a letter from her boyfriend's sister. He was on the U.S.S. Jacob Jones, a destroyer patrolling off Cape May. A u-boat hit them with a torpedo. There were only eleven survivors. He didn't make it. We all feel so bad for her. Last night when I was dancing with a sailor, I felt sort of strange wondering what chance he has of surviving this war. The boys we meet and talk to are the grandest ones on earth. They don't want to talk about the war, but they can go on for hours talking about going fishing back home.

These big old jeeps and trucks we have take a beating. If we have any trouble, there's always a bright young mechanic to fix anything. I declare, sometimes I think they break something just so they can fix it.

I get the impression your little friend, Bertie, is a little dickens. She'll keep you company when Joe works late.

I received a letter from the folks. Mother enumerated all her "causes" and said she couldn't understand why our father doesn't take a more active role in the community. Any idea? I guess you don't see much of them.

Give my love to Joe and take care of yourself.
Lovingly,
Kate

Julia read with blurry eyes. Tears spilled on the letter when she read the part about Kate picturing her and Joe on a blanket by the water. She and Joe had picnicked many times at Buckroe Beach when they were courting. Sometimes they rode the trolley to the beach; sometimes they would ride bikes.

Do I still have that old ragged blanket
we took to the beach?
If it hasn't been tossed,
it may be in Mother's attic.

When the war's over,
will we be like we used to be?

The door to the apartment opened.

I don't want Bertie to feel she can
just come in without knocking.

Julia went to the top of the stairs.
"Joe?"
"Were you expecting someone else?"
"Well, I thought it had to be Bertie and I... never mind. You're home. I don't know what I can fix for dinner, but I know I have something."
"Don't bother. Mrs. Bryan has invited us to dinner. I accepted."

He accepted a dinner invitation
when we haven't had dinner together in weeks.

"But aren't you tired? Wouldn't you rather just have a quiet dinner up here – just the two of us?" she asked.
"I accepted the invitation. Think of it as saving on ration stamps."
"You're so seldom here, I don't often run out of stamps."
"Are you ready? I think Mrs. Bryan has the dinner on the table."
"Maybe they've already started. I could whip up something in no time."
"Mrs. Bryan is expecting us."
As they went downstairs, he was a few steps ahead of her, she asked him, "Honey, do you know what happened to that old blanket we used to take to the beach?"
"No idea. Why do you ask?"
"I thought we might go picnicking sometime this summer."

Nothing. Not even a maybe. He said nothing.

As the couple came down to the center foyer, Mr. Bryan and Bertie came to show them into the dining room. "We've been meaning to do this ever since you moved in. We're so glad you agreed to join us tonight."
"I waited outside for Joe," Bertie whispered to Julia. "You said he might be early tonight."
"Yes, I did. And you SPIED him."

Mr. Bryan led Joe and Julia into the dining room where other guests had already been seated.

"And this is Mr. and Mrs. Keegan," Mrs. Bryan welcomed them. "Mr. Keegan is at the NACA out at Langley Field. I'm sure you gentlemen are familiar with that organization."

"Yes, indeed." Four men in uniform stood. They shook hands with Joe.

"Mac Prescott, good to meet you." And nodding, "Mrs. Keegan."

"Frank Mitchell... Mrs. Keegan."

"Warren Slater, nice to meet the two of you."

"Miles Thornton, good to meet you and your lovely wife." He nodded. "Mrs. Keegan."

"It's a pleasure having you all here," Mr. Bryan said. "We speak for the community when we say how proud we are of you young people. All of you. It's a great responsibility that has been given to you – to protect and defend democracy." He raised his glass, "I toast the United States. God bless us."

"Hear ye! Hear ye!" And everyone touched glasses, Bertie stretching to get her milk glass amongst them.

"Well, don't just sit there," Mr. Bryan continued, "help yourself and pass it!"

Immediately the serving dishes were rotated around the table.

"Mrs. Bryan, you must have spent your entire day in the kitchen to prepare this feast for us," Warren said. "This is the best eating I've had since I left home." He paused, "It is so nice of you people to invite us."

"Where is your home, Mr. Slater?"

"I believe you should address this young man as a private, Caroline."

"Yes, of course. Where is your home, Pvt. Slater?"

"I'm from Indiana – a little town west of Indianapolis. This is the first time I've seen the ocean. And it looks like I'm going to see both sides of it before I get back home."

"Don't get me wrong," Frank said, "but I'm not looking forward to being packed on a ship going across that ocean with German u-boats on the prowl."

Mac cleared his throat. "Tell the Bryans about your hometown, Pvt. Mitchell."

"Yes, sir. I mean excuse me for... well, you know. Where am I from? I'm from Pretty Prairie, Kansas. Out there we don't have oceans, or mountains – just wheat fields as far as the eye can see. But when the wind blows across that golden wheat, what a beautiful sight it is! I reckon that's how it got its name, Pretty Prairie, Kansas."

"And Pvt. Thornton is a Nooyaker. Right?" Mac asked him.

"Wrong. I'm from New Jersey. And, no, we aren't a suburb of Manhattan. I'm from Trenton. We're a whole lot closer to Philadelphia. Pvt. Prescott is from the other side of the country. He doesn't know the whole East Coast isn't one big state of New York."

"I'm from Warrenton, Oregon, a small seaside town just south of the Washington state line. When I came east, it was the first time I'd seen the sun rise over the ocean. Got me kind of turned around at first. Out West, our states are bigger. We have counties the size of New Jersey."

"The Atlantic's no stranger to me," the man from Trenton said. "We vacation at the beach every year. You fellows should spend a day on the beach just listening to the waves breaking on the shore. Watch the seagulls diving for fish. Let your feet sink into the wet sand."

"If you're here in July you boys will have to come to the regatta," Mr. Bryan said. "This will be our fourteenth annual race."

"Power Boats?" someone asked.

"Why do you young folks think of power boats? The Hampton One-Design sailboat is a boat a man can build himself. Now that's boating. The Hampton is the most beautiful racing class on the Bay."

"Calm down, dear," Mrs. Bryan said. "You'll have to forgive my husband. These yacht club boys are like youngsters when it comes to sailing."

"You have your own boat?" one of the young men asked.

"I'll show it to you, before you leave. It's in the garage."

"And you built it yourself?"

"I did. This wasn't my first, but I learned a lot with my first. Couple of years ago I made a very respectable showing – came in seventh."

Not knowing how many boats competed, the men smiled.

Hunt's Fishing Boat *Cheyne's*

"How's the fishing around here?" one of the guests asked.

"Not bad. Croaker seem to be good this year. We have good crabbing... and the clams are more plentiful this year than usual."

"What kind of shells -?"

"That big pile of shells are oyster shells," Bertie answered before the man could complete his question. "Mr. Darling's oyster shells."

"The business has been passed down to the third generation," Mr. Bryan said. "Old J.S. Darling started it back... maybe fifty years ago. It's become the largest such firm in the world – the only seafood firm that deals exclusively with oysters. They process two hundred thousand bushels of oysters a year. That mountain of oyster shells has become a landmark."

"So that's how the man made his money," Pvt. Slater said. "Once they get the oysters out of the shells, what do they do with the shells?"

"They throw some of the shells in Back River for new oysters to anchor upon," Mr. Bryan answered. "And they use shells for paving roads around here."

"Have you been to the Darling's home, Pvt. Slater?" Julia asked.

"Mrs. Darling has extended her welcome to all the men at Ft. Monroe," Pvt. Mitchell answered. "I've never experienced such hospitality as you people have shown."

"Well, we're all in this war together," Mr. Bryan said. "Do you know where you'll go from here?"

"Not where, nor when," Pvt. Thornton answered. "There's a good chance we'll be split up."

"That would be a shame," Mrs. Bryan said.

"Mr. and Mrs. Keegan are from Hampton. I've known Mr. Keegan's family for many years," their hostess continued. "We thought he was going to be leaving us, but NACA snatched him before the Army could. Isn't that fortunate, with a little one on the way?"

"My little woman's expecting, too," Lieutenant Mitchell said. "The baby's due next month."

Mr. Bryan interrupted a brief silence, "Well, congratulations! Will this be your first?"

"Yes, sir. Have you had one, sir? I mean, has your wife had one?"

"Yes, Pvt. Mitchell. And we have the proof setting right at the table."

Everyone laughed and looked at Bertie, who didn't understand why she suddenly received so much attention. She was glad to make the most of it.

"Do any of you think there are German spies in Hampton?"

"You have been behaving so well, Bertie," her mother said. "Why must you bring up such a subject at the table?"

"They told us at school... they really did. There could be spies right here."

"I wish they wouldn't fill your head with such thoughts," Mr. Bryan said. "Such things are not for children to worry about. You and your friends are doing a good job collecting materials for the war effort. That's all you need to be doing. Now, I don't want any more talk about spies."

"Can they answer me first?'

"Very well," her father said. "Have any of you reason to believe there are German spies in town?"

"No." "No." It went around the table until it finally came to Julia.

What can I say?
The poor child looks so disappointed

"If the Germans have spies, and I think they would, they could be here as well as anyplace. I'm sure the school is trying to teach the children not to talk to strangers."

"I'm sure they mean well," Mrs. Bryan said. "But there is an ocean between us and all that kind of goings on. I think having a man patrolling right out in front of the house rather... unpleasant."

"She's talking about the army outpost down here on the Boulevard," Mr. Bryan explained.

"I just don't see the necessity. There's military all around us. Do we really need to have men with guns in our neighborhood? It's not enough now that we keep our lights low, they want us to get blackout curtains and hang them over my beautiful windows. And they frighten our children with talk of spies."

"Mrs. Bryan," Pvt. Prescott answered, "all the military around here makes this area more of a target. The Army would be irresponsible if it didn't recognize the susceptibility of any waterfront properties. We hope such things aren't necessary, but it's better to be overcautious than to be caught unprepared."

"I suppose I'll get used to them," she answered, "I just hope it will never be necessary for our patrol to do anything but get his exercise along the water's edge. Now, I have some pie for dessert. Could I interest any of you in a slice?"

"If we had known you had a pie in the kitchen, we'd have sent a patrol in there to guard it," Pvt. Thornton said.

"Then you must have great trust in your patrols," Mr. Bryan said. "I wouldn't trust a man to guard one of my wife's pies."

When dinner was over Julia helped remove the dishes from the table, but Mrs. Bryan refused to let her do anymore. "You're our guest tonight. Run along and spend some time with your husband."

It had been nice. Julia had enjoyed visiting. She thanked Mrs. Bryan for inviting them and hurried to catch up with Joe. He had started up the stairs.

Once they were back in their apartment, Joe asked, "Did you know the Army was coming to dinner?"

"Yes. I thought you did. Didn't they tell you?"

"No, they didn't tell me. Do you think I would've gone, if I had known?"

"Bertie was sent up to ask me earlier. I told her I – we couldn't come. I didn't expect you home early and I wasn't going without you."

"You should have said something."

"I practically begged you to let us have dinner up here."

"But you didn't say – oh, never mind."

"It's still early, Joe. Can we put a record on the phonograph?"

"You do what you like. I've got some reading to do."

Do what I like?
What I'd like is to do anything with you,
Joseph Keegan.

Oh, did the baby just kick?

She put her hands on her rounded stomach.

No, it was probably the pie kicking.

Julia put a record on the Victrola of *These Foolish Things Remind Me of You* - the theme song for a motion picture Joe had taken Julia to before he went away to college. She sang along until she came to a line that went - "What fun it is to be with you!"

Julia lifted the needle from the record, shut the phonograph and went to bed.

Six

When at last Julia had an opportunity to go back to the "haunted house," she hoped the cat would still be there.

"Here, kitty!" She called. "Here, kitty, kitty, kitty. I brought you a treat."

"There you are! Did you think I'd forgotten you? No, I course I wouldn't forget you. I've a new letter from Kate to read to you today. You're such a good listener.

"Okay, first I'll rub your tummy. You like that, do you? You don't seem to be starving... in fact, I'd say you must be finding lots of handouts. Well, that's all right. I'm just so glad you're still here. I would have been most disappointed if you weren't here today.

"Let me give you your treat. You're not interested? Well, I guess not, with that full tummy you have. Let's go in the back. I'll leave it on the kitchen sink for you."

Julia walked into the kitchen with the cat at her feet. "My goodness! You're so friendly, but I can hardly walk." She placed the small container on the draining board and reached down to pick up the cat. That's when she saw muddy footprints. Lots of muddy footprints. She looked to the counter. The pecan shells weren't there. Julia knew,

Someone is in this house.
No wonder children think it's haunted.
Someone's living in this empty house.

Okay, Julia, calm down.
If this person wanted to harm you,
it would have happened already.

Just do what you did before.
Sit on the steps and read the cat Kate's letter.

"Come, Kitty," she said. "You want to hear Kate's letter?"
"Dearest Julia..." The young woman read the letter – right through what Kate had written about the picnic blanket and the boy on the Jacob Jones – only this time Julia just read the words and didn't feel them as before. While she read, she listened for any sound from the upper floors. There was none.

Oh, I'm just a lily-livered coward.
Whoever's been feeding this cat
brought the mud in
when he came over to take care of the cat.
There's no one here now.
Am I so lonely I'm imagining people?

"You going to show me around, kitty? I like these old houses. Someday, when the war's over, maybe Joe and I can get a place like this."
The proud cat led his houseguest to the second floor. The walls were dark in the upstairs hall. Julia went into the first room and looked out the wide window above the porch roof. She followed the cat into the next room and checked the view towards the Boulevard. The floor of the third room was covered with newspapers.

Maybe there is someone here, she thought

as she read the large headline from a current paper: TOKYO BOMBED. She turned to find the cat.
"Where did you go, kitty?"

I'm leaving.
I'll just call out to the kitty as I've been doing
and then I'll go down the stairs and out the door.

"I've got to go now, kitty. Bye."

Only hesitating to see she still had Kate's letter, Julia slipped out the door, the cat rushing out, just as she pulled the door to. She crossed to the other side of the street.

Don't look back.
Don't look back.
Okay, look now, but make it quick.

She turned and there in the window – the one she had viewed the Boulevard from – was a man. He had to know she saw him, but he didn't move. The cat circled her feet. For, maybe ten seconds Julia looked up at the person in the window. "Go home, kitty," she said. Julia turned around and headed to the Bryan's house.

Julia saw Bertie coming towards her on the Boulevard. The cat was still scampering along with her. "Go! Go! Go back to the house!"

Oh, if I told Bertie about the man in the window,
she would love it!
She'd say the man was a German spy!
No. I can't tell her.
She'd have the whole army after him...
and the FBI.
No, I should tell the authorities myself
and hope Bertie never knows anything about it.

"Julia, we've been looking for you."

"Is something wrong?"

"No. Joe's mother came to visit. She's been here for an hour and we couldn't find you."

"Did she leave?"

"She's still in the house – talking to Mother."

"Well, I look a sight."

"You look very pretty. Mother says women are their prettiest when they're expecting a baby."

"I'm pleased to hear that, though 'pretty' isn't how I feel."

"Trust me. You look nice."

"Thank you, Bertie. You're a special friend."

Julia hurried in the house and unintentionally interrupted.

"We were just having a little heart-to-heart," Mrs. Bryan explained while her friend dried tears with her hankie.

"Mother Keegen, are you all right?"

"Of course. Caroline and I go way back. We were just ... the truth is I've been very hurt that you and Joe haven't come to see me for so long. And when they couldn't find you, I thought perhaps you were avoiding me."

"I had no idea you were coming. I'm so sorry I caused you to worry. And, please believe me, I would not wish to avoid you. I'm happy to see you."

"Where have you been? Did you do some shopping?"

"I was out walking. The rainy weather we've had kept me in most of the week. I guess I was out longer than usual today. I am so sorry."

"It's all right. How is Joe?'

"He's very busy at NACA. Since this last promotion, he's been working extra long days and he's teaching a class in the evenings. I was surprised when he got home early enough that we could join the Bryans for dinner last evening."

"Yes, Caroline told me you had dinner with them. She said Joe didn't have much to say."

Julia turned to her landlady, "Mrs. Bryan, it was a lovely time. Joe's so tired when he comes home, he seldom says much to me. I know he enjoyed the meal. He was so pleased you asked us.

"Would you like to come up to the apartment, Mother Keegan? I wish I could tell you I expect Joe soon, but I rather doubt it."

"No, I think I should be going. I don't want to miss the streetcar."

"May I walk with you to the stop?" Julia asked.

"You've already had your long walk."

"But I'd so enjoy a chance to visit," Julia said.

"May I go with them, Mother?" Bertie asked.

"What a splendid idea!" Mrs. Keegan said. "Then Julia will not have to walk back alone and I won't feel so bad her walking the distance with me. You sure you're not overdoing it, Julia?"

"If the two of you don't start running, I can keep up."

"I think my running days are over." Mrs. Keegan looked back at her friend, "What do you think, Caroline?"

"Indeed, mine are. I think Bertha's the only one you need to worry about – but she'll be so busy running her mouth, she's more likely to trip over her tongue," the mother looked at her daughter, "You may go, but mind your manners. Give the ladies a chance to talk."

"I'm so pleased the sun decided to shine on us again, Bertie," the older woman spoke to the child. Julia walked behind them with her own thoughts.

Should I try to talk to Mother Keegan about Joe?
She never saw how deeply Joe idolized his father –
that he wanted to be like his dad.

Time Will Tell

    Mr. Keegan couldn't have been a soldier
        for very long before he was killed.
    But to Joe, that's what he was.
    That's how he had a father.
    He's told me that
    when he was a boy he'd play soldiers
    and imagine his father was with him on the battlefield.
    If I told her about this,
        would she be able to understand?
    Would she understand his anger
        about being classified 4F?
    If Bertie hadn't come, I could –

"Julia, are you sure you're all right?" Mrs.Keegan asked. "Perhaps I should send Bertie back with you now. You look tired."

"No. No. I'm fine," she insisted. "I'm afraid I was thinking about something... else. That was rude of me, I apologize. What were you saying?"

Darling family home   *Cheyne's*

"We were talking about Mrs. Darling's Easter egg hunt," Bertie answered. "Did you go, when you were a child?"

"I never missed one. Every year Mother would make Kate and me matching spring outfits. We'd get up on Easter morning and she'd braid our hair and put pretty ribbons in it the color of our dresses, shiny patent-leather shoes on our feet and we'd walk to St. John's. People would say we looked like two Madame Alexander dolls just out of the boxes coming to church. We kept our Easter outfits on through lunch without getting a speck of anything on them. Oh, but after the egg hunt, we were a mess! We had so much fun on the Darling's lawn. It's hard to believe Mrs. Darling still does that for the children."

"If you knew Molly Darling the way I've known her, you wouldn't be surprised," Mrs.Keegan said. "Do you know she invites servicemen over to picnic on the lawn, go canoeing on the river, come in the house to sing and dance, and play pool at that grand old Victorian pool table they have upstairs? She does – every week.

"We were laughing the other day when she told us these boys don't sing as well as the boys of the Big War. She says they don't have the kind of songs they had then. Songs like *Over There, Pack Up Your Troubles* and *There's A Long, Long Trail A Winding*. She thinks the popular songs now are not as patriotic, more sentimental, she says. Nevertheless, Molly Darling is going to open up her home for these boys, just like she did for the others."

"Julia," Bertie said pointing to the sentry, "look at that gun the soldier has. Suppose he started shooting?"

"Now, why would he do that?"

"Maybe he sees a German spy down in the water?"

"Bertie, your father doesn't want you thinking about German spies. So, let's agree not to talk about them. Okay? What have you and your friends been collecting for the war effort?"

"Last week we collected coat hangers. I don't see what our soldiers are going to do with them. Do they give them that many uniforms to hang up?"

"The hangers will be made into other things the army needs," the older Mrs. Keegan explained before she noticed the sly smile on the little girl's face. "Why, you were pulling my leg – you knew that."

Bertie snickered.

"Speaking of the Darlings – Ann Darling and the Amory girl come around collecting something all the time," Mrs. Keegan said. "She has a pony cart. Cutest thing I've ever seen. They've just about collected all I have to give them. Well, that was good timing, here comes my trolley."

"Thanks for coming by, Mother Keegan." Julie said. "Joe will be sorry he missed you."

"You tell that young man, he's not to forget he has a mother."

A mother, a wife

and a baby on the way, Julia thought.

"I'll tell him you said so."

Julia watched her mother-in-law get onto the streetcar and take a seat. As the streetcar pulled away, she looked back at Bertie who was eyeing everyone who got off at the stop with a suspicious once-over.

"Stop that, Bertie," Julia corrected the child. "A spy has to be discreet. Don't stare."

"Did you see that woman? I think she was wearing a disguise. She might have been a HE."

"Bertie, where do you get these ideas?"

"I'm a natural. You might say I have a nose for it."

"What you have is a passion for trouble. How old are you?"

"I'm almost nine. I've a birthday in August."

"When I was nine I played house, not espionage," Julia said. "Kate and I and our little friends built a hut out of pieces of old wooden planks down by the marsh. We made mud pies and dug about to see what people had discarded in the marsh."

"Did you ever find anything good?"

"Well, now, that's in one's perspective, isn't it? People threw all kinds of things in the marsh, but they were certainly broken – or they wouldn't have thrown them away. We had a helter-skelter hut. Or as my grandmother would say, it was catawampous. We were quite pleased to furnish it with junk. We had a three-legged table and wooden boxes to sit on. And we had a baby carriage missing one wheel."

"So everything was cataumptious?"

"Catawampous. It means crooked. Yes, everything."

"What did you do in there?"

"It was our clubhouse. We had a secret word we had to say when we wanted to enter. And we swore never to tell anyone what it was."

"Swore?"

"Well, we promised."

"You swore. Did your mother know about your hut in the marsh?"

"Well, goodness, no. If she ever caught us in the marsh she'd have whipped our behinds."

"If I tell you something, will you promise not to tell my mother?"

"Oh. I can't make such a promise. You'd best not tell me."

"But I want to, Julia. Please, promise me."

"I cannot make such a promise. You may tell me you've been up to some dangerous shenanigans. I'd be surprised if you haven't. I'd rather not know."

"It's only about a place Ricky and I found."

"A place where you weren't supposed to be in the first place, I suppose."

"Yeah. I could take you there – if you promise. You kept secrets from your mother."

"Your mother's expecting us back now," Julia said. "I want you to promise me you'll not go to this place until we have time to talk again."

"I didn't think you'd be so picayunish," Bertie fumed as she followed Julia up the front walk to the house. "All right then, I promise not to go back until you go with me tomorrow." She gave Julia a broad smile and ran past her into the house.

"Julia, I'm glad you're back," Mrs. Bryan met her at the door. "I just hung up the telephone. Your mother's sending your father over to get you. She says she needs you there tonight."

"Did she say what -?"

"She's giving a dinner party for some of the officers from Ft. Monroe and, apparently at the last minute, someone cancelled on her. She sounded frantic, poor thing."

Mother always sounds frantic, Julia thought.
I can't go to her dinner party.
She wouldn't want me there looking like this.

"I'll sit on the porch and wait for my father, Mrs. Bryan. Thank you."

Whenever I call Mother, she isn't home,
Or she's on her way out and can't talk.
Now she suddenly wants me to fill a chair
at her dining table.
Kate's the one she needs and Kate's not here.
So she calls me.

Mr. Walters parked in front of the Bryan's home. Julia rushed out to his black Chevrolet sedan. "What's this?" she asked pointing to the headlights.

"That's what everyone is going to be asked to do," her father explained. "The civilian defense people don't want us driving at night unless it's absolutely necessary. If we do drive, we're supposed to cover the top half of our headlights. We got some of these at the dealership today. I thought I'd impress our dinner-guests by being one of the first to try it."

"Your dinner-guests – I'm sorry, but I couldn't possibly go home with you tonight. I have no idea when to expect Joe home."

"Joe can take care of himself. Your mother is counting on you."

"But I'm a mess. And I've nothing suitable to wear."

"Your mother's one step ahead of you. She noticed your dresses were getting a little snug, so she sent over some things she borrowed for you."

"She thinks of everything."

"She does need you this evening, Sweetheart. You know how upset she gets when things don't go the way she's planned. Now, hurry up and get dressed. I'll wait on the porch."

Julia took the small suitcase he handed her and climbed to the upstairs apartment.

How upset she gets!

She opened the suitcase. As she held the clothes up to her and looked at her reflection in the mirror, Julia said to herself,

"This might work.

"Yes, this one is a better color.

"I'll try this first."

"Julia!"

"Yes, Bertie. Come on up."

"Your father said for me to hurry you up. Oh, I like that. You look pretty."

"You always say so. Do you like this one better?" She held one of the others in front of her.

"I like the rose color."

"I need to put my hair up and I'll be ready. It does feel good to have on something that's big enough. I wish I could stay here and surprise Joe. I don't like Mother's dinner parties."

"Are they boring like ours?"

"Bertie, your mother's dinner was very nice. I enjoyed it. Didn't you?"

"Only 'cause you came." Bertie watched Julia brush her hair up into a bun on top of her head. "I wish you could eat with us every night."

"That's sweet, but sometimes it's more special when we do things once and a while. Should I wear my pearls?"

"Yes. They're beautiful."

"They were my grandmother's. She gave them to me when Joe and I got married. They do look nice with this neckline. Okay, you say my father said I must hurry."

"Yes. And I got you ready, didn't I?"

"You did. Let me write a quick note to Joe – in case he gets home before I do:

> Joe,
> Father came for me. They insisted I have dinner there tonight. Sorry I had to leave in a hurry.
> Love,
> Julia

"Ready?" she asked the child as she propped the note up on the table.

"Ready. Julia, do you think Maurice Chevolet is a Nazi collaborator?"

"His name is Chevalier. Probably not. I don't know. I've always liked him."

Julia's father told her she looked very nice. He asked about how she felt and how Joe was doing. She said she was fine and Joe was doing well at NACA. "You know he got another promotion?"

"Yes. Joe has plenty on the ball. Do you know what he does at NACA?"

"Classified. Most of what he does is classified. Though I'm sure I wouldn't understand it if he could tell me."

"You're probably right. The organization has certainly grown in these last several months. I'm told their work is vital to the war effort. Joe got in at a good time."

"Well, don't try to tell him that. He still thinks he's supposed to be in the military."

"Be patient, Sweetheart. He'll get over it."

"He can't. Everywhere he goes, at Langley or in town, there are men in uniform. Will this war be over soon?"

"The President said in his fireside chat this will be a long, hard war. He said the Nazis and the Japs fight dirty – that Germany was behind the Japanese attack on Pearl Harbor. We're going to have to do without things for some time."

"It's not doing without things. It's doing without people – people who are serving in the military, people who are devoting their lives to the war effort, people who cannot be what they would be because of this nasty war."

"Kate writes us about wonderful young people she's getting to meet – courageous men and women sacrificing their lives for our country's

Time Will Tell

defense."

"Our President said that was not 'a sacrifice, but a privilege.' And Joe would say he was right. Joe was denied the privilege to serve his country. He can't wear the uniform of the courageous. With everyday the United States is at war, Joe gets more cantankerous. I can't talk to him about it. I shouldn't be talking to you about it. I'm sorry. How are you doing?"

"Fair to middling, I suppose. I'm hoping to get enough auto repair jobs to keep us going. Once I sell the cars we have left, that's it."

Army Goods Store　　　　　　　　*Cheyne's*

"Oh, Father, it seems so incomprehensible. Just when people start thinking they can afford automobiles, the industry is taken over by the war. Why couldn't we stay out of it?"

"You're going to have to change your tone at the dinner table tonight," her father said. "The officers who will be our guests have no choice but to be committed to the war. This country is at war and nothing we can do or say can change that. This is a time for patriotism, Sweetheart."

"Do you know you always called me 'Sweetheart' when you'd say something... to correct me?

'Don't stand on the seat, Sweetheart.
　Get your fingers out of your mouth, Sweetheart.
　　Help your mother, Sweetheart.
　　　Stop whining, Sweetheart' "

"I did?"

"Yes, you did.

"When you say 'Sweetheart,' I feel like a little girl who's being naughty."

"Well, that's a shame. I always think of you and Kate as my little sweethearts. You know, Sweetheart, sometimes you..."

"Caught you! You were about to do it again," she laughed.

"So I was. Maybe I'll call you 'Little Buddy'," he suggested.

"Your Little Buddy will try to make you proud of her tonight."

Julia was introduced to the four men in uniform. These men were all lieutenants.

Mother wouldn't ask for anything less.

Each of them told of his family and hometown. Julia tried to pay attention, but all she could think of was her aching feet.

Isn't it time to sit down to dinner?

When Evelyn Walters announced dinner, she instructed each of her guests where to sit. Across from Julia was Mattie Tyler, the youngest and only single member of her mother's garden club. An officer was seated to either side of the girls. Evelyn and her husband were at opposite ends.

Once seated, Julia couldn't see Mattie through the enormous centerpiece.

Mother has set out her best china.
She's going to make this
a most auspicious occasion.
If she'd realize that these men want to relax,
and serve them
... sandwiches and beer,
it would surely please them.

"To our guests and the great country they serve," Julia's father offered and everyone sat down watching for signals from Mrs. Walters and responding to her lead. There was an awkward silence.

"Mrs. Keegan, where is Mr. Keegan serving?" the lieutenant to her right asked.

"My husband is with NACA. He couldn't be here tonight because he teaches a class in the evenings."

"Oh, I beg your pardon, I assumed..."

"I understand, Lieutenant."

"Mr. Walters told us Mr. Keegan was with NACA when he introduced Mrs. Keegan," one of the other men offered. "Does your husband think the war will be won in the sky?"

"Well, no, or I don't know. We haven't discussed it."

"Lieutenant Dillard," Mr. Walters said. "As civilians, we would very much like to hear your opinion."

"I come from a long line of cavalry men. The wise old military men have seen to it that the War Department purchased 20,000 horses this year. Wars are fought on the ground by men meeting the enemy face to face."

One of the men from the other side of the flower arrangement said, "I think it's going to take land troops, the navy and the fly boys. We'll give them whatever it takes."

"Mrs. Walters, the roast is delicious," Mattie said.

"Indeed, it is."

"Delicious."

"Yes."

"Just like my mother cooks her roast."

"How long do you expect to be at Ft. Monroe?" Mrs. Walters asked the men.

"I'm at Langley Field, Mrs. Walters. In fact three of us are. The only foot soldier at this table is Lt. Dillard."

"Do you know each other? I mean, did you before tonight?"

"Many times I have had the misfortune of hearing Lt. Dillard boast that the man on the ground is going to fight this war."

"But how did you get together?" Mr. Walters asked.

"He has to report to my office," Lt. Dillard answered.

"It's more like his office needs us. When they need someone to fly over to check things out, they call us."

"I have to admit, he's right, but it bugs the... bugs me that they get all the credit."

"Lt. Dillard has been all hot and bothered since the local paper quoted me on the front page. They sent me up over the area back in December to see how effective the blackout was from the sky."

"Oh, you're the one, Lt. Hane," Mr. Walters said. "You gave a fine report."

"I could only report what I saw. If the citizens hadn't been so responsive, I would have had to report that there were lights beaming."

"The people of Hampton," Mrs. Walters said, "are going to do our part, I assure you. We have had wonderful response from our citizenry. General Sunderland is our civilian defense coordinator. He's retired army.

Not a native, but he's spent a lot of time here. Everyone knows him.

"Our women have signed up to work in shelters and to be spotters. We all want to help. Agnes Connolly – right next door – has been getting training for emergency medical service. J.S. Darling is a warden."

"Evelyn," Mr. Walters broke in when his wife paused, "Lt. O'Neill was telling us they don't expect a massive invasion in this area. The big concern is acts of sabotage, right Lt. Arnold?"

"Yes, sir. There've been numerous industrial disasters in this country over the last several years. Some of these can be attributed to accidents; some to disgruntled workers; but there may well have been enemy agents working in this country to sabotage our factories. England wouldn't have lasted this long without Roosevelt's Lend-Lease Program. The Nazis know this. That's why they've been sinking our ships – so that we couldn't get supplies to England. Now that we are officially in this war, we must be concerned that agents could target our military bases. It's important that everyone on the Virginia Peninsula be most alert."

"Lt. Arnold," Miss Tyler said, "did you know Capt. Kelly?"

"You mean Capt. Colin Kelly? The pilot who dropped a bomb down the stack of a Japanese battleship?"

"Yes. Well, I suppose that's what he did. Did you know him?"

"No, I can't say I ever met him."

"Well, it was nice to see someone score for our side, for a change," Mr. Walters said. "Sorry he had to die doing it. If you'll forgive my saying this, it seems the newspaper is always reporting our ships being sunk."

"The United States has followed the British policy in the Atlantic," Lt. Hanes answered. "The British Admiralty has suppressed reports of victories by Allied vessels because, if Germany knows, they can replace their sunken submarines within a few hours."

"Then, you're saying, the Allies have been sinking ships, but not reporting these sinkings to the public?" Mrs. Walters asked. "We need to be told when we sink a German ship. We're getting a cockeyed picture of the situation."

"The Navy Department is considering making such announcements within a week or ten days from the sinkings – for that very reason," Lt. O'Neill said. "In March Secretary Knox announced that we'd sunk three subs in January and February. You're right, though. It would be heartening if people, particularly on the coast, received reports of successes as they occur. Besides, the Nazis couldn't replace a submarine over here so quickly."

"You think they're going to change this policy?"

"They're talking about it.," Lt. Arnold said. "But it's the Navy's call."

Julia tuned out the table conversation and drifted into her own thoughts.

> All their talk about sabotage makes me wonder
> if I should tell them about the man in the window...
> I certainly can't say anything in front of Father...
>   or Mother...
>   they'd scold me for going there.
>   What if there was more than one man –
>   a team of saboteurs...
>   or maybe there was a girl in there with him...
> perhaps a local girl's having
>   an affair with a soldier...
>   much more likely than saboteurs.

(Julia laughed at herself)

> ... maybe I didn't see anyone...
>   could have been my imagination...

> Mother is so involved in the wartime programs...
>   it's like she's in another world.
>   No, it's me. I'm the one who's not in touch.
>   Mother's in the middle, doing her part.
> Should I volunteer?
>   And be thrown in with military wives.
> No.
>   But if Joe didn't feel as he does, perhaps I could.
>   Do military people actually think that NACA
>   is a bunch of draft-dodgers?
>   Did Lt. Dillard purposefully try to humiliate me
>   when he asked where my husband was serving?
>   Had he heard Father say Joe was with NACA?
>   I'd like to think Kate was sitting behind this
>   floral abundance in the middle of the table.
>   I can't believe I talked her into leaving me.
>   She'd like Lt. Hane.
>   Why did I tell her to seek adventure?

As they rose from the dinner table, the guests proclaimed it a perfect meal and Evelyn Walters accepted their praise graciously. Julia's father brought out the wraps for the girls and placed her shawl over her shoulders. Something was askew. Julia had missed something. She and the other guests were all leaving, and her father was telling her goodbye.

"But aren't you taking me home?" Julia asked.

"Where have you been? Lt. Arnold insisted that he drop you ladies off."

"It's looks like he and Mattie hit it off," Julia's mother whispered. "While the rest of us were talking they had their own conversation going."

"That's sweet. But what does that have to do with Father taking me home?"

"You didn't hear any of the conversation, Sweetheart?"

"Nothing about this."

"Well, you'll just have to go along," her mother answered. "Lt. Arnold will drop you off at the Bryan's. And, thank you for coming, dear. You look lovely. I knew Hallie's things would fit you."

"Julia, you must take the front seat," Mattie said. "I think it's so wonderful you're having a baby."

"Thank you, Mattie." (The only other option would be for Julia to be the girl squeezed in the back seat with three lieutenants.)

"Where to?" Lt. O'Neill asked as he climbed in the driver's seat.

"Go up to Victoria and make a left, I'll tell you from there."

"Will Mr. Keegan be home now?"

"I don't know."

"Well, Miss Tyler and Lt. Arnold and ..."

"I'll just need to be dropped off, Lieutenant. Make another left at this corner."

One of the men in the backseat started singing:

"Don't sit under the apple tree with anyone else but me"

The other's joined in singing the popular song. Even Julia sang while she thought,

> *If that were Joe, wearing a uniform*
>   *and driving a government car,*
> *he'd be euphoric...*
>   *and I'd be scared stiff*
>   *he wouldn't be coming back*

"Praise the Lord and pass the ammunition!" Lt. Arnold sang out.

"What did you say," Mattie interrupted the singing. "Pass the what?"

"Don't tell me you haven't heard this one?" Lt. Arnold looked surprised.

"It's a song?" Mattie asked. "Praise the Lord and pass the ammunition?"

"Yes, it's a song... inspired by the Japs attacking us at Pearl. The words are easy – join in will you? Come on, Praise the Lord and pass the ammunition." He tried to wave his arms as if to lead the choir, but the back seat was too crowded. The others followed his lead anyway.

"Okay, now – Praise the Lord and swing into position."

They sang.

"Now – Can't afford to stand around a wishin'. Praise the Lord and pass the ammunition."

Lt Arnold continued prompting them – "Praise the Lord; we're on a mighty mission... All aboard we're not a goin' fishin'... And we'll all stay free!"

They were all singing the ghastly lyrics and laughing so that Julia had to shout to get the driver's attention. "This is it, right here!"

"Sorry, Mrs. Keegan," Lt O'Neill answered and slammed on the brakes causing the crowd in the backseat to become completely scrambled on the floor.

"I'll just jump out," Julia said.

"I can't let you do that," Lt. O'Neill answered. "It would be a court-martialing offense, if an officer of the United States Army did not open the door for a lady."

He came around the car and opened the door. Julia stepped out, "Thank you for the ride, Lieutenant."

"Bye, Julia... We'll meet again (The men joined Mattie singing.)

> Don't know where,
> Don't know when,
> But I know we'll meet again
> Some sunnnnnnnnny day.

"It is we who thank you, Mrs. Keegan. It was a pleasure meeting you."

While Lt. O'Neill saw her to the door, the others got out of the car, marched around it to the tune of "When Johnny Comes Marching Home Again" and resettled so that Mattie and Lt. Arnold were now in the front seat.

Julia laughed, "Do hurry back to the car before they forget you, Lt. O'Neill. If the Army tries to court-martial you for running off, I will

speak on your behalf."
She watched the young officer dart for the car as it was already rolling away.

I cannot blame them for wanting to have a good time.
As Bertie would say,
dinner with the Walters was boring.

Climbing the stairs Julia hummed "When Johnny Comes Marching Home Again." Her tempo slowed as the climb got more difficult for her aching feet. At last in her living area, she collapsed onto the couch with a "Hurrah!"

I'd like to wait up for Joe –
show him my 'new' borrowed clothes –
but I'm so tired;
I'd certainly fall asleep anyway.

Picking up the shoes she had kicked off and removing the note she'd left on the table for Joe, she made her way into the bedroom with only the moonlight to help her avoid bumping into things.
When she got in the bedroom, she realized Joe was there.
"Joe, how long have you been home?"
He didn't answer.
"Joe, are you asleep?"

If he's not asleep, he's not answering me.

She remembered the clothes she had left tossed on the chair in her hurry to get ready.

I'll hang everything up in the morning, she thought.

She threw the things she'd worn on top of it all. She slipped into the bed and fell instantly asleep. But she slept only a short time. She awakened with a start.

Was Joe awake when I came home?
If he saw the car and all the merriment,
what is he thinking?
Is he awake now?
My note was where I left it.

> *Did he see the clothes flung all over the chair?*
> *Perhaps he didn't see the car.*
> *Maybe he didn't like my going to Mother's.*
> *They insisted.*
> *I had to go.*

"Joe?" she whispered.

She got no answer and very little sleep. She kept repeating the same questions in her mind. Had Joe seen her come home in the army vehicle? Was he only pretending to be asleep?

At last daylight filled the room. Joe sat up and threw his feet out onto the floor.

"Joe. I tried to wake you last night when I came in," she said.

"I came in, saw your note and went to bed. How was the dinner party?"

"Like all of mother's dinner parties – pompous and scrumptious. (That was something Kate used to say.) I missed you."

"I'm sure you did," he answered and walked out of the room.

> *That sounded curt.*
> *Was he awake last night?*
> *If he'd say he was, I could explain.*

"Mother borrowed these clothes from Cousin Hallie. I wanted to show you last night... I'm getting bigger. We may be able to feel the baby kicking soon," she continued... "Father's put caps on his headlights. He says they'll be asking everyone to do that."

"Doesn't affect me. Does it? Being as I don't have a car." He was moving about getting dressed.

"Well, no... Do you think you might get home early tonight?"

"Not likely. You go ahead to your dinner parties."

"I don't like dinner parties, Joe. Not without you."

"Then stay here," he answered, "but don't expect me. Look, I gotta go. There's an early meeting."

She called out, "Bye" but only heard him close the door at the foot of the stairs.

Seven

Julia put on one of her old dresses to go into town. She would save the loaners for times when Joe would be home –

> *whenever that will be.*
> *I'll see if Herbie Goldstein has a good cut of beef*
> *that even I can't ruin.*
> *I'll rest this afternoon*
> *and prepare a good meal for Joe*
> *no matter how late he gets in.*
> *He may have seen me come in last night –*
> *I don't know.*
> *If he did, he could have thought –*

"Stop it, Julia. Did he seem mad this morning, or preoccupied? I think he had something on his mind and I don't think it was me, the baby, or caps on headlights.

"Ou-u-u," she sighed looking at her reflection. "Maybe my poor husband looked at me. He couldn't leave fast enough. I'm too young to have bags under my eyes, but I do.

"What does it matter if I wear this to town?" she asked herself as she changed into one of the dresses her mother had sent over. "I can put it back on tonight, after I've rested. I'm so tired. I hope I can catch the streetcar without a long wait. There, this feels better and maybe people won't notice how pale I am."

"Good morning, Julia," Mrs. Bryan said. She was sweeping the porch. "I don't believe you'll need a sweater today. Now that the newspapers don't give much of a forecast, it's hard to know what to expect.

I know they don't want the enemy to benefit from the reports, but with the seasons changing, it's difficult. I'm sure I dressed Bertie too warmly this morning."

"The sun does seem hot today, but this dress has such a little sleeve. I think it'll look better if I keep the sweater on."

"Well, it does look nice."

"This is a dress of my cousin's. She's loaned me some things."

"Why haven't I thought of that? I still have some things I used when I was carrying Bertie. They're not the latest fashion, but you might want to see if there is something you can use."

"Yes, I'd like that, Mrs. Bryan. You're very kind."

"They're just hanging in the closet getting old. I'd be pleased if you could use them."

"I'm going to the market," Julia said. "I want to have a good dinner for Joe tonight."

"Of course. I'll get Bertie to bring the things up to you when she gets home from school. Did you have a nice time at your mother's yesterday evening?"

"It was very nice. I don't think I'll ever be the cook my mother is... or you, Mrs. Bryan."

"You'll learn. It takes practice."

Julia hurried along the Boulevard and up LaSalle Avenue. She saw the streetcar on Electric Avenue, but she couldn't get there in time to catch it. She would have to wait. In a few minutes several other people gathered at the stop.

"Look here," one man said to the other. He read the headline of a newspaper article. " 'Naval Officer Says Japs Shot Men On Rafts'."

"Let me see that, 'Japanese warships torpedoed raft loads of unarmed and helpless survivors from sunken Dutch destroyer.' "

"If that had been American sailors in those rafts, the Japs would be in serious trouble."

"You're right. Our military wouldn't let the Japs get away with that. It says here, it happened in February in the Dutch East Indies."

"That's the way the Japs fight. They snuck up on us at Pearl Harbor while pretending to be making peace negotiations in Washington. It shouldn't surprise us that they would shoot defenseless men in rafts."

"Aren't you one of Evelyn's girls?" Julia turned around to see the lady who spoke to her.

"Yes, Mrs. Kelsey. I'm Julia. I'm married and living on the Boulevard now. Kate is with the Red Cross in England."

"Someone told me that. Quite a brave thing for a young woman to do. Have you heard from her?"

"She writes often. She's in love with the whole U.S. Army."

"I'm sure your mother's glad that you're here."

"I had dinner at the house last night... Here's the streetcar. Are you going in town to shop?"

"No, I have an appointment with Dr. Jones," she answered as she stepped onto the trolley car.

Mrs. Kelsey sat in the first available seat. The seats to either side of her were occupied.

"It was nice seeing you, Mrs. Kelsey," Julia said as she spotted a seat next to one of the men she'd overheard talking.

The man looked at Julia and said, "I hope the baby's daddy lives to see him. Is your husband in the Pacific, dear?"

Julia shook her head negatively.

I don't want to talk to this man, she thought.
He gives me the willies.

"Well, you can be glad of that." He paused. "But then the Germans aren't going to pay any heed to the Geneva Convention either. What we need to do is shoot to kill until we've killed them all."

When Julia didn't respond, the man directed his oratory to someone else. "What we should do..."

Please, won't someone stop him, Julia thought.

"Our enemies won't play by the rules. Why should we? Day after day, we read..."

Julia pulled the bell cord. She got off early and walked the rest of the way.

I hate talk of the war, of men away from home,
or men who won't come home...
of Japs and Nazis
and air raids and ships being torpedoed.
What I really hate is being alone
in this overcrowded place.

Julia came to the corner of Armistead Avenue and Queen Street. She was a bit frazzled from the heat of the early season. What air moved seemed only good enough to wrap the strong smell of seafood (an odor every citizen of Hampton was well familiar with) around her. She crossed to the far side of the street and went directly to St. John's.

There's no need to hurry to the market.
I'll sit with Lizzie and read Kate's letter.

Julia entered the first gate into the church grounds. There were gravestones of all sizes and shapes, winged angels and towering crosses – some dating back to the seventeen hundreds. But there was one grave she would visit. Along the edge of the grounds stood a magnolia tree, and under the tree, the grave of Lizzie Burcher. Julia didn't know anything more about Lizzie than what was on the stone: "Who departed this life May 28th 1848 in the 23rd year of her age." There were no other Burcher family members buried near her, but the inscription suggested that Lizzie had been loved.

> Dearest Lizzie, thou hast gone
> to thy rest not made with his hands
> eternal in the heavens;
> and we rejoice at thy far more exceeding
> weight of joy but ever mourn thy departure,
> for thy magnanimity of soul
> and pre-eminent worth.

Julia had sat beneath the magnolia tree many times and talked with Lizzie. There were confidences she shared only with her – thoughts she hadn't even expressed to Kate.

"I'm twenty-three – I've finally caught up with you, Lizzie," she said when she approached the grave. "But, I will always seek your counsel for you are my 'magnanimous, pre-eminent' friend. I'm married now – to Joe, of course. And I'm expecting a baby. There's a war. The whole world is at war. Kate has gone to Europe to serve doughnuts to the soldiers. I have a letter from her. George Goldstein is a flyer. The town has been taken over by the Army, but the Army refused to take Joe. So really, the whole world minus Mr. and Mrs. Joseph Keegan is at war. My dear, sweet Joe is angry. He will not talk about it. What can I do, Lizzie?" She picked up a fallen magnolia leaf and circled the tree.

"When I was twelve and read your tombstone, I thought twenty-three sounded pretty young to die. I went home and looked up the meaning of magnanimity. I understood then that you were a martyr. But why and how did you sacrifice your life? How did you die so young?

"Lizzie, what would you do if you were in my place? How can I get through to Joe?

He's so miserable. He has a good job. He's been promoted. But he hates that he isn't in the Army. Sometimes I think he hates me because he isn't in the Army."

Julia sat down in the shade of the tree. "Oh, Kate's letter...

> Dear Julia,
>
> Today we were out in the English countryside. It rained, and when it wasn't raining, it was foggy as soup. The winding country roads are beautiful in the haze. Some of them don't seem as wide as the trucks we're driving.
>
> Tonight we were invited to a party given by some British Naval officers. It was in a splendid old building. They treated us like royalty. The British know how to do that. There I was in this grand place and I was dressed in my Red Cross uniform – my hair still very kinky from a day in the rainy countryside – and I met a very charming British lieutenant. He looked gorgeous! But I'm determined not to allow myself any heart entanglements. One of our girls married someone over here and the Red Cross sent her home. Besides, how could I choose just one? They are all so adorable!

"That's my sister! I miss her, but I wouldn't want her to know Joe is still so moody. That's why I came to talk to you. I want Joe back. I'm lonely"

The church bells reminded Julia she needed to get on to the market.

"I must be going. Lizzie, what would be written on my tombstone if I should die at twenty-three? I need you to help me to do and say what is good for Joe."

Julia walked by the tall monument honoring "Our Confederate Dead." The statue of a Southern soldier stood on top with his rifle at rest.

> *Why must a man die in battle*
> *to be remembered as a hero?*

She closed the cemetery gate behind her.

"All right, Lady. What were you doing in the churchyard? You're under arrest!"

"Now, Charlie," another voice said, "we can't arrest a lady for

Time Will Tell

visiting the church."

"She's taking something."

"It's only a magnolia leaf, Charlie," Julia said. "May I put it back?"

"I'll be watching," he said.

Old Charlie only thought he was a police officer. Chief Curtis let him wear a hat and a badge, and he carried a cap gun. Locals would play along with Charlie,

> *but what will happen*
> *if he tries to arrest a stranger,* thought Julia.

He did watch and when she returned he warned her, "I'll have to take you in if I catch you doing that again, Miss."

"Thank you, Officer Charlie," she said.

Julia smiled and gave a little thank you nod to the man who had coaxed Charlie into not 'arresting' her. They didn't know each other, but everyone knew Charlie.

Cheyne's

The Sunshine Market was across the street from the church. Julia thought it was becoming the most fascinating store in Hampton. This was the place to get unusual items. In recent months people had moved to the Peninsula from all over the country. The Goldsteins made sure they had items that couldn't be found anywhere else in the area "Just tell Herbie Goldstein what you want. He'll get it for you."

Julia didn't know what a lot of the stuff was, but it was fun to look in the refrigerated meat counter, or watch when a customer ordered fresh lobster from Boston, or pickled pigs feet from...

> *where I don't want to know.*

"And what will you be needing today, young lady?" Herbie

Goldstein asked.

"I want something special. I'm quite sure I have plenty of stamps."

"Sounds like you need to talk to the head butcher." Daniel Goldstein had studied anatomy before deciding to come into the grocery business with his brothers. He was the man who knew his cuts of meat.

"What's your fancy, Miss Julia?" the butcher said. "I have steak and lamb chops. I could ground up some beef for you. I have chicken and fresh fish. And soaking in a barrel of brine, I have some corned beef."

"Corned beef. Can you give me some hints on how to prepare it?"

"Well, little lady, we have to ration our hints, you know."

"Julia, pay no attention to him.

"Get the lady some corned beef," Herbie Goldstein said, "and I'll tell her how to fix it just like Ma does.

"Is this a special occasion?" he asked Julia.

"I just want to surprise Joe. Make him a good dinner."

"Perhaps a little candlelight?"

Julia blushed. "I wrote Kate that George and Gene are in Europe."

"Tell us what you hear from your sister."

"She experienced her first 'lovely little air raid in London.' That's what she called it, but I don't think she thought it was lovely."

"No, I wouldn't think so. Tell her to watch out for my brothers. They like doughnuts. They might be stuffing them in their pockets when she isn't looking."

****

With her sack filled with corned beef, cabbage, potatoes and carrots, Julia left the store reciting the instructions she'd been given. "Don't rush it," he had concluded. "Let it cook for about three hours, turning it every thirty minutes."

Julia was hungry and hot and tired. She made it across the streetcar tracks just ahead of the streetcar. There were no empty seats, but there was room for her to stand. With the war on people gave up their seats to men in uniform – not pregnant women. At the next stop the car gained as many passengers as it lost, but Julia was able to slip onto a seat. When she sat down she had a strange sensation.

The baby kicked!
I know that was the baby kicking.

Time Will Tell

> *Oh, again!*
>
> *Can anything be so thrilling*
>   *as to feel a life inside of you?*
> *Here I sit on this crowded streetcar –*
>   *not one familiar face on the car –*
>   *They have no idea what I've just felt.*
>   *Baby, you've made me so happy.*
>   *Wait until we tell Daddy!*

The flutter repeated itself. She refused to shift at all, thinking she might not feel the baby's kicking if she did.

> *Oh, I wish Joe were here.*
> *You'll kick for your daddy, won't you Baby?*

Other passengers moved about her. They talked, but Julia didn't hear them. All she heard were her own joyful thoughts.

> *I've got to stand up soon, Baby.*
>   *The next stop is ours.*

Julia walked home with renewed energy – forgetting her hunger, how tired she was, or how hot the day had become. She skipped along and sang...

> Just Joey and me
>   And Baby makes three
> We're happy in myyyy blueueueue heaven!
>   Dah – de – dah – dah, dah, dah
>   Dah, dah , dah, dah – dah, de, dah, dah...
>   Dah – de – dah – dah, dah, dah
>   Dah, dah , dah, dah – dah – dah –
>   daaaaahhhh...
> Just Joey and me
>   And Baby makes three
> We're happy in my blue heavennnnnn!

Julia slipped quietly into the house hoping to avoid Mrs.Bryan and Bertie. She wanted Joe to be the next person she saw.

I'll put the meat on to cook slowly
        as Herbie said to do.
While it's cooking, I'll rest,
        but I must remember to turn the meat.
When Joe comes home,
        Baby and I will have a surprise for him.

Julia was too excited about the baby kicking and too anxious about her cooking to get any rest. When she heard Bertie at the door, she didn't answer. After she heard the child leave, she opened the door and picked up the box of clothing Bertie had left there. She tried on the clothes. Mrs. Bryan's things would do fine. After her warm trip to town Julia choose a light summer dress to keep on.

She put her hair up and then decided to wear it down. She found candles for the table and selected a couple of records for the phonograph. All the time she tried to find that special little kick... until she began to worry the baby wasn't going to kick for Joe.

Joe opened the door.

He's home. I must look a mess.

She rushed over to pull the phonograph lever for a record to drop. Ethel Merman sang "I Get a Kick Out of You."

I wonder if he'll catch on?

Julia met her husband at the top of the stairs, but it was he who surprised her. "For my beautiful wife – I love you!" he said handing her a bouquet of flowers.

"They're lovely, Joe. But, Joe, how did you know?"

"Know?"

"Baby kicked today. Put your hand here. Maybe you will feel him. Let's sit down."

"Yes, sit down," said Joe assisting her to the couch. "I'll take care of the flowers and then we'll sit there together until the little quarterback makes his move."

"Joe, on the streetcar this morning, I felt him move. It was so wonderful, Joe. You're going to be a daddy."

"Perhaps, if you sit more like you did on the trolley, he'll kick again."

Julia sat up straight. The two of them waited.

"Do you like the song? Kick out of you? Wait... there," she said, moving his hand.

"Yes, I felt him kick," Joe said.

"Why did you say 'him'?"

"You did, too."

"Did I? It could be a girl. Would that be all right?"

"If she looks like her mother."

"Joe, I have dinner almost ready. I'm so glad you didn't have a late class tonight."

"Benny Newman is going to be teaching my class."

"Good, we don't need the extra money, Joe. It will be so much nicer your coming home earlier."

"Julia..."

"What, Joe? Why have you given up the class?"

"The Army asked for a couple of NACA engineers."

"What do you mean?"

"I mean I'm going overseas as a civilian with the Army. I'll still be connected with NACA, but I'll go where the Army needs me. This is my opportunity to get out of here. I can't stay here any longer. I've been terrible to you."

"You haven't been yourself, but we're okay now, and the baby..."

"Julia, I've got to go. And I have to do it now. There's a rumor going around they're going to start making any of the NACA guys who enlist come back to Langley as privates. This is probably my only chance. I'm just lucky NACA is willing to let us go ... though I suppose no one says no to the Army."

Julia went over to the stove. She stuck a knife into the meat to test its doneness.

Why does he have to go?
Why?

She lifted the meat from the pan, drained it and placed it unto a platter. She spooned the vegetables onto the platter and placed it all in the oven set for 300 degrees as Herbie had said. "About ten minutes – to dry out the exterior a little," she remembered him saying.

Joe needs to feel the baby kick again.
I can't change his mind, but perhaps the baby can.

"It's all arranged," Joe said.

"Your meeting this morning?"

"Yes. I wanted to tell you, but when you went to your parents last

night, I couldn't stay up. I had to be sharp today."
Julia lit the candles.

I don't want him to see I'm crying.

The record kept spinning though the song had ended moments ago. It repeated it's "swish, swish, swish," the needle trapped in that circle at the center of the record.

"I hope I've cooked the corned beef enough. Herbie said it's difficult to overcook it."

"Smells good," he answered. "Let me change the record."

Julia set the food on the table. She watched her husband as he moved around the apartment.

It will be so awful without him.
I don't want him to go.
Why has he done this?

Joe sat across the table and reached for her hand.

He has never been more handsome
than he is at this moment.
The candle glow makes him radiant.
No, it's not that.
Joe's finally doing what he wants to do.
I must accept it.
Oh, Lizzie dear, if he doesn't come back,
I wish to die at twenty-three.

Eight

"Go down, Moses. Way down in Egypt land
Tell ol' Pharaoh, Let my people go."

Rose went to meet Samuel when she heard him singing outside. Twice a week he went over to Hampton Institute to sing with the "Crusaders," a group of shipyard men. "Mama, there's not two of us alike in the whole chorus. Most of us aren't musicians. We don't know one note from another. Mr. Flax insists that every voice does his part in the group – the good and the bad. He says we all blend in together. How that man makes us sound so good... it's magic."

She hadn't known what to think of it at first, but she'd noticed his singing was getting pretty good. "So," she said to Thomas, "if he wants to go singing, what's wrong with that? He's not having to pay."

"And he's not getting paid," Thomas pointed out.

"Come Thomas, listen to the two of them. There's another boy coming along with Samuel."

They were both dressed in suits and ties. They harmonized:

"Oh, Israel was in Egypt land...
... Let my peeeeeple gooooooo."

"Mama and Pop, I'd like you to meet my friend Jesse Nelson," Samuel said. "Jesse works in the shipyard. He's a welder."

"Nice to meet you, Jesse. I guess you're in the Crusaders, too?"

"Best time I've ever had, Mrs. Washington. Did Samuel tell you Mr. Flax passed up an opportunity to go on stage professionally? He's a baritone – has a pair of pipes, he does. He passed up his chance so he could stay here and teach his kind how to sing. He's a character. We have the best time."

"No, Samuel hadn't told me, but I knew the man was something special when he got my boy singing. Would you come in, Jesse? I have a fresh pitcher of lemonade in the ice box."

"I'd best be going on home, Mrs. Washington. Back to the yard in the morning, you know."

"So what's so different about him?" Rose asked Samuel. "You said you were all so different. He seems like a nice young man."

"Mama, they're all nice. I was just saying there are about thirty of us now and we have little in common. Some of the men are Pop's age. Some of them are roughnecks. There are carpenters, riveters, electricians; some from the Newport News shipyard and some from the Norfolk yard. They started a couple of years ago with just twelve men and it keeps growing. I guess 'Go Down, Moses' is Mr. Flax' favorite song. When he gets us all singing it, he probably has that ol' Pharaoh turning over in his pyramid."

Rose laughed and went in the house to get the lemonade, leaving her husband and son on the porch.

Hampton Institute   *Cheyne's*

"Pop, they had a notice at the school about some training."

"If you're talking about military training, you know what your mother will say."

"That's why I waited to talk to you."

"I see. Well, tell me what this notice said."

"In July the school is offering a $500 training course for just $45."

"That so? What kind of training?"

"Flying. I could get my CAA certificate. The course is the one prescribed by the government. The Army won't train colored so Hampton Institute is offering civilian training for us."

"Do you think the Army Air Corps is going to take you with this training?"

"That's the idea. We're going to show them what we can do and they'll have to take us."

"Son, there's nothing the government has to do but what it wants to do with a colored man. No, sir, they'll more likely have you shining the pilots' boots."

"Come on, Pop. We have to try. Isn't that what you've always said? Jesse and I know we can do this. They're drafting colored. You know if we let them get us that way, we'll be issued mops instead of guns."

"You check this thing out, Samuel. We don't need to upset your mother until we know all the facts. I can't say I feel good about aeronautics – it's too new."

"Thanks, Pop. I've made an appointment with Mr. Frank and Major Brown in the morning. Mr. Frank started the flying school. Major Brown's been running the school's ROTC program for years. Hampton Institute isn't going to let the Army continue treating us like we're of the social and mental level of Uncle Remus."

"I've brought you two some lemonade," Rose said. "What were you saying about Uncle Remus?"

"Mama, if you had been there tonight you'd have been crying tears of joy. There were some people visiting from one of the national magazines taking pictures and talking to school staff. I suppose the students were curious. They were following the magazine folks about the campus. When they started taking pictures of us, the students all stood around humming along with our singing. It was glorious, Mama. Their humming and our singing – it was glorious."

"No wonder you and that other boy were coming down the street like you were in a parade. Does my heart good to hear you singing."

"Sammy," Thomas said, "there was the funniest story in the Daily Press yesterday. I about busted my sides laughing so hard."

"What on earth are you talking about, Thomas?" Rose asked.

"I'm telling Sammy about this article in the newspaper. You see, son, a white man stole a lot of jewels. The police said he was the brains of the 'Madame Lady Finger Gang.' But he disappeared and they couldn't find him for near a year." Thomas paused to chuckle.

"Well, Pop, what was so funny?"

"This man sat under a sun lamp to darken his skin. And then he took burnt cork to make himself look really dark-skinned. You see, he hid out disguised as a Negro for a year."

"Did they catch him?"

"Sure did. But I was thinking how funny it would have been if some KKK had decided to string him up from a tree just because they didn't like the looks of a nigger."

"Thomas!"

"That's one for the books," Samuel said. "I never thought I'd hear about a white man posing as a Negro. A colored man is likely to be blamed for a robbery just because he's within ten city blocks of it. What was that white dude thinking?"

Still chuckling, Thomas answered, "Can't say I've figured him out."

"That's enough of that," Rose reprimanded them.

"I can tell you about another story that's not so funny.

"According to the paper," Thomas continued, "a U.S. sentry was walking his post in Bermuda. He called out for a worker to halt and claims the man made a move towards his back pocket. The soldier pulled his gun and fired eight shots at the man. Hit him at point-blank range six times."

"The worker is dead?" Rose asked.

"Six bullets hit him, Rose. He's more than dead. They asked the soldier why he'd fired so many shots and he said he might have 'gotten excited.'"

"This war is an awful thing," Rose said. "Killing doesn't ever solve anything."

"The point I was making was that these men had no dispute. The soldier just lost his head and now a man is dead. A colored man."

"What are they going to do?" Samuel asked.

"The paper said they were having an inquest, but I don't expect anything will be done. Now if the worker had been a white guy and the sentry a colored fellow, it'd be a different story."

"Thomas, can't you find something pleasant to talk about?"

"They say about a hundred stalks of bananas washed ashore in Florida."

"Where did they come from?"

"They're guessing it was the cargo of a torpedoed ship. Anyway, everybody was rushing to get free bananas. That's about all the good news

I could find in the paper and I suppose it wasn't good news for the cargo ship."

Samuel laughed.

"What's this world coming to when they're shooting down boats of bananas? And the two of you sitting here laughing. I'm going over to help Claire."

"Why? What's she doing?"

"She has her grandmother who needs help getting in the bed. I told her I'd come over to help her." Rose left the porch.

Thomas watched her until she was out of hearing distance. "She's right, Son. War is ugly. Always has been. The enemy is shooting down defenseless cargo boats and you want to take flying lessons."

"What do cargo ships have to do with my training for the Air Corps?"

"Shows how crazy this war is. It's a war between governments. It's not the Negro's war, but if we get into it, we'll go down in the crossfire just like that banana boat."

"You're not telling me I can't take the flying course at the Institute. Are you, Pop?"

"I'd like to tell you that," Thomas admitted. "It wouldn't stop you, though."

"I suppose the colored man has his own war, Pop. Maybe we can finally win the Civil War if we join up and prove ourselves. I know I can learn to fly just as good as any of those white boys at Langley."

First thing the next morning, Samuel came to the kitchen wearing his suit and carrying a bag of work clothes.

"Well, la-di-da and lardy-dardy! Samuel, do you have a date this morning?" his mother asked.

"I'm just going to see someone at the Institute."

"Well, she must be something special. You're dressed up like a plush horse. Where are you going? You haven't had your breakfast."

"I'll be fine, Mama. I'm in a hurry," he called back to her as he left the yard.

"Thomas," Rose sat at the kitchen table, "what's Samuel up to? That boy doesn't skip his breakfast."

"I guess we'll have to wait until he's ready to tell us."

"Tell us what?"

"I don't know. What he's up to."

"Thomas, you do know. What's going on?"

"Rose, we didn't want to say anything until he found out more.

Samuel has an appointment this morning at the Institute."

"Tell me, Thomas."

"There's a notice up at the school offering training for the Army. Samuel feels that if he waits to be drafted he won't be given a chance to do anything. He going to talk to Major Brown about taking a course – so he'll be trained before the Army gets him."

"Trained at what?"

"He can get his pilots license. He wants to go in the Army Air Corps."

"Lord, have mercy! Thomas, go after him. Tell him he can't do this. If men were meant to fly, God would have given them wings. Go after him, Thomas."

"I'm not going after him. The boy is going to have to learn for himself."

"The very idea of him flying in one of those awful machines is scary. But to go to war in one, that's beyond belief."

"I can't say the major won't let him take the course, Rose, but the white man's army isn't going to let him fly in the war. That much, I know."

"How can you be so sure?"

"A few months ago the Navy sent out letters to some Hampton pilots asking them to seek appointments as aviation cadets. When they found out the boys were Negroes, they quickly turned around and said it was against Navy regulations."

"What was against Navy regulations?"

"It's against Navy regulations for a Negro to serve in any branch of the Navy other than the messman branch. The Navy needs pilots, but they don't want any of our boys in the cockpit."

"Did you tell Samuel this, Thomas?"

"I told him they wouldn't take Negroes, but he wouldn't listen. I was just like him. I thought I could change the world. All I needed to do was get an education. But we found out a black man's education doesn't mean a lot. We have to let Samuel find out for himself. No, the government will give him some menial job, but he'll feel better about himself if he knows he can pilot a plane"

"I hope you're right. Why can't he keep his feet on the ground like God intended him to?"

"Don't you worry about Samuel. He's a man now. He must make his own decisions"

"Thomas, Samuel is our only child. God blessed us with one beautiful child. You men go on and on about changing the world. Well, I'm Samuel's mama. And I'll be his mama when he's thirty, forty, fifty...

The world might not ever change, but I'll always be his mama. And I'll never stop worrying as long as you men keep talking about changing the way things are.

"The streetcar's coming. Here's your lunch. Goodness, Samuel didn't even take his lunch with him."

Nine

- Summer of 1942 -

"It's not necessary that you buy a new carriage for the baby," Julia said. "I'm quite sure I can find someone to loan me one when the time comes."

"Brittingham's Furniture has a number of them to choose from," Joe answered. "It may be the only wheels we can buy until the war's over. I don't think it's a foolish expense. We can afford it. I have to report tomorrow and I want to know my wife and baby are going to be moving about town with a snappy rig. It'll be fun shopping for the carriage together... I think, being as you're pregnant," he continued, "you ought to move in with Mother. I don't want you being alone."

"I want to stay here. I'll be lonesome without you, but our place will be here for us when you return," she insisted. "If we give it up, we might not be able to get another. Apartments are so scarce."

There was truth to what Julia said. Builders couldn't keep up with the demand for living space to house all the new military and shipyard people. Hampton was getting its first apartment buildings and communities of duplex housing units. They were occupied as soon as they were built. Many people had rented rooms in their homes to accommodate the men. Even the colored institution was asked to share its living quarters with white officers.

"If I'd known you were going to get pregnant right away, I wouldn't have taken a place on the third floor. Just promise me you won't stay here when it gets too much."

"It won't get too much. I'll be fine. I want to stay here."

"Will you ask Elizabeth to come when the baby's due?"

"Of course. I know how much you think of Elizabeth. Mother

knows several women who've had her as their midwife. She must be very good."

"She'll be a lot of help to you. I'll feel much better knowing she's here."

"Then you'll let me stay here with the Bryans?"

"If that's really what you want."

The couple left for town to go "buggy shopping." They met a group of army men in uniform walking the other direction on the Boulevard.

One of them pointed across the water and asked Joe, "Is that the Norfolk Naval Base over there?"

"It is," Joe answered. "One of the finest harbors in the world."

"Is this the ocean?"

"This is Hampton Roads. This is where the James River, the Elizabeth River and the Nansemond River flow into the Chesapeake Bay."

"Is Buckroe Beach on the ocean?"

"Buckroe is on the Chesapeake Bay. The bay feeds into the ocean between Cape Charles and Cape Henry."

"Oh. Well, how do we get to the ocean?"

"You'd take the ferry over to Norfolk and then... "

"We don't have that much time. Is this the way to Buckroe Beach?"

"No. The new Port of Debarkation and the Newport News Shipyard are on up there. You're going the wrong way. You'll have to go back through town. You can take the streetcar out there."

"Thanks. We have less than forty-eight hours before we have to report to our unit. We want to see the beach. Do you people live here?"

"I'm shipping out tomorrow," Joe said.

"That so? Well, best of luck to you. Thanks for turning us around."

Sad as she was about Joe leaving, Julia saw and heard the pride in his voice when he told the men he was shipping out. She hated that he was leaving – that he'd be going "over there" – but it had taken that for him to be himself again.

"Buy a poppy, mister? Help the families of veterans."

Joe dug in his pants pocket. He handed the young girl two coins, "One for my wife too."

"Yes, sir. Thank you, sir," the girl was delighted with her double-sale.

"You're so good, Mr. Keegan," Julia said.

"Now we can go in town wearing our poppies and not have them all after us to buy one."

"Is that really why you bought them?"

"Truth? No."

"Go on."

"I thought the girl was cute."

"Joe."

"The truth is Mom's always told me they helped her when my father was killed. She's always had me buy them on Poppy Day."

"They're made by disabled veterans, aren't they?"

Joe walked over and put a penny in one of the new parking meters.

"Why did you do that?"

"It was expired. Mr.Curtis's man would be along soon to write a ticket," Joe said. "I read in the paper where Herbie Goldstein had gone before the city council asking that the meters be removed. People are shopping where they don't have to pay for parking. It's hurting his business."

"Do you see any others that have expired? Let's find them," Julia said.

"I may run out of pennies, but we can use what I have."

"And I'll bring pennies with me when I come to town while you're gone."

"You better not let Mr. Curtis see you."

"Why? Why should he care whose penny it is?"

"If it expires, the city gets much more than a penny. I'll buy you a soda at Woodward's if you'll quit looking at the meters."

"One soda; two straws?"

"Deal."

The couple went to a booth – their booth. Immediately Julia rubbed her fingers across the etched lettering on the table. J.K. – J.W. with a heart shape between them. "How old were we?" she asked.

"I don't remember. Eleven? Twelve?"

"It was the first time – just the two of us."

"I paid Harry to distract Kate so I could get you in here alone."

"You did? How much?"

"Oh, probably a stick of gum."

"A stick of gum and one soda for two. You were quite the big spender."

"I had to sell a bunch of papers to get that much money. You were the first girl I ever spent money on."

"Oh, Joe!" Her laughter turned to tears. "I'm going to miss you so much."

"I'll be back and we'll come to Woodward's."

"I hear you're..." The counter boy started to speak to Joe, but Joe shook his head. The boy understood Joe was telling him this wasn't a good time to talk about his joining up.

"One soda, two straws," Joe said.

Julia managed a smile. When the soda came, Julia was eager to wash the lump out of her throat.

Don't get all weepy, Julia.

Brittingham's Furniture   *Cheyne's*

Refreshed, they waited for the streetcar to pass and then went over to Brittingham's. "Someday I'll bring you back here and we'll pick out a dining room suite," Joe said.

"First, we'll need a house."

"I'll build you a house with a curved stairway just like that," he said pointing to the grand stairs that went to the balcony of the store.

"What can I help you young people with today?" the salesman asked.

"We're looking for a carriage."

"A baby carriage," Julia added.

"What's this one cost?" Joe asked going to the most elaborate, silk-lined one on the floor.

"We don't need all those frills. What if this is a boy?" Julia asked him.

"Then how about this one? Nothing prissy about this one. It has steel axles and springs and an automatic brake."

"Looks like an army tank," Julia answered. "Let's get something simple. This baby's going to walk before he's a year old. Then I'll have to store the stroller. This one over here will do fine." She'd selected the least expensive on the floor.

"I can see the little lady knows what she wants," the disappointed salesman sighed. "Where would you like us to deliver it?"

"There's no need for you to deliver it. We can walk it over to my folks. Right, Joe? They'll keep it there until I need it."

They strolled out of Brittingham's, past another furniture store and the Presbyterian Church. People passing by stretched their necks to see the baby in the carriage and then they grunted as if Joe and Julia had meant to trick them.

"Are you sorry you didn't let the man deliver this thing?" Joe asked.

"They act like we're guilty of some flimflam stunt," Julia answered. "It's not like we ask them to look at a baby."

"Give me two minutes," Joe said and he ran across to the five and dime.

Joe returned with a bag of baby blankets. He pulled one blanket from the bag and wrapped it around the bag and placed it in the carriage and they proceeded along Queen Street. When people looked in for a baby, he'd whisper to them, "He's sleeping," and they'd whisper back, "Oh, how dear!"

Julia's mother greeted them waving a letter from Kate. "The mailman's just been. Come in and we'll see what Kate's been up to. Oh, a baby carriage! I had one in the attic. I thought you knew."

"Joe wanted to do this. Can I store it here until I need it?"

"Of course, you can. I hope you didn't buy anything else. We have everything you'll need."

Mrs. Walters tore open the letter. "I'll read it aloud."

Dearest Mother and Father,

There's nothing like an ocean and a little war to make one homesick. Don't misunderstand me, I love the girls I'm working with and I certainly do love the men, but sometimes I find myself missing the smell of pungent steamed crabs. And I miss sunshine. But most of all, I miss my family.

I feel I can tell you now that my first impression of the British was not good. They seemed to have no heart. They looked tough and shabby – for which I couldn't blame them having gone through the blitz. But they wouldn't look us in the face. I felt they resented us. I didn't understand.

Yesterday I spent some time with a local girl. Boy did I learn a thing or two! She showed me where her father's house stood before the bombings. She showed me her church that had lost its roof. She took me into the underground where they spent their nights for most of a year. She talked of how strangers helped one another, of heroic efforts to rescue people from the rubble. She told of when the air raids stopped and things got quiet again. Now they had time to look at the chaos around them. Time to feel hunger. Time to mourn.

Then Rosemary said the most unusual thing, she said 'I sometimes wish they'd come back.'

Well, I wasn't sure I understood her.

Then she said, "We've lost our spirit. We need something to shake us up again."

Imagine me at a loss for words! Oh, I pray this war will end soon

Rosemary and I shared some special moments. We each got a kick out of hearing the other speak English. And she gave me my very first official London afternoon tea... and what she called a biscuit.

I hope you are well and that Hampton and neither of you change one little bit while I'm away.

Your loving daughter,
Kate

"Your father will be so pleased to hear from her." Mrs. Walters placed the letter on a hall table where her husband would see it when he came in the door.

"Now, I insist that you two stay for dinner. I called at the house, but Mrs. Bryan said you'd gone to town."

"Mother, not tonight."

"Of course, tonight. I had Mr. Goldstein send over a pot roast. You want Joseph to have a good meal before we send him off. I've invited your mother, Joe."

I don't want to share Joe tonight.
It's been a perfect day until now.

"I'll be in the kitchen. Perhaps you would like to go out by the water?"

"I don't want to be here tonight, Joe. I want you to myself. Mother shouldn't just tell us we're staying."

"We have to stay for dinner, but I'll insist we leave early," Joe answered. "Remember when we used to take the boat over to Ft. Wool?"

"I never told Mother we went over there. I wonder if she knew."

"Remember when we went up to Indian River Creek and some children up there challenged us to a race around an island?" Joe asked.

"Only they didn't warn us about the sandbars and we swung in too close and got stuck," Julia said, laughing.

"I was so embarrassed and all you did was sit there and laugh, just as you're doing now," Joe said. "You could have helped."

"That was the time we discovered Mr. Carmine's Candy Shack." Julia reminded him. "We'd take the boat up there and give him pennies for as many fire balls and Mary Janes as they would buy."

"Then we'd come back around Blackbeard's Point. Somebody always shouted they saw the pirate's head under the water and we'd pretend to be scared and we'd take off as fast as that little fifteen horsepower engine could go – with Blackbeard chasing us. Sometimes I almost believed it," Joe said.

"Joe, I remember when my folks finally agreed that I could go down to Buckroe Beach on the streetcar with you. Kate and Henry went with us that first time. We rode the 'Dips' and you held your hands up when we went over the big dip and I thought you were the bravest boy I'd ever seen. We named every horse on the Merry-go-Round. Shadow was your favorite. The man that ran it would let it go extra long for us. And the man on Monkey Island would let us feed the monkeys raisin bread.

"I wonder what it's going to be like down there this year," Julia mused. "Somewhere I heard they told them they could keep it going but they'd have to put tin cans over their lights to keep them from being visible from the water."

"The hotel's been taken over for military housing," she said. "They probably won't be able to bring in the excursion trains from Richmond. The war is ruining everything."

"We couldn't do much swimming after the jellyfish came in, but we'd catch them in buckets."

"The Dips" *Cheyne's*

"You'd catch them," Julia said. "Disgusting slime was all they were. I didn't want anything to do with them. I remember when you tricked little Sammy Atkins into picking one up off the beach."

"I told him the jellyfish was dead. And it was."

"But they still sting if you touch them," Julia said. "Sammy's hand was one big red welt from picking up that jellyfish."

"When I told him he could make a jellyfish sandwich," Joe said, "I didn't think he'd try to do it."

"Do you remember spending a whole morning looking over the fence at Bay Shore?" Joe asked. "I remember you asking why the Negroes wanted to be out in the sun. 'They'll get darker, won't they?' you asked."

"And you said, 'Maybe if they peel they'll turn white.' I thought about that a lot. If they peeled and turned white they could come to Buckroe. I decided that was the thing for them to do. Finally, I asked Fran."

"Who?" Joe asked.

"You remember, Fran, the colored girl Mother used to have come do her cleaning. She'd been coming since before I was born. One day Mother told me Fran had a little girl. Oh, was I jealous! All the time I'd thought Fran belonged to us. How could she have another family?"

"Did you ever see her daughter?"

"No but after Fran left, Mother told me her little girl was blind. Fran had moved to Hampton to be near the Negro school for the deaf and blind. I think she got a job out there and that is why she left us.

"What did Fran say when you asked her about colored people peeling down to white?"

" 'Young lady,' she said as sternly as she ever spoke to me, 'white folks don't become Negroes when they get sunburned and colored folks don't peel and become white folks. God made us the way we are. We are all God's children.' "

"Well, God's children on the other side of the fence make better music than we do," Joe said. "I've always wished I could go to Bay Shore to listen to them play and watch them dance. Peter and I got off at the Bay Shore streetcar stop one time. We were going to go see what we could see."

"What was it like? I wish I'd been with you," Julia said.

"The motorman said, 'This is not your stop, boys. Get yourselves back on the streetcar.' So, we got back on. Maybe he thought we wanted to stir up trouble."

"Well, the motormen had reason to think you two were up to something," Julia said.

"Do you think it's like Buckroe?" she asked.

"Did you really ask Fran if she'd peel would she be white?" Joe asked.

"If Mother had known I did, she'd have whipped me good... Joe, will you write me?"

"If you don't expect long letters like Kate writes, I'll..."

"Everyone's here now and dinner is ready!" Mrs. Walters called.

"I wouldn't expect you to write long letters, Joe. You never wrote but a note from Blacksburg. That was okay. But you'll be over where the war is. I'll want to know you're safe."

"Don't get all upset if you don't get a letter – I mean, like a week passes and you don't hear from me. Overseas mail sometimes gets backed up. Now, we better go eat your mother's pot roast."

"Wait, Joe. The baby's kicking. Put your hand here. Feel him?"

"If that's not a boy, it's Rosie the Riveter!" Joe said. "He's not hurting you, is he?"

"Not yet. Truly, it feels wonderful. He's probably, like you, excited about Mother's dinner."

"You know I'd rather be in our place with you," Joe said. "My mother is so angry with me, I hope she doesn't cause a scene."

"Can we help it if we love you?" Julia asked.

"No, I guess you can't," he said with a laugh.

A houseful of family and friends greeted Joe and Julia when they went inside. "We had planned a baby shower, but we decided to have it while Joe's here," Mrs. Walters said, "and have everyone here to see Joe before he leaves."

Julia looked around the room and forced herself to smile at these people before them. There was Mrs. Kelsey who she had talked with at the streetcar stop. Mrs. Kelsey who recognized her only as one of the Walters' girls. And there was Mrs. Hanson who had lived across the street from them years ago. Julia knew who she was because people had always talked about her dying her hair. It was an odd shade of purple. Each of these women had brought along her husband who Julia and Joe had only a second-hand acquaintance with.

There were several couples from the neighborhood who had always responded with lovely gifts for the girls' graduations, from kindergarten to high school. Julia felt embarrassed that they had been asked to give again.

Both of her mother's parents and the senior Walters were there. Joe's mom was there moving about in the background.

Poor Mother Keegan.
She's obviously trying to keep herself too busy
to think about Joe's leaving.

Julia pulled Joe across the room to speak to her cousins, Hallie and Mable and their mother, Julia's Aunt Bernice. "Your Uncle Bob wanted to come," the aunt explained. "He's lost several men to the draft, so he's having to make deliveries himself."

"But how did you get here?" Julia asked.

"We came across on the ferry. It was a lovely day."

"Yes, it was," Julia agreed, "but the ferries and streetcars are so crowded now."

"It's a pleasure getting away from Norfolk," Aunt Bernice said. "That Gypsy Rose Lee and her kind have given Norfolk a notorious reputation."

"Is she the one that does the strip-..."

"She and others like her."

"I heard she has a classy act," Mable said.

"Where did you hear that?" Mable's mother asked her.

"Oh, I don't remember. I just heard ..."

"There is no such thing as a 'classy act' in those sleazy places."

World War I had left scars on the City of Norfolk. The citizens didn't have good feelings about the military. They tended to expect more of the same unmanageable expansion they had seen during the First World War. Public utilities would be strained beyond capacity. The housing situation would be impossible, with the population growing by leaps and bounds. Public transportation would be overcrowded. The harbor would be filled with ships flying flags of every nation waiting to unload or take on freight. The citizens of Norfolk remembered how their town had become a major city in just a few months – once the Navy Department decided to make Hampton Roads the greatest naval base in the United States. When World War One was over Norfolk had a red light district and an assortment of lurid businesses. Citizens saw this as the direct result of the presence of the military. In 1918 Norfolk had given the victorious soldiers and sailors a hero's welcome, but in the '40s they weren't ready to give their city back to the disreputable behavior of men in uniform.

Ferry Station   *Cheyne's*

"Last year they shut down the bordellos. We thought that was a good thing. But now East Main Street is a row of beer joints, penny arcades, peep shows and shooting galleries," Hallie said.

"And tattoo emporiums where sailors pay to have pictures of naked women burned onto their skin," Mable added.

"You're lucky you live on this side of the water," Julia's aunt told her. "I'm afraid for my girls to go to town in broad daylight."

"Did you receive my note, Hallie?" Julia asked. "It's so nice having clothes that aren't too tight. I'll take good care of them and get them back to you after the baby."

"Have you picked names for the baby?"

"If it's a boy," Julia said, "I want him to be a junior."

"And, if it's a girl?"

"We haven't decided. I was thinking of naming her after Kate."

"She'd be thrilled, if you did. What have you heard from her?"

"When the war is over she never wants to see – or smell – a doughnut again."

"What does she have to do?"

"The girls make and serve coffee and doughnuts to the troops. Each day they start very early making fresh doughnuts. Kate says her hair and clothes are so penetrated with the fumes of melted fat and doughnut flour that GIs lift their noses and say, 'a Clubmobile girl, I suppose?' "

"Is that what she's called?"

"When they're not working in one of the canteens in the cities, they take the doughnuts to the men in a 'clubmobile.' "

"How close does she get to the war?" Mable asked.

"I'm sure they stay away from the firing. Kate doesn't tell me the names of places she goes. She says she often doesn't know. There are no signs in all of England. They took them down so they wouldn't help the enemy."

"I think we ought to be as considerate of the boys that are stateside," Mable said. "You know, give them doughnuts and be friendly."

"I know what you're getting at, young lady," Aunt Bernice said. "Mable thinks we should invite the boys to the house for dinner."

"Well, in Hampton, the people invite the servicemen to dinner," Mable said.

"I see quite enough bell bottoms without inviting them to dinner, thank you."

"But they have no place to go."

"They flock to those flophouses like bees to honey."

"Mother thinks," Mable said looking to Julia and Joe, "the good Lord is going to destroy Norfolk like He did Sodom and Gomorrah in the Old Testament."

"Hallie, where is Matt now?" Julia asked thinking it best to change the subject.

"I think he's been all over, but I never know where. He's not allowed to say. It bothers me to think that our mail is being read by strangers before it gets to us."

"I tell her," Aunt Bernice said, "the censors aren't interested in the personal stuff. They look for things that might give the enemy information. She shouldn't be embarrassed to write what's in her heart."

"Who are the censors?" Hallie asked. "Who would want to read other's mail?"

"It's their job. There aren't many jobs related to the war that people want to do. You mustn't take such things personally."

"Well, if you two," Hallie looked at Julia and Joe, "have something private you want to say to each other, you'd best say it now. Soon you'll be talking through the United States Victory mail system."

"Does Matt say anything about what it's like over there?" Julia asked.

"He says he gets seven packs of butts – that means cigarettes, four candy bars and seven sticks of gum. That's his ration."

"What if he didn't smoke?"

"Matt says the guys who don't smoke make out like bandits. Those that do are willing to trade them most anything for another pack of 'butts.' Some guys are even willing to work extra duty for cigarettes."

"Julia," Mrs. Walters called to her, "you young people come to the table."

"Joe, I put you there beside your mother. Julia, I want you next to me. I apologize that we don't have more elbowroom, but isn't it nice having us all together? I was afraid I'd have to send your father out combing the streets of the city looking for the two of you, and then there you were coming up the walkway with the baby stroller. Before you leave, I must get a picture of that. Hazel went to…"

> *Oh, Mother!*
> *This is Joe's last day home and you've trapped us here –*
> *at opposite ends of your dinner table –*
> *with all these people.*
> *I know you mean well, but couldn't you have asked me first?*
> *You did the same thing to Kate when she came home for her day*
> *off before leaving Camp Pat.*
> *You invited everyone*
> *who was available for a big send-off.*
> *Kate wanted time with her family; not a party.*
> *And right now I want to be with Joe.*

Around the table the conversation progressed:
"Did you hear Eddie Drummond is alive?"

"No, last I heard he was missing in action."

"Rhonda got a letter from him saying he had participated in several engagements with the enemy, but he's all right."

"That's wonderful. I know she must be relieved."

"So, how do you think this war is going to change American women?"

"They're taking over the jobs of men in all the factories. In many cases they're getting the same pay the men got. We're fooling ourselves if we think they're going to give up their jobs when the men return."

"You're darned tooting, we're going to do no such thing. We're proving we're capable of doing just about everything a man does. And we look better in pants than most men do."

"I cannot disagree. But you look better in skirts and we'd look like hell in skirts. Someone has to wear skirts."

"The paper said people at Virginia Beach can see ships out in the ocean that have been struck by torpedoes from German u-boats."

"It must be terrifying for our boys who are assigned to ships with those u-boats sneaking around sinking everything in sight."

"I never thought they'd get in this close to our shore."

"I've heard talk of German agents being brought to our coast."

"We should have entered this war before the German's gained so much power."

"There're still people who think we shouldn't be involved now."

"Would they wait until the Japs have infiltrated the west coast and Germany has landed on the east?"

"If the nation hadn't voted Roosevelt in for another term, we might not be in this thing."

"How do you figure that?"

"Like Wilkie said, Roosevelt was leading us into war, trading battleships for bases."

"If the President hadn't stepped up our rearmament program, we would have been up the creek without a paddle."

"If you ask me, the President put us in the war with that Lend-Lease Program of his. Our merchant ships were carrying arms to England. That's what got us into this submarine war. Hardly a day goes by without a report of another torpedoed ship. I'm quite afraid the German's u-boats are going to blow us out of the water for good."

"The nation must pull together now and support the war effort. It's too late to stop what's already in motion. Our young men are being sent overseas to fight. We must stand united."

"But of course, we will. I just wish there was some other way to handle international disputes…"

"There's talk some Nazis may be working inside our unions stirring up trouble."

"That wouldn't be hard to do."

"Don't you think you'd know a Nazi if one was working with you?"

"If the fellow spoke German, I certainly would be suspicious. But there are a lot of Germans who were educated in the States. I suppose they could fool people."

"Yes, they're not like the Japanese. You can tell a Jap when you see one."

"Can you tell a Jap from a Chinaman?"

"The Japs have a broader face with a flat nose."

"That doesn't help much. I still wouldn't know one from the other. I heard the actors who play Japanese in the movies are Chinese. That doesn't help."

"On this side of the country, we don't have many Japanese. It's the Germans we have to worry about."

"We have some very prominent citizens in Hampton who are from Germany. Quite a few. The Berghoffs, for instance."

"They caused some ill-feelings during the last war when they insisted on flying the German flag."

"Yes, but I'm sure they have no sympathies with the Third Reich."

"On the West Coast the government rounded up all the Japanese after they discovered they were marking their fields so the Japanese navy would know where to strike. When they shelled that oil field in California the Japs were only ten or fifteen miles out."

"Some of those people our government rounded up were United States citizens. Can the government force them out of their homes?"

"The article in *Life* magazine said the people were settled comfortably and prepared to wait out the war in 'willing internment.' They will have their own democratic government in each camp. And schools… and stores…and theatres and whatever they need."

"Speaking of *Life* magazine, I don't understand why the government allows them to print some of their articles. There was an article about a new machine gun that's supposed to revolutionize warfare. They showed every detail of how the gun is made and what it can do. I hope the Axis governments don't subscribe to *Life*."

"It's hard to know what the government wants the enemy to know.

They say we must be careful not to talk too freely as 'someone may be listening.' Then the papers and newsreels seem to tell it all."

"If you pay close attention, most of what they say happened weeks earlier."

"Did any of you hear about the people who were rescued by a US destroyer, the USS Roper? A woman had given birth to a baby boy in a life raft after the Germans torpedoed the ship she was on. Can you imagine?"

"Noooo," Mrs. Walters said. "Oh. We have gifts for Julia to open. Shall we all go out on the porch? We can have cake out there."

Julia's mother relocated her guests, but the war remained the topic of conversation. Julia unwrapped, and acknowledged as best she could with so much talking going on, the precious things that had been brought for the baby.

"I want to tell you, Joseph Keegan," Mr. Hanson said, "I, for one, am very proud of you. It's shameful what some young men do to avoid the draft. I don't know if it's true or not, but I heard one man was found dressed in women's clothes – passing himself off as a female."

"Some of the boys break away from training. Then they're on the run. If the military finds them, they'll be charged with treason."

"Isn't that a bit harsh? Some of them may never have been away from home before this."

"When your country's at war, you answer the call. Do you know that anyone hiding a deserter could be sent to prison?" There's no place for a deserter to go. His family can't hide him. He'd be better off serving like he's supposed to."

"War is such an ugly business."

"Well, it's young men like Joseph here, who is determined to serve his country, that are going to bring this thing to an end."

"Yes, we are all proud of Joe."

"Were you surprised at the findings of the presidential commission investigating why the U.S. was caught unprepared at Pearl Harbor?"

"I never thought they'd find Admiral Kimmel 'in dereliction of duty.' It's terrible that a man in such a high position could be so negligent as to allow the deaths of so many of our men. But it says something for our government that they moved quickly to see where the blame should be placed."

"I heard some of the families of sailors who died have said that the man should be executed for treason."

"Both Admiral Kimmel and General Short... or at least court-martialed. The report said they should have been aware of what the Japs were planning and they failed to prepare for an attack which allowed the Japanese to have complete success."

"We should direct our anger at the Japs. When the war is over, we'll have time to consider what should be done with Kimmel and Short. The important thing is they are no longer in command of any of our troops."

"If your son had been killed at Pearl Harbor, I think you wouldn't be satisfied waiting until the war is over."

"Thank you all for the lovely gifts," Julia said. "It was nice of you to come. Joe and I appreciate it. Thank you."

"Yes, thank you," Joe said. "Now, if you will excuse us, Julia and I have only hours left before I must report."

"Oh, but you didn't have any cake," Mrs. Walters said following them as Joe swept Julia towards the door. "And I wanted to take your picture."

"I'm sorry, Mother. Dinner was very nice, but we must leave now. I'll come by in a couple of days to pack the baby things out of the way. Thank you for dinner and all."

"I'll drive you home," Mr. Walters said.

"Joe, where's your mother?" Julia asked. "You have to see her before we leave."

Joe found his mother and through her sobs she told her son, "Your father would be proud of you and ... I'm proud of you."

"I'll be back, Mom. I promise."

Ten

Julia had closed the windows during the night to keep out the storm. She awoke in a sweat. She opened the windows and discovered the stickiness in the aftermath of the storm would do little to cool her. There was a haze on the water that hid the Norfolk side from her view. Foghorns conversed, their deep tone playing a lovely haunting song as they alerted each other of their presence.

What is it like, being on a ship in such a heavy fog you can't see what's ahead of you?
You hear another ship's horn.
Do you move this way, or that?
Is there some kind of code ship captains use?
It all sounds like the same low moan.
How is it they avoid ramming each other?

How can Kate stand one rainy day after another?
At least there's hope the sun will break through this.
She's had weeks of rain.
Is that where Joe will end up?
What are the chances Kate will be serving doughnuts one day and Joe will step up?

I'm sure the Bryans aren't awake yet.
It's so hot up here. I have to get out.

Julia slipped on one of the dresses Mrs. Bryan had sent up to her. She dismissed the idea of carrying an umbrella. "There was a beautiful rainbow yesterday. That means the sun will come out today," she told herself.

> *Joe's been gone two weeks.*
> *I can't keep moping about.*
> *I've gone to St. John's everyday since he left.*
> *I thought talking with Lizzie*
>   *would help me be strong.*
>   *I wonder if it isn't morbid.*

> *Today, I'll see if my cat friend can cheer me up.*

Julia tiptoed down the stairs trying not to disturb the Bryans.

> *I don't want to wake Bertie.*

The front door wined when she opened it. She slipped out and down the porch steps and then she saw Bertie.
"Bertie, what are you doing in the bushes?"
"Sh-h-h-h"
"Does your mother know you're out here in your nighty?"
"Don't tell her, Julia. Where are you going?"
"I couldn't sleep. I'm going to take a walk before it gets too hot."
"May I come with you?"
"Certainly not in your nighty and not without asking your mother."
"They're still asleep."
"Then we'll do it another day."
"Promise?"
"Promise. Don't step on your mother's jonquils."

As Julia rounded the corner, she admitted to herself,
> *I'm going to the house*
> *and if the man I saw in the window*
>   *is a draft dodger I'm ...*
> *I'm going to try to help him get away.*
> *If they catch him, he'll be charged with treason.*
>   *That's what they said at Mother's.*
> *I haven't been able*
>   *to get him out of my mind since.*

> *They also said anyone who helped deserters*
> *could go to prison.*
> *Why am I getting involved?*
> *I don't even know the boy.*
> *Right, I don't know the boy.*
> *If he's hiding from the draft,*
> *he might deserve what they do to him.*
> *But I don't think so.*
> *I think he's wrong... but he might be scared.*
> *Certainly he's scared.*
> *I agree with Aunt Bernice.*
> *It's too harsh to charge him with treason.*

Julia continued towards the house telling herself the government wouldn't send a pregnant woman to jail for aiding a draft-dodger. She would do what Lizzie would do.

The newspaper boy was the only one she saw on the street. She waited until he made it to the end of the street before she approached the house. This time she didn't go to the door. She circled the house trying to see in the windows.

> *If he's still in there,*
> *he may be crazy with hunger, or fear.*
> *If I startle him, he could react violently.*
> *I shouldn't be here.*
> *Maybe Dad would help him.*
> *No, I can't ask Dad to get involved.*
> *If I want to be magnanimous,*
> *I must do it myself.*

The back door was wide open. Julia climbed up the porch steps and, there in the middle of the kitchen floor, was the man she had seen in the window. He was asleep. He had a beard. His clothes were ragged and wet. He looked like someone had dragged him through the river. Was this a scared boy, or just a bum?

Julia was about to turn and tiptoe away, when she spotted the cat. It saw her too and squirmed. The man scolded it muttering something Julia couldn't understand. He was holding the cat down.

"What are you doing to that cat? Let go of him," she ordered.

The man opened his eyes and focused on the girl standing over him.

"Hello," he said. "The cat got its foot caught in a piece of wire.

He's got a nasty cut and, having nothing to wrap it with, I've been holding it so he won't lose more blood. Could you take the cat? See that its foot is taken care of?"

"Oh, kitty, you are hurt. Here, may I pick him up?"

The man handed her the cat. "We were both caught out in the storm," he said. "Actually, I heard him cry and went out to find him. There he was caught in a wire fence unable to get loose. I had to pull hard to free him and then the foot started bleeding. There was nothing I could do but hold it. It's stopped bleeding, hasn't it?"

"Yes, it seems to have, but it seems sensitive to the touch. I think it needs to be cleaned good and then bandaged."

"Can you take care of him?" the man asked. "I can't stay. He's not my cat. I must go."

"You don't look like you're ready to go anywhere. I saw you here before. You've been hiding here, haven't you?"

"I have. I'm ready to turn myself in," he added.

"No. I mean, that may not be wise," Julia said. "I'm guessing you're a draft dodger. Do you know that's considered treason? Not just desertion, but treason."

He didn't respond.

"If you turn yourself in," she continued, "I'm not sure what they'll do to you. You shouldn't have run, but I don't think you can go back now. Not now. If you want me to, I'll try to help you."

"I want you to help this poor cat. If you want to help me, forget you've seen me. Please, take Snarls."

"If he's not your cat, why do you call him by name?"

"That's just something I called him while we were hanging out together."

"I can't take the cat to the place I live," Julia said. "If you'll stay here with it, I'll go home and get something to clean the wound with and a bandage."

"And the authorities, if you're smart."

"I'm not smart," she said smiling.

"You could get in serious trouble for not turning me in."

"If you don't tell me you're a draft dodger, I can't be responsible for knowing that you are. Let me take care of the cat before you decide what to do," she urged him. "Will you wait here with him?"

"I'll wait with the cat. You take care of him. Forget me."

"I'll be back as soon as I can," Julia answered. "I don't live far from here. I think he'll be all right. What did you call him?"

"Snarls. That's what he did when I first met him. I suppose I scared him. I woke from a nightmare with this cat all hunched up about to attack me. He snarled and the hair on his back was standing straight up. It was soon obvious that he was more scared than scary, so I named him Snarls."

"Not a very affectionate name for such a sweet cat."

"A manly name. Wouldn't you agree?"

"I think I'll call him Kitty, if you don't mind."

She left by the back door making sure it was closed.

I cannot tell how old he is.
With the beard he has, he can't be so young.
I don't know how long he's been hiding.
Whatever can I do?
Maybe put off the inevitable for just a little while.
Once I take care of the cat,
I can find some old things of Joe's
and some scissors would be helpful.
He can trim up a bit so he doesn't look ...
like Rumpelstiltskin.
I have my own little Red Cross.
I'm neutral.
I give care to any in need of it –
two legged or four legged.

Then she thought of Joe joining the Army when he didn't have to – so eager to serve his country. This man should feel that way.

Take care of the cat. Forget him.
If I didn't know they would
charge him with treason for deserting,
I might even hope they'd catch him.
Other boys are serving
and surely they are scared.

I didn't want Joe to serve.
How is that different from this boy
not wanting to go?
It seems he needed the 4F classification
Joe didn't want.

Julia hurried to the house and up two flights of stairs. She had her first aid kit all assembled. She tossed it into the small suitcase her father had used to bring her clothes. She went to Joe's wardrobe and grabbed a shirt and pants from the back.

Joe hasn't worn these things since we were married.

"A towel, a washrag, scissors, what else?" She put things in the case. "If I had a belt, that might help. But I don't."

Julia hadn't had much appetite since Joe left. She hadn't been to the market. Mrs. Bryan had baked cornbread and sent some up to her. Julia put the cornbread and a couple of apples in with the other things and closed the case.

"I'll clean up Kitty's foot and give the clothes and food to the man. He's going to get caught. I can't help that. He shouldn't have tried to run. But if he could avoid getting caught until the war is over, perhaps they'll go easier on him."

Halfway down the stairs, Julia recognized Bertie's familiar knock on her door. "Just a minute, Bertie," she called, and she climbed back up to her living area and shoved the case behind the couch.

"I'm coming, Bertie. I locked the door."

Julia came down the stairs to unlock the door. She felt faintish. She sat down on the steps and invited Bertie to join her.

"Julia, I heard you up here. I thought that you might like to do something."

"Do something?"

"School's out for the summer and Joe's gone. I can keep you company so you don't get lonesome."

"Perhaps, if we ask your folks, you could go to town with me."

"Now?"

"No, tomorrow. I'm not going to town today."

"What are you doing?"

"I'm going to see a friend. In fact, I was just getting ready to go."

"Will you ask Mother?"

"About our going to town tomorrow? Yes, I will."

"She's in the backyard."

"Bertie, I'll see her this afternoon. I really need to go now. You may tell your mother I'm going to be asking, if you like."

"I will. I'm sure she'll say yes." Bertie left Julia on the steps.

Now, I must go back up to get the suitcase.
Hopefully, I can leave without Bertie following.
I'm too tired to be sneaking around.
It's getting very hot. I'm exhausted.

Julia found the cat alone on the landing of the stairs. He moved his head ever so slightly acknowledging her. "Oh, Kitty," she said, "it does hurt, doesn't it? And he left you here alone. I suppose he didn't believe me. I'm going to take you to the kitchen where I can put you on the counter." She lifted him as she spoke.

"I've something in my first aide kit that should clean that paw. I promise to be very gentle. Oh, you poor little thing.

"I shouldn't have bothered with stuff for the deserter. Now, he's deserted you. I only asked him to wait with you."

Julia picked up the suitcase while holding the cat. When she did the cat wiggled and she nearly let him fall.

"Kitty! Oh, have I hurt you?"

The man appeared from the back of the house, "Let me help you."

"I thought you were gone," she said. "Yes, I need you to carry the case into the kitchen. I almost dropped the cat just now."

"That would have done him no good."

"I realize that."

The man followed her with the case. "Is there anything else you'll be needing me for?"

"If you're not in too big a hurry, you could hold him while I clean the wound."

"Of course." He placed his hands around the cat.

Julia rubbed the paw with a cotton ball soaked with iodine. "I don't see any inflammation yet. Hopefully this will take care of it. Hold him still. I'm going to wrap his leg with gauze. Try to keep it clean."

"This is not my cat, lady. Don't tell me to keep it clean. I won't be here."

"I wasn't telling you to keep it clean. I said, I'm putting the gauze on to keep it clean. Run. Go. Do you really think they won't find you?"

"I told you earlier," he insisted. "I'm going to turn myself in."

"What is the penalty for treason? Death?"

"I'd welcome death," he said.

"If you have no fear of death, why didn't you enlist... or why did you run?"

"Just get Snarls fixed up and I won't be here."

"There are some clothes in the case. They belong to my husband. When we're through with Snarls, take the case and clean yourself up. There's some cornbread and fruit, too. You don't need to worry about my saying anything. I won't. I don't like what you're doing, or what you've done, but that's your affair."

"You don't know what I'm doing or what I've done."

"There, I think that will stay on the leg," Julia said. "I'll come back and check on him. You can put him down on the floor," she said.

The two people watched the cat try to steady himself on his feet.

"It's going to take a little getting used to, Kitty," she said. "I'm sorry."

"He's going to be all right," the man said. "I'm glad you came. I feel better leaving him."

"But he's not your cat, you said."

"No. He's not. Well, bye, Snarls. Do what the doctor says."

He started towards the back door.

"I told you I brought you some clothes to change into."

"And I told you not to try to help me."

"Don't be a fool. If you're going to turn yourself in, at least try to look like someone they won't shoot on sight. There are some scissors to shape up your beard. Take the case."

"I'm not what you think," he said.

"It doesn't matter what I think, does it?"

"You think I've deserted."

"I don't know, or care why," Julia said. "Just take the case."

"I was on a boat. We were spotted. There was no way of maneuvering out of their range. We fired one torpedo that just missed them. I gave the order to abandon ship. Then they killed the boys in the water. They moved into them and killed them," he repeated. "All I could do was watch."

"It must have been horrible," Julia said. "You are the captain?"

He didn't reply. She didn't need a reply.

Of course, he is. He said he gave the order.

"I heard of a Japanese ship that opened fire on men in rafts," Julia said.

"People say the enemy is ruthless. But it's so hard to believe they would kill defenseless sailors. And your men weren't even in rafts?"

The man said nothing.

"Do you blame yourself for what happened? Is that why you hide? Well, the Navy won't blame you, I'm certain, they won't."

"You don't know what you're talking about," he said in a murmur so low she thought he hadn't meant her to hear.

Julia stood there silently trying to understand what he was thinking.

He doesn't care what the Navy thinks.

He's not going back – he's deserting.

"Do you understand?" she asked. "It has been on the news, our government is going to treat deserters as traitors. If you turn yourself in, they will send you back. If you refuse to go back and they find you, they may kill you. If they see you looking like this, they will shoot you on sight."

"You don't understand. I was the captain. I gave up my boat and then I watched helplessly as the destroyer moved into my men in the water. The boys were shouting for help – for mercy. I can still hear their cries. You think you know about war. You know nothing," he said.

"I know," Julia started to defend herself. "No. You are right. I know very little. Tell me about it... about your men."

"War is too ugly for your delicate ears," he answered.

Julia felt the sting in his remark – an insinuation she chose to ignore.

"I'm not telling you what you should do," Julia said. "I'm not saying you should go back. I only want you to take these clothes that you may run, hide, or turn yourself in. It's your choice."

"And I'm telling you, you don't know what you are doing," he answered.

"Me? I'm doing nothing. I'm not hiding you. I'm not turning you in. I'm just begging you to think about what you are doing."

"You don't know what you're talking about," he told Julia.

"Perhaps, I don't. But my husband has just gone overseas. Maybe your story is more real to me than you think."

"I must go," he said.

"Please, take the clothes." Julia said. "And the food."

"I can't. You still don't understand."

"Stop!" she shouted. "I'm going, but I'm leaving the case. I hope you'll take the things. I'll come back tomorrow to check on the cat."

Julia went out the back door determined to exit before the man did.

He'll come to his senses when I'm gone.

Was it the heat, the exercise, the anxiety of the conversation with this stranger, or all of this? Julia felt herself go faint.

She was unaware of his carrying her back inside. He found the towel in the case and rolled it to put under her head. With a great deal of noise he opened the windows downstairs trying to get an airflow. And then he sat on the floor next to her and waited.

Ann Davis

When she came out of it, he was there with the cat on his lap.
"I think I should take you to a hospital," he said.
"I only fainted."
"And do you faint often?"
"No. But I've had a lot of exercise this morning and it's terribly hot today."
"And you've been very busy doctoring a stray cat and arguing with a stray man. I think I should get you to a doctor."
"I'm the doctor, remember. I don't need a doctor, but you could help if you wouldn't argue with me."
"I can't do what you say," he said.
"Why can't you?"
"Because I am... I was the captain of a German u-boat."
"I don't believe you."
"Oberleutnant Eberhard Greger," he said and gave her a salute.
"But you've been speaking English. You can't be German."
"Actually I seem to be a man without a country – a captain without a boat – a two legged creature without a suit of clothes."

Eberhard Greger   Dr. Fresenius

"And I suppose you made up that horrible story of how they sunk your boat." Julia said.
"I wish it was a story. My boat was sunk as I said... And I was a German captain serving in the Fuhrer's navy."
"Then I really do not understand war. Why would the Germans sink your boat and then kill their own men?"
"I didn't say the Germans sunk my boat. I said the destroyer did."
"Whose destroyer?"
"In war, neither side plays fair."
"I don't believe you. I don't."
"I don't ask you to. It doesn't matter what you think – isn't that

what you said?"

"I must go," she said.

"You should sit up a while before you try to stand. You don't want to faint again."

"That was a horrible lie you told me," she sat up as she spoke. "I was believing your every word."

"If you take it slowly, I believe you'll be all right. Are you sure you don't want me to help you to a hospital?"

"I'll be fine."

"I'll leave you and Snarls to take care of each other," he said.

"Where are you going?"

"That is another thing that doesn't matter. Didn't you say they will shoot me on sight?"

"Then why didn't you take the clothes and let me continue thinking you were an American boy running from the draft?" Julia asked.

"Oh, now you believe me?"

"I don't know what I believe," she said.

"You don't need to worry about it then. I will walk out of here and you can forget you ever saw me. You're not hiding me. You're not turning me in."

"Please stay. Tell me about what happened to your boat."

"You want me to try to convince you I've told the truth?"

"No. I only want to hear your truth. I want to know what happened to you."

"I think you shouldn't be here. I think you should find a real deserter you can give your husband's clothes to."

"Oh, you are so...."

"German? Yes, I am. If you want me to take you to the hospital, I will. Otherwise, I will get out of here and you can..."

"I don't want to go to the hospital. But would you mind staying until I get my balance?"

"Now that you believe I'm German, you want me to stay so you can turn me in to your military?"

"No."

"Why not? I'll let you turn me in."

"I said, no. Where did you go to school?" she asked.

"My mother's brother lived in New York. I lived with them and got Americanized."

"Why did you go back to Germany?"

"My parents said they wanted me to return. They said things had improved in Germany."

"Is your uncle still in New York?" Julia asked.

"I don't know."

"Maybe you could find him," she suggested.

"No. If my uncle is in New York, your government agents will be watching him. If I went anywhere near him, I'd be the kiss of death."

"Do you want to die?" Julia asked him.

"I told you I did. Can you not believe anything I say?"

"You shouldn't want to die."

"As long as I'm alive, I will relive the sinking of my boat. I will hear the screams of my men. I don't want to live with this."

"Then why are you here?" she asked.

"I am here for my men. God has kept me alive for some reason."

"Tell me. Tell me what happened," Julia said.

"Clausewitz would not have been pleased with the captain of the sunken U-85, the only survivor, Eberhard Greger," he said.

"Is he your commander?"

"No, he was a great man. He died in 1830... something. Carl von Clausewitz."

"A German?" she asked.

"Yes, a German. Germany has had many great men. Bach and Beethoven, for instance."

"Clausewitz was a composer?"

"No, Germans have many talents. Martin Luther started the Reformation. Gottlieb Daimler made the first motorcycle. Gutenberg perfected the printing press and many Nobel Prizes have gone to German scientists."

"So what did Clausewitz do?"

"He wrote a textbook on war, 'Vom Kreige.' "

"An awful subject..."

"But full of wisdom. Clausewitz never had a command of his own. He served mostly in a staff capacity recording the history of warfare. He saw that success in a battle had a lot to do with the leader's ability to recognize the importance of accidental factors that elude exact calculation. 'Since we are always open to attack,' he wrote, 'we must at every instant be on the defensive and thus should place our forces as much under cover as possible.' He wouldn't have parked his boat in enemy territory and let them sneak up on him. He wouldn't have needed to have his men abandon ship and watch them die... They're all dead."

"As you survived, isn't it possible others did?"

"I relive that night over and over. I watch the ship..." he stopped.

"Go on," she said.

"It is too ghastly to put into words. It is horrid."

Julia sat still.

"This was my third cruise," Eberhard said. "For some of the boys, it was their first. They didn't get to see much of the world down inside that steel tube. There were no skylights, or portholes. It doesn't take long before the stench of the boat can drive a man to madness. I tried to rotate the men so they'd each have time on the conning tower. Clausewitz taught the importance of morale.

"The new guys were so proud to be assigned to the u-boat flotilla. It's quite an honor. Nothing is too good for the crew of the u-boats when we're in port. We're treated like high-ranking officers. All the wine, women and song a man could dream of. Dream. That's all a man can do once the u-boat leaves port. Squeeze in between the sausages and eels and try to escape into la-la land."

Julia wanted to ask questions (*What's an eel?*), but she wondered if he was even aware of her.

Best keep quiet.

"Some of the guys were just kids. They didn't even know how to hold their liquor. They'd probably never had a fistfight, or made love to a girl. But before we left port, they had lost their virginity and a couple of them had black eyes. Hell, they didn't know what they were doing – pretending to be men – just a bunch of asinine boys wanting to be heroes. Maybe not even sixteen. They didn't understand they were in for the nastiest duty in the German Navy. They were so proud. I can see the drunken, pompous expressions on their faces as the band played and people waved and cheered when we pulled out of the bunker at Saint-Nazaire."

The captain looked at Julia. She nodded for him to go on.

"The boys were soon feeling the sickness of being submerged for two days straight. When we're submerged there's no way for the vile smell to escape. As one of the youngsters finally stopped heaving, another started. It was the same on every cruise once they started recruiting kids. The smell of vomit so strong even some of the older men couldn't hold their stomachs. Vomit, aging sausages, moldy bread, diesel fuel and sweaty men – the stinking smell of a u-boat.

"When at last we no longer heard the sound of depth charges in the distance, I decided it was safe to proceed on the surface. We had one day of smooth sailing before the heavy seas made the going rough. The torpedoes were shifting causing a great deal of trouble. Still I had to order drills. I wanted the men prepared for whatever was to come. I drilled them until they could slip through the submarine like tadpoles between the stones in a brook.

"I wanted them prepared. They were. They were terrific. But it didn't matter. They're all dead now." He stopped.

"Captain Greger," Julia said. "You shouldn't blame yourself."

He turned to face her.

"What do you know? I had the boat sitting on the surface recharging the batteries when the destroyer snuck up on us. Why did I sit there? Why didn't I see them coming? I was in enemy waters, for Christ's sake. The lucky sons-of-a-bitches just happened upon us."

"You didn't..."

"The first week we found one lousy steamer. We sunk her. But then we found nothing more. When we reached American waters, the crew got excited as they expected some action. It would have helped morale if we had only spotted something to sink. We were ready to attack, but we couldn't find a target. Sometimes we could see lights on the shore, but no ships in the very waters that had been yielding easy pickings. The damned eels kept the men pinned in so tight, they were getting at each other. The men were crazed. We had to stay submerged once we were within sight of the coast. Our food supply was spoiling, but we couldn't put it out as it might draw attention to us."

Am I to feel bad he couldn't find a ship to target?
What am I doing? Julia thought.

"The men needed air. We couldn't go home until we'd used all the torpedoes. This was going to be an extended cruise. The men had to breathe. I was so foolish! I thought we wouldn't be found off the coast of North Carolina, the 'Graveyard Coast.' I thought we were away from shipping lanes. I brought us up and sat there like a moron. Strobel, one of the older men, got the boys singing – trying to boost their moral. While the destroyer snuck up on us, my men were singing."

"Singing about being the 'master race'?"

"Singing about a lady. Lily Marlene...

Vor der Kaserne

Vor dem GroBen Tor

Stand eine Laterne..."

"But that's a British song," Julia interrupted

"It was first a German song. Now it's a soldier's song. Soldiers want to get home to their women. Without a woman to dream about, the soldier is pretty much worthless."

"Your u-boats have been notorious. You strike at anything. Merchant ships. Passenger ships. You care nothing about the lives of your victims." Julia exploded with anger.

"Our victims? Merchant ships carrying supplies to Europe.

Passenger ships carrying weapons."

"How can you know what's on the ships? You shoot them down indiscriminately. Women and children – makes no difference."

"Think what you will. It was my job to sink boats. That's what I did. At least I didn't kill survivors."

Kill survivors?
He's suggesting that our ships shoot survivors?

The two people looked away from each other.

"Yes, I was the captain of a u-boat. I am German. You should go home now. There is no way you can understand. Go."

Julia stood looking at the German who had turned away. Her eyes were full of tears.

Why am I tearing? Why have I let him upset me so?
It is time for me to go.
Why am I here?
Why did I come?

Julia turned towards the door. She could think of nothing to say. Her steps across the floor were uncomfortably loud. She wanted to slip out quietly. Just disappear. At last she was outside. She looked about to see if anyone was there to see her.

"All clear," she whispered to herself and she started towards the Boulevard. Now her mind took off in all directions.

He's despicable. He's the enemy.
He and his u-boat sunk American ships.
Should I take pity
they couldn't find anymore to shoot down?
Everyone says the u-boats show no mercy.

Why didn't he just take the clothes and leave?
He didn't even eat the food.

He looked so strange
sitting on the floor with the cat.
What has he been feeding it?

Where did he get the newspapers?
What is an eel?

How did he survive?
What really happened to his crew?

Julia went back to the house. She found the German talking to the cat.

"Okay, Snarls, I'll see if I can catch a fish for you after dark. But this is it. You're going to have to find yourself a home. You could go hungry as a stray."

"Where will you go?" Julia asked.

"Why have you come back? You left your case. It's still there," the German said as he pointed to the case where she had put it.

"I have questions. I need you to answer them," Julia said.

"Ask then. But I know nothing you want to know. Why do you insist?"

"I need to know. Are you a Nazi?" she asked.

"No. No, I'm just a u-boat captain. I've no interest in politics. Frankly, I don't understand the effect Hitler has on people. He helped Germany for a while, but now everyone says 'Heil Hitler' – it's against the law to say 'Guten Tag' as we used to say."

"You said you served Hitler. Hitler is a monster."

"Power makes monsters of men. Perhaps he is a monster."

"Then why would you serve him?" Julia asked.

"I answered my country's call. I do not understand why we chose up sides with someone named Hideki Tojo. I've never been to Japan. I've never met a Jap. I don't speak Japanese. I do not understand why the United States teamed up with Joseph Stalin. Since when were Russia and the United States friendly? Just a few months ago our orders were to avoid conflicts with U.S. vessels. Then Japan attacked the U.S. fleet in Hawaii and Germany aligned itself with that little island on the other side of the world. But a man in the service of his country isn't supposed to question command."

"Did your country order you to kill innocent people? To sink ships full of women and children? To run up and down our coast targeting anything you could find? Terrorizing the whole East Coast. Sneaking ashore to sabotage our factories."

"My orders were to keep ships from getting to Europe with supplies. That's what I was doing. I regret that innocent people have suffered as a consequence. Tell me, why, in God's name, were they on those ships in the middle of this mess?"

Julia couldn't think of anything to say.

"Have I answered your questions?" he asked. "Is that all?"

> *No, that isn't what I came back to ask*, she thought.
> *What happened to his men? Julia.*
> *That's what you want to know.*

"Take your husband's clothes and get out of here," the German said.

"No, I won't leave until you tell me what happened to your men."

"My men were killed. I watched as they were murdered."

"You mean..."

"I mean, they were slaughtered. There was no way for them to protect themselves."

"You want me to believe that our men stood on the deck of an American ship and shot at ..."

"I don't care what you believe," he walked away from Julia.

"No, tell me. I will listen. Please, tell me," she spoke quickly, not wanting to be dismissed.

Eberhard Greger sat on the steps, his elbows on his knees, his hands cradling his head. Neither of them spoke. The cat rushed to the German apparently thinking he had sat down to pet him. But the man did not acknowledge the cat.

> *Why did I come back?* Julia asked herself.
> *Why do I need to know?*
> *What do I expect him to tell me?*
> *Why would I believe him?*
> *I know I should go, but I can't. I just can't.*

> *He is trembling.*
> *Is he crying?*
> *What am I to do now?*

Julia was standing in the middle of the empty room. She didn't want to make a sound. Slowly she backed over to a windowsill and propped herself against it.

Eberhard Greger looked up to where she had been standing. He didn't notice her across the room. His body went limp and slid down to the foot of the steps. He curled himself up and wept.

Julia waited until she thought the man had fallen asleep. She moved very slowly and, with each step, the boards of the old house made their creaking noises under her weight.

She jumped when the German spoke, "I didn't know you were still here."

"I am so sorry," Julia was shaking her head and moving towards the door. "I didn't mean to be. I didn't want to disturb you. I, I, I ..."

"Do you think I am embarrassed that you should see me cry?"

"Well, I didn't... "

"They dropped depth charges on them! They drove the ship into them chopping them up with the propeller. The men were screaming for mercy. The destroyer shone bright spotlights in their faces. I could see their looks of terror and hear their cries for help. Those who had life jackets on were holding the others up. They were in a straight line, holding their shipmates up. Still the destroyer moved into them. What kind of seaman would drop depth charges on men screaming for mercy? Did he think they had torpedoes in their armpits? I heard their cries. I still see their faces."

"No. No."

"No? You say 'no'?"

"Forgive me," she said and moved closer to the door. His words repeated themselves in her head.

Depth charges. Propeller. Cries.
Depth charges. Propeller. Cries.

"What happened?" she screamed.

When Julia screamed, the German seemed to snap out of the stupor he had been in. He noticed Julia was unsteady and he rushed to support her. "Come sit on the steps," he said helping her along. "You shouldn't be here. You are expecting a baby, are you not?"

Julia nodded.

"You must take care of yourself," he said. "You shouldn't get worked up like this. You don't want to hurt your baby."

Julia shook her head.

"It is not necessary that you should know any of this," he said looking down at her. "You must rest and then go home. Forget about all this. It doesn't concern you. War is ugly. It is not for women to know the grotesque things men at war do to each other."

The day was passing. Julia had to get home. But she was weak from this encounter. They both knew this and he wouldn't allow her to leave like that.

"I must go home. The Bryans will worry."

"Then I must go with you."

"Perhaps, you're right," she said. "If you'll clean up your whiskers and put on those clothes, I think no one will notice us. Of course, I can't let you go in the house with me, but I'd feel better if you got me to the corner."

"Yes, I will do what you ask. You wait here with Snarls. You're right, I couldn't go with you if I look like this."

The man had collected rainwater to wash with. He made the most of the little he had left. He trimmed his beard. The pants were slightly big in the waist and longer than were they his own. "Your husband is bigger than I am," he said when he returned after having changed.

Julia looked at him wondering how old he was.

> *He has the ruddy complexion of a seaman.*
> *But he's not so old.*

"Can we eat something, before we go?" Julia asked.

"Yes, let me get it for you."

Julia insisted he eat something too.

"You have gotten your way. I'm dressed and fed," he said. "Now, you must let me get you home."

"We shouldn't go out together," Julia said. "Someone may see us."

"We'll slip out the back, and I'm holding onto you. I'm not going to let you fall down those steps again."

"But the neighbors," Julia said.

"Mrs. Hubbard is out front sweeping. It's a daily ritual. And the MacAdoos will be gone all day and Mr. Black, also. If we go out the back, no one will see us."

"You know the neighbors?" she asked.

"Of course, not. I only gave them names, like I call the cat Snarls."

"You are a strange man. What do you call yourself?"

"You wouldn't want to hear what I call myself."

"No? Well, what did your mother name you?"

"Eberhard Greger. I told you."

"If we run into anyone, I will introduce you as Greg. Okay?"

"Okay. But you haven't told me your name."

"What have you been calling me? You named everyone else. Surely I merited a name."

"Yes, Snarls and I called you, Miss Hello."

"You needn't try to place any of the blame on Snarls. Why Miss Hello?"

"You came in the house calling out hello. Would you like me to call you something else?"

"It would hardly do for someone to hear you call me Miss Hello. You may call me, Julia. I'm Julia Keegan."

"Julia Keegan," he repeated.

The German captain held onto Julia's arm and they started down the back stairs.

"Greg, where did they sink your boat?" Julia was practicing saying the name.

"We were off the coast of North Carolina. With its Outer Banks it is a treacherous coastline. I figured there wouldn't be any traffic there to spot us. We could sit there while we recharged our batteries and let the men have an opportunity to breathe real air."

"How many men were on your boat?"

"There were forty-six men and a dozen torpedoes, and other supplies to last for six to eight weeks on the seas."

"A u-boat must be larger than I thought."

"Probably not. U-boats are not designed for human comfort. We're packed in with the eels and our food supplies..."

"Please, tell me what an eel is," Julia said.

"An eel is a long slimy fish. But, in this case, an eel is a torpedo. That's what the men call them."

"Can the men stand up inside the boat?" she asked.

"Well, not all forty-six at one time. They sleep in shifts. A man sleeps alongside the torpedoes and with moldy loaves of bread, sacks of potatoes and lots of sausages hanging all about him. The food supplies go bad after awhile and add to the already disgusting odor of diesel fuel and ... I apologize. This is not what you need to hear."

"It's all right. I believe I asked. Tell me about your men."

"My men were ready for anything. I drilled them on what to do in case we were being attacked. There's not room for more than one man in a hatch at a time. I had them practice so many times they moved like a single unit during evacuation drills. Each man knew he was supposed to leave everything. Just pull on his lifejacket and escape lung.

"Some of them had lucky charms." Eb told Julia of the boy who went back to get his number thirteen. He smiled remembering little things about them: the pride of the young boys with new tattoos, the boy who did card tricks, the one who got letters from several girls at one time, the one who was always humming. "Jesus Christ, they were too young to die!"

A string of six army vehicles approached Eberhard and Julia on the Boulevard. The men waved as they passed.

"Keep talking," Julia urged.

"I should stop them," the German said.

"You said you would help me home."

"They could take you home."

"No, they can't."

The last green army vehicle passed. "See?" she asked.

"See what?"

"They didn't even find you suspicious. You don't have to turn yourself in."

"You said you were off the North Carolina coast. How did you get here?"

"I lucked upon a power boat someone had left unguarded and I followed the boats that pulled the bodies of my men out of the water. I thought God had kept me alive for some purpose. I had the crazy notion I was supposed to do something for my men.

"Clausewitz said, 'Even when the likelihood of success is against us, we must not think of our undertaking as unreasonable or impossible for it is always reasonable if we do not know of anything better to do, and if we make best use of the few means at our disposal.' He said we must be determined to find a glorious end."

"But now?" she asked.

"Clausewitz said something else – he said, 'Great strength is not easily produced where there is no emotion.' I seem to have lost my emotion."

"You don't seem to be without emotion."

"Now, well, what can I do? They're dead. Perhaps I could turn myself into a human torpedo and go after the ship.

"Tell me about your husband," Eberhard said.

"At first the Army didn't want him. He had an eye injury and is nearly blind in one eye. He was miserable because they wouldn't take him. He wanted to be a soldier. He found a way of going to work as a civilian for the Army. He shipped out two weeks ago."

"How old are you?" she asked.

"Why do you ask?"

"I've been wondering. You look a great deal younger now that you've cut away some of those unruly whiskers."

"So how old do you think I am?" he asked.

"Maybe, thirty?"

"I guess I need a razor," he said rubbing his beard. "I'm twenty-seven."

They had come to within the block of the Bryan's house. Julia saw Bertie running towards them.

"Oh, no. She's seen us!"

"That little girl?"

"She's my landlady's child. Please, let me do the talking," Julia told Eberhard.

"Bertie, did you ask your mother about tomorrow?"

"She said I wasn't to make a nuisance of myself."

"I'll talk to her. This is a friend of Joe's, Bertie. This is Greg Street."

"Are you coming to the house?"

"Greg was just saying he has to run catch the streetcar. I'll be home in a minute."

"Do you live over here?" Bertie asked the German.

"No."

"Greg used to live near Joe's house, but he doesn't anymore."

"Well, where do you live?"

"Bertie, Greg is just passing through. You go on home. Greg was telling me something."

"I'm making a nuisance of myself?"

Julia smiled.

Watching the girl run down the street Eberhard Greger said, "She's like my cousin's child."

"Oh?"

"Yes, Germans have little girls and boys."

"Look. I don't think you should turn yourself in. I will come back to the house tomorrow to check on Snarls. Please, be there."

"Are you all right now?"

She nodded.

"Then go on home and forget about me." He paused. "But Snarls will need someone to check his paw."

Eleven

Clock Tower   *Cheyne's*

From the start of the war, Hampton Institute began a program insupport of the nation's war effort. They cancelled formal mid-year examinations and set aside the time to train the student body in civilian defense skills. Curriculums for courses taught were changed and new courses, such as Water and Food Supply, were offered that might better prepare students for the crisis. The light inside the Clock Tower of the Memorial Church on campus was turned off in cooperation with area dimouts.

"Mama, Dr. MacLean says it's important we show the nation what we are," Samuel said. "He says this is our opportunity to prove ourselves. He says, 'We are on the spot from here on out. We are daily being put to the test.' "

"And what test is the college president talking about? He was the one who cancelled the exams for the students because of the war."

"You know, Mama. You're just being difficult."

"Son, the Negro has been trying to prove himself to the white man for ages. Dr. MacLean means well, but he shouldn't be filling young folks heads with any notions of the whites ever letting you do anything besides mop up after them."

"Mama. You should go over to the campus. It's jumping with activity. The Institute is going to play a major roll in setting up the defense of this area... Mama..."

"Dr. MacLean is from up north somewhere," Rose interrupted. "He doesn't know what he's talking about. The Negro is discriminated against in this part of the country and in the military. You won't be allowed to serve on equal terms with the whites. They'll continue to treat you like you're not good enough to stand beside them."

"Dean Brown isn't from the North. You know him, Mama. He agrees with Dr. MacLean. And Mr. Flax. He's the chairman of the committee who developed the activities on campus related to the war effort. Mama, I'm going to serve in the military and I won't be just swabbing decks. I'm going to be a pilot."

"You think you can turn the world upside down. Your father says we must let you learn for yourself. He knows what it was like during the Big War, but he says you've got to find out for yourself."

"He's told me how the military treated them. All of that's going to change."

"Oh, you think so, do you? Won't you give up this idea of the Air Corps? I can't stand the thought of you in one of those contraptions falling from the sky."

"We're getting the best training, Mama. We won't be falling from the sky. Here at the Institute they're training us on Piper Cubs, but when we get to Alabama we'll get time in the real thing."

"Lord have mercy! The real thing. You're going to get yourself killed. And there's not one white man who's going to come to your funeral."

"Mama..."

"Don't mama me no more," she said. She looked up to the sky and prayed, "If he must prove something, Jesus, let him prove me wrong. Oh, Jesus, let me be wrong."

****

"I was outside a restaurant in Hampton yesterday. A bunch of Negro soldiers walked right on in as if they owned the place." Freddie Nelson told Samuel.

"And did they get thrown out on their ears?"

"That's what I expected was gonna happen. So, I crossed to the other side of the street and waited. I didn't want to get involved, but I would've bet the shirt on my back they'd be coming out in short order."

"Well?"

"You won't believe this. I saw them through the window. They were seated like they were white as lilies. Those colored boys sat right down and I couldn't believe my own eyes. I didn't know what to make of it."

"I remember asking to buy a cup of coffee at the Langley."

"They wouldn't serve you, would they?"

"The white fellow told me, 'Sure, boy, it'll be five dollars. You got five dollars?"

"Five dollars! Holy moly. I suppose you told the man to keep his cup of coffee?"

"No. I was determined. I had five dollars and I took it out of my pocket and slapped it up on his shiny counter."

"And did he get you the cup of coffee?"

"He didn't want to. But he did.

"Well, I left the place feeling I'd out-smarted that fellow. Then I realized I'd given him all the money I had. Just like that."

Freddie laughed. "I hope that was a good cup of coffee."

"It wasn't that good and, to this day, I don't know which one of us out-smarted the other."

"If you don't know, I won't tell you," Freddie was still laughing.

"Anyway, I waited until those boys came out of the restaurant," Freddie continued. "I had a longer wait than I expected. When they came out one of them was saying, 'My ma needs to teach the cook how to make grits.'"

"He told the restaurant people that?"

"No, sir-re. He was talking to his buddies. So I asked, 'You boys aren't from here, are you?' as if I wasn't sure they weren't.

" 'We just came in from Michigan, they answered.'

"So I asked them. I said, 'White restaurants don't serve colored around here. How'd you get in there?' "

" 'You see this gold service-school S on our uniforms?' one of them said.

" 'What is it?' I asked."

" 'That's our key to the town. They told us at the Institute, as long as we were wearing it, we were welcome anywhere in town.' "

"I told Mama, things are going to change," Samuel said. "This time they're going to let us fight for our country."

"I hope you're right. I sometimes think there're white men in America who'd rather lose the war than see any change in the *status quo*. What if we join the fighting and get ourselves shot up? Is the government going to take care of us? Or are we going to be like old Mr. Banks, trying to make a living selling fish and moving about town on a board 'cause the war took his legs?"

"If the Allies loose this thing, we could end up with the Nazis. Hitler is calling for the destruction of all non-Nordic races. Whatever they are – I'm sure we're non-Nordic. We wouldn't have a chance with the Nazis."

"This land of democracy doesn't practice what it preaches. The Navy says they can't put Negroes on their ships 'cause there wouldn't be room to segregate us on ships. The Army wants to keep us in service, or labors units. You don't think it's bad enough having to 'yes sir' these white folks all the time? What's it going to be like when you have to salute them?" Freddie asked Samuel.

"You may be right about that, but Mr. Flax says this is the only country in the world with a constitution that states all races have a right to equal freedom and opportunity."

"So?"

"The ideal is written in the constitution. We have reason to hope, unless Hitler wins this war. If he does, Negroes will be the losers.

"It's not as though you can refuse to serve, you know," Samuel said. "I say you ought to go over to the Institute and talk to them about getting some specialized training. You don't want to be a Negro draftee."

"If you think I'm going to try to fly a plane, you're crazy," Freddie said. "Pilots are killing themselves before they get over to the fighting. Crashing in cornfields."

"Don't say that around Mama. I'm afraid she's going to kill me for trying to get in the Air Corps as it is." He laughed. "Imagine that, Mother kills son so he can't get in an airplane and kill himself.

"They have a school of mechanics at the Institute. Mr. Gilliard and Mr. Burrell are running it. You had classes with both of them when you were in school."

"Don't rush me," Freddie said. "I have to think about this."

Twelve

Julia spoke with Mrs. Bryan about Bertie going to town with her.

"Bertie has taken quite a liking to you, Julia. She can make a pest of herself if you let her."

"I'm fond of her, too. She's such an inquisitive child."

"If that's a polite way of saying she never stops asking questions, you're absolutely right. And she has such an imagination – I don't know where she gets it from. Her father likes to tell people that when she was born, the doctor smacked her bottom and she asked 'Why'd you do that?' and she's been asking questions ever since. I'm afraid she wears my patience thin sometimes."

"It would be nice to have her come with me when I go to town. Would you mind?"

"But, of course, I wouldn't mind. Please don't let her talk you to death. Oh, when will you be going?"

"In the afternoon."

"Bertie has a piano lesson after lunch. Perhaps another day?"

"No, I promised Bertie. Could she go in the morning?"

"Yes, that would be fine. Bertie will be so pleased."

In the morning, Julia didn't want to go to town. At first her thoughts were of the cat –

Is his foot okay? Is he hungry?
Who's going to take care of him?
Should I try to slip out early to check on him?
If Bertie is up, she'll want to go with me.
And what if Eberhard is still there?
Then what?

Then Julia started thinking of the German captain –

> *Has he already turned himself in?*
> *What will happen to him?*
> *Was he lying about his boat?*
> *If he was going to lie,*
> *why did he even tell me he was German?*

And finally, Julia concluded –

> *I have to take Bertie to town this morning.*
> *I hope the cat will be okay*
> *until I get there this afternoon.*
> *If I was sure Eberhard was gone,*
> *I could let Bertie go with me, but*
> *she's already seen him and*
> *it wouldn't do for her to see him there.*

With thoughts arguing in her head, Julia opened her door to find Bertie waiting in the hall.

"Have you been sitting here long?" she asked the child.

"Somehow she managed to get up and dressed early this morning," Mrs. Bryan said from a room across the hall. "She never moved so early on school days."

"I made my bed, too," Bertie said. "Is that a letter for Joe?"

"Yes, and one for my sister. Do you want to be the mailman?"

"If you're going to the post office, could I give you money to pick up some ink from the stationery store for me," Mrs. Bryan asked. "You'll have to carry my ink jar in for Mr. Wornham to fill."

"Certainly, I'll be right there. I'm stopping at Sunshine Market. Can we pick up anything for you there as well?"

"I wouldn't trouble you about the ink if I hadn't let myself run out."

"It's no trouble. I'll enjoy seeing Mr. and Mrs. Wornham."

"It'll be something for you to carry."

"I think I can manage a little jar of ink. I don't need much from the market and Bertie will help."

The haze on the water wasn't nearly as dense this morning. Julia could see the ships at the Norfolk Naval Base though they looked further away than on some mornings. Julia thought –

I've lived by the water all my life,
*　　　but I never tire of Hampton Roads.*
It has a new personality for every day.
Today there is barely a ripple on the water.

Some days there are waves so big
*　　　I can hear them breaking on the shore.*
At times the water looks brown, or green
*　　　and on a clear day it is beautifully blue.*

What is it about water that seems so peaceful?
There's a sentry walking along the water's edge.
Nothing but military vehicles
*　　　passing along the Boulevard*
and the navy base on high alert
*　　　in the mist across the way.*

But I still get a sense of peace from the water.
*　　　It's hard to think of the war –*
*　　　to believe men are shooting at each other.*
*　　　Surely there won't be shots fired here.*

Then Julia thought of the German.

"Julia, you're doing it again," Bertie said. "You're thinking."

"What is it, Bertie?"

"Some children in Newport News got their names in the newspaper because they collected scrap rubber for the war effort. There were ten of them and they collected fifty pounds. I was thinking that me and my friends could collect sixty, maybe, a hundred pounds. Maybe we'd get our picture in the paper."

"That's a good idea."

"Mother won't let me."

"I'm sure she has good reason."

"She says I've been knocking on people's doors too much. She's embarrassed to meet people in the market. But Julia, only one lady gave the Newport News children her girdle. I figure that if I asked the ladies to give us their girdles, I could get a lot of them. Most of the ladies have girdles."

"Why do you think the other children only got one?"

"They were probably too shy to ask for them. I'm not shy."

"No, I don't think you are. Maybe, since your mother doesn't want you to do collecting anymore, you should look for something else you could do."

"I suppose.

"Julia, there's that man. The one who has no legs. Sometimes Mother buys fish from him. He never acts friendly."

"Perhaps we wouldn't be friendly either if we had to get around without legs."

"I wonder what happened to him. Does he have any family?"

"I don't know. He used to have a goat. The goat would pull him along."

"What happened to the goat?"

"I don't know."

"I wonder how he eats."

"Just like we do. He can chew. He just can't walk."

"But how does he reach the table?"

"I bet he's made a table that's just right for him. The way he gets around is really incredible. I do worry with all the crowds on the sidewalks now. It must be more difficult for him."

"How does he go to the ... you know?"

"Bertie, you're shameful. I'm quite sure the man has that figured out for himself and we have no need to know."

"Have you ever seen any of the children from the school for the deaf and blind?"

"Of course."

"I think it's funny to watch them wave their hands," the child said.

"It looks funny to us, but that's the way the deaf children can talk to each other. It's called signing. As they can't hear and, some of them can't speak, that's their way of communicating."

"But the blind children can't see them."

"That's right. The blind children have to use their fingers to see. They are taught what things look like by touching them. They even read with their fingers."

"I'm glad white children aren't deaf and blind," Bertie said.

"That's not the case. The school in Hampton is for the Negro children. There's another school out in the mountains for the white children who are deaf and blind."

"How do they get that way?"

"Lots of times, no one knows. It just happens. Some babies are born unable to see or hear."

"And some children look directly at the sun and are blinded," Bertie said. "Right?"

"You certainly shouldn't look at the sun, Bertie. But I don't think that's what happened to these children."

"What then?"

"Why don't you ask your mother to explain that to you? Let's change the subject."

"I saw some children once that were white all over. Their hair, their eyebrows, everything. Their shin was as white as marshmallows!"

"Yes, Bertie."

"What happened to them?"

"They have no pigmentation."

"What's that?"

"Bertie, when one doesn't have pigmentation it means they have no color and we call them albinos."

"Do Negro children... I mean, are there colored al - what-you-said?"

"I don't know, Bertie."

"Ask Mother?"

"Yes."

"There are some midgets who live down by the water."

"Yes, Bertie, I know."

"You don't want to talk about midgets, either?"

"I don't know how to answer your questions. Bertie, there's one thing everybody has."

"What's that?"

"Feelings. We would all like to be beautiful and blessed with all our senses. You and I are more fortunate than some, but that doesn't make us better and doesn't make them less. We should be careful not to stare, or say things that might hurt them."

"Do Japs and Nazis have feelings?"

"Oh, Bertie, do you ever stop asking questions.? Look, here comes the streetcar."

Thank Heavens! Julia thought.
Oh, there's that same man
who wanted to talk about the war.
I don't want Bertie hearing what he has to say.
I'll get more questions than I can handle.

"Let's sit over here," Julia directed Bertie as far from the man as there were available seats.

"When do we get off, Julia?" the child asked.

"We'll stay on to the other end of town and get off at the post office. Do you still have my letters?"
"Right here."
"Thank you. That's good."

Did that man say something about
a German u-boat? Julia asked herself.

"Julia, can we go..."
"Sh-h-h-h."
"Why?"
"Just don't talk right now, please."
"Are you mad?"
"No, Sweetie, I'm not mad at you. Sh-h-h."
The child finally stopped talking. Julia heard the man say 'cemetery in Phoebus.' The motorman mentioned April and a government secret. That was all she heard. The man got off the streetcar. The motorman started up a conversation with another passenger.
"Julia," Bertie whispered.
"Yes, Bertie?"
"May I speak now?"
"Of course. What do you want to ask?"
"That man..."
"What man?"
"The man you were staring at. Do you think he's a spy?"
"Of course not. Was I staring?"
"Bertie, let's move up front. He's getting close to our stop."

If the motorman would stop talking to that lady,
maybe I could ask him... what?
There is nothing I can ask him.

"Julia, can I pull the cord? The next stop is the post office."
Julia nodded and the child gave the cord a long pull.
"Let go, Bertie. I think he's heard the bell.
"I like to go to the post office first," Julia said when they stepped off the streetcar. "That way I don't loose my letters along the way."
"I wish I had someone to write."
"That's what you can do, Bertie. When next I write Joe, I'll ask him if he knows a GI who needs mail. Or maybe I should ask Kate. She will know who really would appreciate getting your letters."
"Would you write her tonight?"

"Yes, I'll write her tonight."

Bertie mailed the letters and the two of them walked back up Queen Street to Hampton Stationery. "I always like to come here to get my school supplies," Bertie said.

"Yes, my mother used to bring me here."

"My, look who's here!" Mrs. Wornham said greeting them at the door. "I wondered if you had left town, Julia."

"I'm living on the Boulevard. I come to town quite often, but you're usually so busy and I don't need school supplies anymore."

"I suppose we'll see more of you when junior gets to school age."

"Yes, I'm expecting. Though I hadn't thought about sending the baby to school yet. I've got an apartment on the third floor of the Bryan's," Julia told Mrs. Wornham. "Bertie and I came to town together today. She helped me mail my letters. Mrs. Bryan asked that we stop and get Mr. Wornham to fill her ink bottle."

"We can take care of that." Mrs. Wornham handed the empty bottle to her husband. "Tell me about your family."

"Joe left a few weeks ago. I'm like everyone else living from letter to letter."

"It's so awful that we have to send our young men off to war," Mrs. Wornham said.

"I heard Kate is working for the Red Cross. Does she have to put in long hours?"

"Kate's in Europe," Julia answered.

"No."

"She's with the recreation division of the Red Cross. They serve coffee and doughnuts to the American GIs."

"Sounds like a fun way to spend the war but a little too close to the action."

"I think it's more work than play," Julia explained. "They're always cooking, serving, or driving on to the next point."

"You mean they aren't situated in one place?"

"No they're always on the move. We have to trust that the Red Cross on the vehicle is plain to see."

"And your folks? How are they?" Mrs. Wornham asked.

"Mother is very involved with one thing and another. Father tries to stay out of the way."

"I know just how he feels," Mr. Wornham said. "Is your father hoping to keep his business going through the war?"

"Automobile plants have stopped making cars. I'm sure you...

everyone knows that. He's going to try to operate the business as an auto repair."

"Good."

"Now what about Bertie Bryan?" Mr. Wornham asked, leaning down to her eye-level.

"Mother won't let me collect anything else for the war effort, so Julia's going to ask Kate for someone I can write."

"Well, I think that's a fine idea."

Julia and Bertie continued along Queen Street. Julia felt a lump in her throat as they passed Brittingham's. It seemed like Joe should be here as he was just a few weeks ago when they went in to buy the stroller.

"Julia, you're thinking again."

"How'd you like to put a penny in this parking meter?" Julia offered the child a penny. "Now turn this thing and watch the red flag disappear."

"Do you know who parked there?"

"I don't think so."

"Then why did you want me to put a penny in?"

"I'll tell you another time. Let's go find a place that sells penny candy."

Bertie had to stop at all the shop windows. When they got to Leggett's Department store, she pleaded to go in.

"We'll go in, but we have to watch our time. Your mother wants you home in time for you to eat before your piano lesson."

Bertie liked to watch the clerk send the money to the second floor office in a capsule that ran on a track. The cashier would take the money and put the customer's change in the capsule and send it back along the track to the clerk.

"What makes it go?" Bertie asked.

"That's a question for your father. In fact, I'm surprised you haven't already asked him."

"I did, but I didn't understand."

"If he couldn't make you understand, I'm sure I can't. Let's go to the market."

Herbie remembered Julia had taken the recipe for corned beef and cabbage. "How was your dinner, Julia?"

"It was so good, Joe took off for Europe."

"I thought you said he was with NACA?"

"He found a way to get sent overseas."

"Is that why you haven't been in for awhile? You can't stop eating for the duration."

"Bertie's mom hasn't let me stop eating. She either has me down, or she sends me leftovers. I should be practicing my cooking skills. Do you have anymore good recipes?"

"You want to send someone else overseas?"

Julia handed the grocer her list. "I just need small quantities. It's hardly worth your trouble."

"It's no trouble," the grocer insisted. "We're always happy to see you."

"What's that?"

"What's what, Bertie?"

"That." She pointed to something in a jar on the counter.

"It's... something I wouldn't want to eat." Julia spoke softly. "How about you?"

"People eat that?"

"I guess so. The Goldsteins like to carry things people can't get at the Colonial Store."

"It's disgusting."

"Sh-h-h-h."

"Here you are," Herbie said. He took the money and the necessary ration stamps. "You know, you can call us and we'll deliver your groceries, Julia."

"Yes, you've been doing that for Mother for years. I like to get out."

"The summer weather may change your mind. You call us if you need some things and you can't make it in. We'll be happy to send them to you. It doesn't have to be a large order."

"Thank you, Herbie. I may do that sometime.

"Are your brothers okay?" Julia asked.

"You're asking about the two overseas? Yes, they've been good about writing."

"Herbie, do you have any relatives in Germany?"

"A cousin and perhaps some others that we haven't kept in touch with over the years. But all of our immediate family is in the states."

"Julia, the streetcar's coming," Bertie said and they hurried out to catch it.

Stepping onto the streetcar Bertie spotted a friend. "Julia, is it all right if I sit with Sarah? She's in my class at school."

"Of course. Hold on tight to my parcel, or do you want me to hold it?"

"I've got it."
"Okay"
Julia saw that Bertie was seated and then found a seat by a window. She welcomed the little breeze it let in. She could hear Bertie's voice above the rest – "I mailed Julia's letters for her. She's going to..."

> Bertie's so cute,
> but what a relief she's found someone to talk to!
> After they go to her piano lesson,
> I can check on Snarls.
> Snarls. Such an ugly name.
> But I seemed to have picked it up.
> I suppose the cat doesn't know it's meaning.
> What of the German? Did he leave?
> Did he turn himself in?
> What were they talking about
> on the streetcar this morning?
> I wish I had gone to Phoebus,
> But I couldn't take Bertie over there.

The streetcar passed Hampton High School. A flood of nostalgia swept through Julia. How many times she had waited in the schoolyard hoping to see Joe before she had to go to class!

> He'd come running up
> with barely enough time to beat the tardy bell
> and I'd start each day
> with a breathless dash for my homeroom.
> But I simply had to see him.

Julia sat on the streetcar humming the school song to herself...

> I'm a Crabber born
> and a Crabber bred
> And when I die I'll be
> a Crabber dead
> Yeah, yeah, oh
> Crabber, Crabber.
> Yeah, yeah, oh
> Crabber, Crabber.
> Yeah, yeah, Oh
> Crabber
> Yeah, yeah, rah!

"Oh, no. She's thinking again," Bertie said to her school friend. "Julia, we get off at the next stop. Want me to pull the cord?"

"Yes, I'm glad you were watching."

"You were thinking about Joe, weren't you?" The child asked when they were off the streetcar.

"You're a very smart little girl."

"Not so smart. You had tears in your eyes."

Cheerleaders   *Cheyne's*

Thirteen

"Where have you been? Snarls could be dead by now."

"Where is he? Is his leg infected?" Julia asked the German.

"He's in the kitchen. He hasn't shown any interest in the fish I got him."

Julia went to the back of the house. There on the kitchen floor was Snarls, wrapped in her towel and looking lifeless.

"What are you doing?" Eberhard asked.

"I'm going to look at his paw, if it's all right with you."

"Go on."

"Thank you. I will."

"I thought you would come first thing today. Maybe a vet should look at the paw."

"If I had come this morning the little girl would have come with me. I was afraid you might still be here... as you are."

"I told you to forget about me."

"Why are you still here?" she asked.

"I waited outside all morning to see if you would come. I was going to slip away as soon as I saw you."

"I told you I'd come take care of Snarls," Julia said.

"Well, it certainly took you long enough," he said. "I can go..."

"No, you come here and hold Snarls for me." Julia insisted.

He picked up the cat and held him while Julia undid the gauze from his foot. "It looks good," she said. "I think he'll be okay."

"Are you a vet? He hasn't eaten. He's not himself."

"Are you his mother?" Julia asked.

"No. I have no claim to the cat. I just thought you'd show a little more concern."

"Why am I here," she asked, "if I'm not concerned? Put the

cat down. Let's watch him. See if he acts sickly now that the leg isn't wrapped."

On his feet, Snarls gave out with something of a mix between a yarn and a meow and then rubbed up against Julia's legs.

"See, he's all right. Animals don't understand being bandaged up," Julia said.

"You're all right, Snarls," the man said to the cat. "I guess she is a vet."

"We had cats when I was growing up. I was always the one to look after them. The vet used to let me watch what he did when I took my pets to him," Julia explained. "He said it was too bad I wasn't a boy; I'd make a good vet."

"You don't think your landlady would let you take Snarls there?" Eberhard asked.

"She says she's extremely allergic to furry animals. It's not that she doesn't like them."

"He's gotten accustomed to my bringing him fish. I'd like to think someone will feed him. Maybe you can find him a home," he suggested.

"I'll see," Julia said. "But there's something else I want to talk to you about."

"You shouldn't have anything to say to me. I'm a German. Please, just take the cat and find him a home... I figure it would be best if I..."

"I heard something when I went into town this morning."

"You heard they're looking for me?" he asked. "Good."

"Will you be quiet? I heard two men talking about a government secret and the national cemetery."

"I don't know what..."

"Listen.," Julia said. "One of them was talking about something that happened in April. You said they brought the bodies of your men here. Could the government's secret be that they put them in the cemetery?" Julia asked.

"They sent men out in whaleboats," Eberhard explained. "They were shouting back and forth:

'This one's dead,' one hollered.

'So's this one,' another called back.

'They're all dead. Why must we drag them back?'

'Captain's orders,

I suppose they hope to find top-secret stuff on them.'

'The two boats won't hold them all.'

'Then we might have to leave some for the sharks.' "

"You were close enough to hear them?" Julia asked.

"I waited, hoping they would find someone alive. I had on my life jacket and I was dog paddling. By then the water was calm. It seemed to have lost its life in the barrage of depth charges. Though most of the boys were in their life jackets that kept them afloat, they were all dead. All I could do was watch the sailors pull my men out of the water and toss their lifeless bodies, like sacks of waste material, onto their boats.

"The U.S. ships were there for a long time, their searchlights keeping me on the alert, dodging their beams. I figured they were trying to find the Enigma."

"What?"

"The coding machine on the boat. Meanwhile I swam to the shore. Someone had pulled a small motorboat up on the beach. They must have planned to be right back. I jumped in, and when the Navy was ready to leave the sight of the sinking, I was able to follow."

"Couldn't they see you?"

"I kept my distance. If they noticed me, they must not have been concerned. When they turned in towards the naval base, I knew I'd be spotted there, so I came over here. I had to dodge ferryboats to get over to this side, but otherwise there was very little traffic on the water. I climbed out of the boat, set it adrift and snuck up on the shore after the guard passed."

> *I saw him in the moonlight*
> *that night just before Joe came home.*

Julia missed part of what the German was saying, as she recalled noticing something cross the line of moonlight on the water.

> *It was Eberhard that I saw in the water*
> *in front of the house.*
> *I thought something was there. I was right.*

" ... suppose they might have brought the bodies to this side later. Can you tell me how to get to the cemetery?" Eberhard asked Julia.

"You think that's where your men are?"

"You're the thinker, Mrs. Keegan. If they are, then I want to go there before I turn myself in. Can you please draw me a map so I can find the cemetery? I have no right to ask any kindness of you. But it means everything to me."

"The cemetery is quite a long ways from here. It won't be easy for you to get there without being seen."

"Didn't you tell me I didn't draw suspicious looks from the army men who passed us on the street?"

"Probably because I was with you," she said.

"No. You can't go with me."

"Then I don't know how you'll get there. It's on the other side of town – on the other side of Hampton Creek."

"Can you find a boat I could use?" he asked.

"That would be the worst thing for you to try to do."

"You forget, I'm a sailor," he said.

"You forget, they have sentries all along the water."

"How do you think I ended up here? I came by boat."

"I will not stand on the shore and watch them gun you down."

"No. You shouldn't be involved at all. You get out of here. This is my problem."

"You think I'm just going to leave? You're mistaken," she said. "I wanted to go to the cemetery this morning, but the child was with me. Maybe, I'm wrong. Maybe your men aren't buried there. Then I have you chancing your life trying to get there for nothing."

"I can't let you do this. If I'm caught, I'm caught. I can't let you..." he argued.

"You can't stop me. You need my help if you're going to get to the cemetery. Let me see what I can find out tomorrow. I'll go there. I can ask questions if I'm alone."

"No. You cannot ask questions. Don't say anything to anyone that could ever connect you to me. If you go to the cemetery, and I'm sure you shouldn't, at least take some flowers with you. Pretend to be visiting someone's grave. If there are other people around, don't even go near."

"But..."

"Julia Keegan, listen to me. I cannot be responsible for anyone else. My men are dead because I didn't do my job. Let me die before I put you in danger."

"This is America," she said. "Not Nazi Germany. But I won't ask questions. I'll listen and hope to hear something. I'll take flowers and wait until no one is around. I promise, no one will notice me there. I'll be very careful."

"Why are you so bullheaded?" he asked. "Why don't you forget about me?"

"Because if those boys died as you said, someone needs to care."

"Even though they're German?"

"Tell me about the German people."

"All the women are big and jovial. All the men are tough and have little mustaches. When they speak they sound rather like they are riding on a bumpy road. 'Hump, hump, hump, hump, hump.' When they walk they kick their feet out in front of them."

"Why do you tease? I really want to know. My grandparents were from Germany."

"Your grandparents were German?" he asked.

"Yes, they came to the states before the last war. When things started getting bad, they changed their name from Koehn to Kain. They were afraid to have people know they were Germans. My sister and I didn't know they were from Germany until we were almost grown. That's why I asked you about Germans. I wonder if my grandparents sacrificed their ancestry hiding behind a false name. I wonder if they even think about Germany."

"Germans love to sing," he said. "We're a proud people. We're hard workers. Good beer drinkers. By far more honest than the English. More trustworthy than the French. More loyal than the Italians."

"And more irritating than the rest of us." Julia added.

"Careful. You're a bit German yourself. I don't know about your grandparents, though their granddaughter has a strong will that is very typical of the German people. Still, there must be something else mixed in."

"What?" she asked.

"German people have a tendency to mind their own business. I don't see that characteristic in Mr. and Mrs. Koehn's granddaughter."

"Sh-h-h-h."

"What..."

"Sh-h! There's someone outside," she whispered.

"You cannot be found here with me. That could cause you a lot of trouble."

"Just keep out of sight," Julia said. "I think it's Bertie."

"Do you think she knows you're here?"

"Maybe. I don't know. You must stay down and be quiet. Let me... and Snarls take care of this."

Julia picked up the cat and walked to the front room. She saw Bertie and a little boy on the porch. Julia went onto the porch calling to the child, "Bertie, what are you doing here? Is your piano lesson over already?"

"Miss Eloise had a headache, so I had a short lesson today." the child said.

"Did you follow me here? Does your mother know you're here?"

"I didn't know you were in the house. Ricky and I were just looking in the windows. What's in there?" Bertie asked.

"It's really dirty. Lots of cobwebs. And mice and bugs. I think this poor cat was after catching a mouse, but something in the house scared him. And he may have hurt his paw."

"The ghost!" the children exclaimed in unison.

"This house IS haunted," Bertie added. "I knew it."

"I dare you to go inside, Bertie," Ricky said.

"You'll do no such thing!" Julia answered. "That would be trespassing. Bertie could get in trouble."

"But you went inside, Julia."

"Yes, I heard this little fellow crying. He must be lost and I bet he needs something to eat. Poor thing."

"We can't take him to my house," Bertie said. "Mother would have a hissy."

"I have a dog and he doesn't much like cats," Ricky said.

"I know, Ricky," Bertie said. "You could go inside and catch a mouse for him!"

"Eu-u-u-u-u-u!" Ricky replied.

"I don't think either of you need to go inside. Perhaps we can find something for the cat outside."

"I live across the street," Ricky said. "I suppose I could get some scraps for him to eat."

"That would be nice. Why don't you see if you can get something? You can go with him, Bertie."

"I'm not supposed to be here.... at the vacant house," Ricky said. "You won't tell my mother, will you, lady?"

"Promise you won't come back here? Your mother, and yours, too Bertie, knows it's dangerous for children to play around a deserted house."

"What do you think scared him?" Bertie asked.

"Scared who?" Julia asked.

"The cat. Do you think he saw a ghost?"

"Ghosts are invisible," Ricky said.

"Then maybe he could smell it," Bertie replied.

"Maybe the cat is hungry," Julia said. "I don't think he encountered a ghost."

"He could have," Bertie insisted. "Ricky, tell her. He's seen some strange things."

"What have you seen, Ricky?"

"I found giant footprints over by the water... and it looks like something trampled the cattails and broke them. Maybe something is prowling at night and maybe it's inside the house."

"Maybe it's not a ghost. Maybe it's a boogey man!" Bertie suggested.

"Maybe this is not the place for you children to be playing," Julia said.

"Don't say anything to Mother."

"Go. Go see if you can get something for this poor cat."

"She won't tell, will she?" Ricky asked as the children crossed the street.

While the children were gone, Julia went up to the house and whispered into the door, "It's okay I've got to go. Don't take any chances tonight. The boy thinks someone is in here." Then she added, "I'll go to the cemetery in the morning."

Snarls showed he appreciated the free rations. "You were right, lady. He was hungry," Ricky said.

"Now, what can we do with him?" Bertie asked.

"As we cannot take him home with us, I think it best we leave him here," Julia said. "Perhaps someone will come looking for him."

"What if he goes back inside?" Bertie said.

"The boogey man will get him," Ricky said.

"Poor kitty."

Fourteen

Mrs. Bryan had a message for Julia when she came in. "Your mother said your cousin will be at the house this evening. She wants you to come to dinner. I told her I'd have you call her as soon as you came in."

"Thank you, Mrs. Bryan." She accepted the telephone earpiece the woman handed her.

Julia dialed the four digits to ring her parent's home.

"Hello, Walter's residence."

"Hello. To whom am I speaking?"

"Is that you, Julia?"

"Yes."

"Don't you know who this is?"

"I do now! Peter. What are you doing in town?"

"I got an invitation from Uncle Sam that I couldn't refuse. They gave us a few hours before we have to report back. So I called my favorite aunt and asked if she'd feed a man in uniform. I think that was the wrong thing to say. She's been cooking ever since I got here... as though it's going to be my last meal."

"You'd best appreciate it. Judging from what Kate says the boys tell her, they don't get any real food over there – except her doughnuts, of course."

"Your mother told me to answer the telephone. I'm supposed to ask you to come to dinner."

"Of course, I'll come. It will be so nice to see you. How are your brother and sister? And Aunt Lucille and Uncle Maynard? Oh, don't tell me now. I'll see you at the house. This is such a pleasant surprise. I mean, getting to see you, not that you've been drafted."

"When shall I tell your father to come for you? He wants to know."

"Can he come now? I'm impatient to see you."

"He say's he'll be right over."

"See you in a little bit, bye." Julia put the earpiece on the receiver.

"Where are you going, Julia? Can I go with you?"

"Not this time, Bertie. I'm going to another boring dinner. You know how you dislike them."

"When will you be back?"

"Bertie, you cannot be trailing along with Julia everywhere she goes. Her folks want her to help entertain her cousin this evening," Bertie's mother explained. "Now you run along and play with your friends."

"Can I go over to Ricky's," Bertie asked her mother

" MAY I go?"

"Yes, ma'am. May I go to Ricky's?"

"Do I know him?" Mrs. Bryan asked.

"He's littler than me."

"Littler than I am," her mother corrected her. "Where does he live?"

"Just a couple of streets over."

"Not on the other side of Kecoughtan Road. You know I don't want you crossing Kecoughtan."

"No, his house is not even near Kecoughtan. I don't have to cross no big streets."

"Any big streets. You don't have to cross ANY big streets," Mrs. Bryan sighed. "You may go, but don't stay late. You have to do your practicing today. And you need to spend some time cleaning your room," Bertie was running down the street while Mrs. Bryan called out to her.

> *If only I could have thought of some way*
> *to keep Bertie from going back there!*
> *I hope the German heard me say to stay out of sight.*
> *How am I going to go to Phoebus tomorrow*
> *without Bertie tagging along?*

Julia didn't have time to worry about Eberhard Greger. She had to get ready. Her father was coming for her.

> *I wish Peter had come before Joe left.*
> *Peter and Joe used to get into so much mischief,*
> *when Peter lived here.*

I thought they were really going to get it
when someone finally caught them
disconnecting the trolley from the streetcar.
Those two could charm their way out of anything.
Peter didn't sound too happy about being called up.

With Bertie gone, Julia hurried downstairs so no one would have to come up for her. Her father was waiting for her outside.

"I would have let Peter drive over for you, but I was afraid he'd get some notion of taking you on a joy ride," Mr. Walters told his daughter.

"Even with the government saying we're not to do any unnecessary driving?"

"Because the government says no unnecessary driving. He'd do it just to see if he could get away with it. I don't want to have to call my sister and tell her he's in the brig."

"You don't think he's grown up?"

"No, I don't. But the Army is going to knock some sense into him. And if the Army doesn't, it's liable the Krauts will."

"Does he know where he's going?"

"No idea. Lucille is in a state. It's hardest on the mothers, you know."

"It's not easy for the wives. Especially when they go off when they don't have to."

"You know you can come back home. Your mother and I would love to have you there with us."

"Thanks. I do appreciate you, but I want a home – our home – for Joe to come back to."

"Your mother is wondering if she should make a room available for some military personnel. You sure you don't want to come home before your room is taken?"

"I'm sure, but..."

"But what?"

"Do you think I could stay over tonight? Just tonight?"

"Sure you can. Did you bring your toothbrush?"

In the morning I'll go to the cemetery.
I won't have to worry about Bertie
asking to come with me.

Now that that's taken care of
I can enjoy the evening.

Peter still had his mischievous, boyish look.

He looks like he did when he was fourteen.

He greeted Julia with an exaggerated bow and she returned it with a salute.

"Did Joe do that to you?" he asked and waved his hand to her rounded stomach.

"He did. And then he took off."

"The scoundrel!"

"Now, I'll wait by the shore for my lover to return," she said melodramatically.

"Could you get Betty Grable to wait for me?"

"Betty Grable will be waiting for the entire US Army. Perhaps, you should find a five and ten cents store gal all of your own."

"Do they come 34 – 23 – 35?"

"You're shameful! Come give me a hug."

Peter made a joke out of everything during dinner.

It wasn't until he went out on the porch with Julia that she realized he was scared. The sergeant in boot camp had singled Peter out to get the blunt of his wrath: "He'd make me clean the latrine. Then he'd come in with his white gloves, find a spec of dirt and give me a cussing out. For every hurdle the unit did, he'd make me do them ten times, or more. He always cancelled my pass to town. Then he'd have me paint a newly painted hut, or something just as stupid. He was determined to break me."

"But you have moxie, Peter. No one could break you."

"He had the stripes. There was nothing I could do but take all his razzing. Some day I'd like to meet him on common ground. Then I'll even the score."

"That's all behind you now, isn't it?" Julia asked.

"Yeah. Now they'll send me over to Europe and let the Nazis have at me. Jesus, they give a guy every reason to wish he was dead and then they ship him over so the enemy can finish the job. You know, if the Krauts look like Sergeant Penner, I could kill them all by myself."

"His name was Penner? Like Joe 'Wanna buy a duck?' Penner?" she asked thinking of a popular radio comic.

"Yeah," Peter laughed. "But this fellow had no sense of humor. All he ever gave me was chickenshit."

"What?"

" 'cuse, me. That's a military term. You wouldn't know it."

"Whatever he gave you, I hope he taught you how to survive in combat. I've been fretting over Joe going over there. Now, I'll be worrying about you, too."

"He didn't teach me a damn thing.

"But I can take care of myself," Peter was quick to add. "You just concentrate on Joe and that baby you're carrying. If I weren't such a bonehead, I'd have found some war-related job before they called my number."

"Joe had the job, but he didn't want to stay home."

Peter didn't seem to know what to think of that.

"Joe had a job with NACA at Langley," Julia explained. "He volunteered to go overseas."

"I guess I'm not as patriotic as Joe."

"No. You remember how Joe always wanted to be a soldier like his dad."

"What did his father do?" Peter asked. "Win the battles of Cantigny and Argonne single-handedly?"

"To hear Joe tell it, the rest of the troops were just backup. But Mr. Keegan didn't get over there until the war was almost over."

"He might have been killed by friendly fire," Peter said.

"Friendly fire?" she questioned.

"That's when our boys kill our own... by mistake. It happens."

"Do you think this war will be over soon?" Julia asked.

"I wouldn't mind coming back before I get over there," Peter replied.

"Peter, you will take care of yourself, won't you? Forget that contemptible sergeant and take care of yourself. If you end up in England, look for Kate."

"Aunt Evelyn gave me her mailing address. If there's anyway I can get a free doughnut, I will."

"You're such a clown. Take care." Julia turned to go back inside before he could see her tears. She couldn't say goodbye. She went to the window to wave, but Peter was gone.

Take care, Peter.
Come back.

Seeing Peter leaving for the war, made the war so real to Julia. She cried for Joe and Kate and Peter.

The helplessness of seeing people you love
go off to war!
I didn't mean for Kate to get in the middle of it.

> *Now, Peter has to go.*
> *Why, why did Joe think he could find*
> *his long-dead father*
> *by putting on a uniform?*
> *They have to come back.*
> *Please, take care of yourself, Peter. Take care.*

"Let her have her cry," Evelyn said to her husband. "I was weepy the whole time I was pregnant with Kate and I had nothing to cry about. Sometimes a woman just needs a good cry."

"Did she cry like this when Joe left."

"She may have. I don't know. If she didn't, that's all the more reason she needs to get it out now."

"I guess you know what you're talking about, but she's breaking my heart."

"I'll give her a little time and then I'll fix something cool to drink. I'm glad you asked her to stay overnight."

Sitting at the kitchen table with her parents, Julia shared some of what Peter had told her about his sergeant. His aunt was irate. Wanted to call the Army and "tell them a thing or two about Sergeant Penner.

Mr. Bryan told her there was nothing that could be done. Nothing that would be done. "Unfortunately, some of the men who are put in charge of training the troops find morbid pleasure in tormenting the boys. Peter probably set him off from the start with that hoity-toity smirk he wears on his face."

"That's no excuse for that kind of harassment," Mrs. Bryan said.

"Insolence isn't going to be tolerated in the service."

"I know Peter can be difficult, Jules, but it's not right to try and break a boy's spirit like that. And then ship him off to war.

"You don't think Joe had such an experience?" the mother asked her daughter.

"No. He didn't go through the kind of training draftees go through. No. What I worry about is whether Joe and Kate and, now Peter, are going to survive the war. Seeing Peter tonight made me wonder if any of them will come back. I do hope they're back for Christmas. That's not too much to wish for, is it?"

"Certainly not. They could get here for the baby."

"Churchill said the Allies could win once the United States joined the effort."

"The problem is everyone underestimated Adolf Hitler," Mr. Walters said. "He's a little runt with a mighty fist. The German people are hypnotized by him. He tells them they are the master race. He gets them to 'Heil Hitler' like he's a god. It's madness."

"Honey, you're not helping. We're trying to be positive... for Julia."

"Mother, it's time I woke up to what's going on. I stopped reading the paper because I was afraid it would tell me something I didn't want to know. I've been pretending Joe is just – away. Did I really think that if I didn't know about it, it didn't happen?"

"It's probably best not to be reading the papers and listening to the radio accounts of the war," her father said. "I think it was easier on the folks back home during the last war when there weren't so many reports before the dust settled. Joe and Kate have been writing and they say they're all right. That's the kind of news we need."

"And when the letters stop... is that when I should pick up the newspaper?"

"Julia, it's better for Joe and the baby if you don't think too much about the war."

"Daddy, do you think the Germans are evil people?"

"I think they have chosen an evil leader."

"Grandmother and Grandfather Kain were Germans," Julia reminded them.

"Oh, I hardly think of them as Germans," Evelyn Walters said.

"When does one stop being one and become the other?" Julia asked. "Some Japanese, though they are United States citizens, are still considered Japanese since the war started. Could the government decide to arrest your parents just because they were born in Germany?"

"Is that what is worrying you? No, the government isn't going to take your grandparents away," Mrs. Walters assured her daughter.

"Your father tells me he asked you to move back here with us, but you refused."

"I told Daddy I appreciate the offer, but I want to keep the apartment. The Bryans are very nice and their daughter, Bertie, is my little friend. She came to town with me yesterday."

"Then you're sure? I may rent a room, if you're sure."

"Yes, I'm sure. And you should rent a room. There's a real need."

"I'm going to bed, if that's all right?" Julia asked.

"Certainly, you're tired."

"All that foolish crying drained me. I should fall asleep as soon as I touch the bed."

Julia should have fallen asleep before she started thinking –

Peter is so dear.
He tried to hide his misery
       behind that big smile of his.
Mother was going to talk to the Army
          about Sergeant Penner.
I couldn't look at Peter just before he left.
If he'd had tears in his eyes,
      I don't know what I would have done.
Wouldn't it be nice if he does see Kate?
    Wouldn't it be nicer if he didn't have to go?

Is Joe telling me the truth?
Have they really not seen the enemy?
    Would he tell me if he had?
        Could he?

Should I tell someone about Eberhard Greger?
I could be in trouble for
    not saying something first thing.
I shouldn't be helping him.
I won't go to Phoebus tomorrow
      and I won't go to the house again.
If I go to the cemetery and don't find anything,
    I can...
If I do find something...
      I shouldn't go.

It was into the early hours of the morning before Julia got any sleep. She thought of Peter going to Europe. She wondered if Joe still felt the same about serving in the war. She thought about Kate in a country the Germans were bombing.

Gracious, Kate could come face to face
      with a German.
  Well, I suppose, I have.

She thought of the story Eberhard had told her. The destroyer dropped depth charges into the survivors in the water. It ran into some of the boys with its huge propeller.

What did I tell the German?
Someone has to care what happened to those boys.

> *The German has told me over*
> *   and over to mind my own business.*
> *Why can't I?*

At last she decided. She would go to the cemetery at St. John's and talk this out with Lizzie.

In the morning Julia heard her folks moving about the house. Her father would be leaving for work soon. Would her mother be going out? Julia stayed in bed and hoped they would leave thinking she was still asleep. She tried to go back to sleep, but her mind was replaying every thought that had kept her awake most of the night.

There was a light tap on the bedroom door. Julia kept still. The door was pushed opened and then shut again. Julia heard her mother go down the stairs and open and shut the front door. Julia slipped from the bed and saw her mother walking away. She was wearing a hat and gloves.

> *I wonder if Peter has already left.*
> *Poor Peter. Do make it back.*

Julia wondered why she had gotten so upset by Peter's visit. He was undoubtedly one of her favorite people, but that wasn't it. It was that he was being forced to go. It was because she knew if she had looked at him just before he left, he would have had tears in his eyes. And, it was that she resented Joe for not feeling the same as Peter.

> *He's afraid he's going to die over there.*
> *   He could be killed.*
> *   Joe could be killed.*
> *   Kate could be killed.*
> *Will I see them again?*
> *   Oh, if I could stop thinking!*

Julia took off her mother's lime green nightgown she had loaned her and laid it over the footboard of the bed. "That's why I couldn't sleep," she said aloud. "Who could sleep in that ugly thing?"

She put on the dress she had worn to dinner the night before, and went to the kitchen to get a little something to eat. There was a note from her mother:

Good morning, Darling,

    I thought it best to let you sleep. I have a meeting this morning and will be out for lunch. Do not leave without getting yourself a decent breakfast – and lunch too if you're still here.

    Even if we do rent a room, you can come home. We won't be renting Kate's room, or my sewing room. We have plenty of space.

    This war will end and they'll all come home – don't you worry.

    Love,
    Mother

"Okay, Mother. I'll scramble an egg."

"Julia finish chewing
    before you get up from the table."
"That's not enough peas."
"You need your green vegetables."
"Where's you sister?"

"Julia, can I wear your sweater today?"
"Okay girls. Daddy's got to go. Come give me hugs."
"Don't mess up your clothes. We'll be leaving soon."

"I love this house," Julia said. "What a lovely home to grow up in! Kate and I had our arguments over whose turn it was to wash dishes, but most of the time we got along. Now, she's on permanent K.P. duty with the Red Cross and I'm in the old kitchen with my one plate listening to voices from the past that were so ordinary then. I wish she were here. I wish I could expect Joe to come by.

"I want to stay at the Bryans'. This house seems so strange without Kate. So empty."

Julia started to leave, but hesitated long enough to find a pencil and paper:

Mother and Daddy,

    I enjoyed our evening though seeing Peter leave did make me a little teary.

    Thanks for the offer to come home, but I'll wait for Joe in the apartment.

Love, Julia

P.S. This is the most beautiful home in the world!

Taking the footbridge across the creek, Julia came alongside the market and crossed the street to St. John's. She looked around to see that Crazy Charlie wasn't going to arrest her and made her way over to visit Lizzie.

"It's me, Lizzie. I didn't expect to be back so soon. You're the only one I can talk to. If only you could answer me.

"Peter's gone off to the war. Now I have Joe and Kate and Peter, too – all over there. Until I saw Peter leaving, I said I worried about Joe. Somehow I hadn't let the reality of the war sink in. It must be terrible for Kate – meeting all those boys and wondering if they'll make it. Lizzie, Joe may not come back.

"I'm being selfish, I know. Some Americans are going to be killed. I don't want it to be mine. Mother says not to worry – it's not good for the baby. But I worry more because of the baby. Lizzie, what's this war about? Will the world be a better place when the war is over?"

The young woman sat down on the grass beside Lizzie Burcher's tombstone.

"Lizzie," she spoke in a whisper, "I need to tell you something. There's a man who says he was the captain of a German u-boat. He says one of our destroyers killed all his men after they sunk the u-boat. The men were in the water pleading for help and our ship dropped depth charges in amongst them. I think he's telling the truth. I think the Army buried them in the National Cemetery.

"He and his men were torpedoing American ships and still would be if our ship hadn't shot them down. But the German boys – and he says some of them were very young – shouldn't have been killed that way. Should they? They should have been taken as prisoners, or allowed to struggle in the ocean, but not killed when they were defenseless.

"They are no longer Germans. They are simply God's children who called out for mercy and got something else. I pray the other side doesn't fight this way."

Julia had started something she had to see through. She walked out to the street and caught a streetcar to Phoebus.

"Julia Walters." Julia was greeted by a friend she'd gone to high school with.

"Virginia. How are you?"

"I'm fine. I heard a rumor that you married Joe."

"I did. But you all knew I would."

"Looks like it's working."

"Yes, we're expecting. I hadn't thought he was going overseas."

"I heard Joe was with NACA. I suppose you can't believe everything you hear."

Julia didn't want to explain. She left it as it was.

"What are you doing, Virginia?"

"Grumbling mostly. I had a cushy job in a dentist office before the war. Then the dentist enlisted in the Army and that was the end of that."

"So, you're not working now?"

"Like never before! I'm on an assembly line in the shipyard making some part of something and I have no idea what. I wear overalls and a hard hat. I sweat. There's hardly a man in sight who's not old enough to be my father. If I have any energy left when I get home, I go to the USO just to reassure myself all the young men haven't disappeared from the face of the earth. I'm still looking for a guy like Joe."

"Are you off today?"

"I'm playing hooky. There was an ad for a receptionist in the paper this morning. I'm going to stand in line.

"Where are you going?" she asked Julia.

"Just some errands. My life is mostly waiting. Waiting for Joe to come home. Waiting for this baby."

"What do you hear from Kate?"

"There's no shortage of men where she is. Otherwise she's working around the clock and traveling all over England."

"I envy her."

"I worry about her. She's too close to the fire."

"Long as they wave the Red Cross flag, she'll be okay," Virginia said.

"This is my stop. You're not going over to Phoebus, are you?"

"Yes... to the bicycle shop." Julia lied.

"Good to see you. Let me know when the little one arrives." Virginia got off at the last streetcar stop before it crossed the bridge.

The other passengers on the car all sat silent, each at a window seat taking in what little air they could. The smell of seafood was very strong as it always was. No one appeared to have any interest in anything until Julia rang the bell to get off at the cemetery.

"Oh, you don't want to get off here, miss. The bicycle shop is over on Mellon," one passenger said, "you'd have a long walk."

"She's right," a man said. "This ain't your stop."

"The bicycle shop is across from the post office only further down.

You don't want to get off here," another said.

One woman even told the motorman not to stop. "The young lady wants to go to the bicycle shop."

What was she to do? These kind people weren't going to let her off. She couldn't insist she wanted off at the cemetery now. That would make everyone too aware that she did. She rode on and when she got off, she walked towards the shop instead of the cemetery.

I know they're watching me
from the streetcar windows.

When the streetcar disappeared, Julia turned around. The Phoebus area was unfamiliar to her. There were a lot of bars along the street. She wouldn't run into people she knew here, but she felt conspicuously out of place.

Is it that I don't want to be noticed
that I think everyone is watching me?

The brick wall around the graveyard meant she had to walk all the way back to the gate to go into the cemetery.

Oh, I forgot the flowers.
I don't see anyone around.
There is someone sitting on the porch over there.
I should just stroll in, they won't even notice me.
Why do they fence in cemeteries?
To keep in the dead?
There's a whole group of people over there.
Should I leave?
They aren't interested in me.
Just walk about... slowly.

Julia had never been in this cemetery before. It was very different from the one at St. John's. The markers stood in evenly spaced rows, one identical to all around it except for the inscription. There were no elaborate inscriptions, "IN LOVING MEMORY, TO MY BELOVED, MAY SHE REST IN PEACE." There were no towering monuments. No little footstones.

There is something overwhelmingly beautiful

Rows and rows of markers
Like all for one and one for all.
What am I looking for?

Julia scrutinized the rows of stone markers before she realized there were no markers in an open space, but there were graves. This is where many new graves had been dug.

Eberhard's men are buried here.
The government has buried them here

Fifteen

"Has the war taken your loved one already?" Rose asked as she stepped up to the streetcar stop.

Julia didn't realize the woman was speaking to her.

"Are you all right, miss?"

"I'm sorry," Julia answered. "I didn't see you come up. Yes, I'm fine."

"You could hardly be fine. Here you are come with child and you're visiting the cemetery. You can tell Rose. I can see your sorrow."

"I was just walking around in the cemetery. I don't have anyone buried there."

"You've been crying. Your cheeks are streaked with tears."

"I've never been to this cemetery before, I suppose I got emotional."

"It is a sad place. Beautiful, but sad. I live there across the street from the cemetery. I sit on my porch snapping beans and shelling peas – that's what I was just now doing – and I see people come to the cemetery. I've seen a lot of grieving. I noticed you over there. I'd have sworn you were deeply troubled."

"I'm all right," Julia insisted.

"We had one big commotion here in the spring," Rose said. "I haven't gotten over it yet."

"A commotion in the cemetery?"

"Yeah, over there, where you were."

"What happened?" Julia said.

"It's a long story. You sure I'm not bothering you?"

"Please, tell me. Rose?"

"Yes. I'm Rose Washington. My husband and I were sitting on the porch. It was the first evening that was warm enough to sit out. Everything

Time Will Tell

was quiet and peaceful and then along came the army. They used to come by here going to Fort Monroe. This time they stopped right in front of the house. Looked like they were fixing to start a battle right there. The soldiers hopped out of their trucks. We couldn't imagine what they were up to. So, I sent my Thomas over to find out, but all they did was shove him out of their way. Then they got back in the trucks and drove them on into the cemetery." she paused.

Rose dug in her pocketbook. "Whew! I wondered if I'd remembered my ration stamp book. Here it is. I didn't want to go into town without it. Where was I?"

"The army vehicles had pulled into the cemetery," Julia prompted Rose.

"Yes. By now the whole neighborhood had come out to see what was happening. There were a lot of men – looked like prisoners. They put them to work digging. And not just one, or two graves. No, Ma'am. They had them dig twenty-nine graves. I counted them. Twenty-nine. One of the soldiers tried to tell us to get back in our houses. He said it was none of our business.

"I told Thomas we'd best do what they said," Rose continued. "But he kept asking what they were doing. Someone said they were burying bodies of merchant marines who had washed up on shore. Then somebody else said they were burying Germans. I 'spose the Good Lord knows. They took crates out of the trucks and men in dress uniform carried them to the graves."

"Was that the end of it?"

"Goodness, no. Thomas told me to go inside. He ran down to the corner to call the newspaper. Next thing, they fired those terrible guns. I thought we were all going to die. Were they gonna shoot us 'cause we were watching? But they weren't. They just shot into the air like they do. I think they call them blanks, but they're plenty loud.

"It was dark by then. A navy boy played taps. Everybody stood there listening. The sound of that horn was something in the night – no other sound, just the bugle.

(She hummed) Hmmm, hmm, hmm.
    Hmm, hmm, hmmmmm,
    Hmm, hmm, hmmmmm,
    Hmm, hmm, hmmmmm.

    Hmm, hmm,
    hmmmmmmmmmmmm,
    Hmm, hmm, hmmmm,
    Hmm, hmm, hmmmmmmm.

"It was some kind of pretty."

"You hadn't gone inside like Thomas said?"

"With Thomas going off down the street and ...I didn't know where Samuel was. No, Ma'am. I may have been shaking in my boots, but I wasn't going inside alone. All the army men got back into the trucks and they made enough racket to wake up the dead turning those big things around so they could come back out the gate. I was glad to see them leave."

"Did your husband get..."

"Here comes the streetcar. Now, are you going to be all right?"

"Yes, I'm fine. You're kind to be concerned."

The two women got onto the streetcar. Julia took a seat towards the front. Rose went to the back and sat with folks her own color. Neither of them would have been permitted to do otherwise.

Julia wanted to know what Rose's husband had found out when he called the newspaper.

From the way she spoke,
   he must not have learned anything.
Still, I'm sure that's where the bodies
   of the German sailors ended up.
      But why did they bury them at night?
         Under cover of night?

         With a bugle and a gun salute?

The streetcar passed through the downtown district. Though she sat at a window, Julia didn't focus on the people, or the business places along Queen Street. She imagined the propeller of the destroyer moving in on the German boys. She thought of how Eberhard told her they were screaming for mercy, but the ship went right into them. And then the tremendous explosions.

It's a wonder there was anything left of them
   to be pulled from the water.
   Perhaps I should go directly to the old house.
   I can avoid Bertie.
But if I go by my place I can
   get some more clothes for the German.
   If we're going to get to the cemetery,
      he'll need clean clothes.

In the heat of the summer day the walk from Electric Avenue to the Boulevard seemed twice as long as ever before. Julia was pleased to discover a breeze coming off the water that would be with her the rest of the way home. But the presence of the sentry standing in his station by the water, made her uncomfortable.

He's watching me.
Why does everyone notice me?

The freshness of the breeze that had cooled her turned to stickiness as soon as she went inside the house. She didn't see anyone downstairs, so she moved quietly up to the second floor hoping her luck would hold out.

"Julia, is that you?" Bertie asked. "Why didn't you come home last night?"

"I stayed with my folks," Julia told the child. "What are you doing?"

"Yes, Bertha Sue Bryan," Caroline Bryan said. "What ARE you doing? What is that?"

Julia took a good look at Bertie and could hardly refrain from laughing.

"It's 'Liquid Stockings,'" Bertie said. "I was just trying..."

"Give it here," said the mother. "Where did you get this? This isn't for children. You have it all over you. Excuse us, Julia. Oh, here's a loaf of fresh bread I brought up to you."

"Thank you, Mrs. Bryan," Julia said. "You are too good to me."

"It's no trouble to make an extra loaf."

"If you're going to do this, you must let me give you some flour."

"Maybe," Mrs. Bryan smiled at Julia, then turned back to her child.

"Bertha Sue, if your father saw you, he would have a conniption. Let's get you into the bath and wash that stuff off before it won't come off."

"But Mama. I wanted ..."

"Now is not the time to tell me what you wanted."

Julia could still hear their voices behind the bathroom door. She went on up to her apartment.

If I hurry,
   I can gather up some things and be out of here
   before they're through washing Bertie's

stockings off.

*Doesn't the Geneva Convention
    say armies have to take prisoners?
They can't shoot unarmed men.
    Then they can't depth charge men in the water
    or run them down with their propeller.*

Something went wrong.

*The newspapers tell of terrible things
    the u-boats are doing.
Of how they ambush merchant ships.
But we're not supposed to kill defenseless men.
    It's wrong.*

As Julia came to the corner, she saw some boys playing.

I think that's Ricky. I can't let him see me.

    The boys were marching along the edge of the street, their toy rifles across their shoulders. Julia turned back to see the sentry with the real gun making his way along the water's edge. She had to continue on to the next street and circle a block. The bag of things she carried would be difficult to explain.

    Once she turned away from the Boulevard, the sticky heat smothered her. She needed to cool off. Julia walked up in a yard to stand by a shade tree. A woman and a boy came out of the house. They were arguing. Julia felt embarrassed to be caught in their yard, but the woman gave her a wave to say she understood. Another woman was sweeping her porch. She was singing while she worked. Straight ahead of her, Julia could see someone boating in the Indian River Creek. They disturbed a group of ducks that suddenly took flight. Turning back to the old house, Julia was startled by a dog. Barking, he circled her preventing her from moving.

    "Come, Max!" someone shouted. But it took calling him several times before the dog would give up his vigilance. Julia saw a screen door open for the dog to go in.

    Now she would go up to the back of the house where she had discovered the German captain. Hopefully the little army would not be between here and there. If they were, she'd have to make something up. She couldn't keep walking in the heat.

I'll tell them a friend gave me these things...
and I'm on my way home.

Julia didn't meet the boys.

"Hello," she called when she went in the house. "Hello. Where are you?"

He didn't answer.

She went through the rooms of the first floor, "Hello. Please, be here."

I'm too tired to go upstairs.
Why doesn't he answer me?
Surely he hasn't gone.
He knew I was going to the cemetery.
Doesn't he care what happened to his men?

She sat on the steps and wept. She was crying because she was so tired. Had she done all of this for nothing? She was crying for the young Germans. She had stood on their graves! She was crying for Joe, for Peter, for all of the soldiers who were fighting and might never come home. She was crying for her baby. What kind of world would there be for her baby? And she was crying for Eberhard Greger.

Snarls rubbed up against her and purred.

"Oh, Snarls, you poor, poor kitty. I've got to find you a home. If I could, I'd take you home with me. The German captain liked you too. I didn't want to believe him about the destroyer running over his men and dropping depth charges, but I'm sure it is so. I went to the cemetery. A woman there told me about the Army burying them. I don't understand why they..."

"You talked to someone? You should not have done that." Eberhard Greger spoke as he descended the stairs.

"Why didn't you answer me? I thought you were gone."

"I was about to leave when I heard the dog barking at you. I've been watching to see if anyone noticed you coming in the house."

"Don't you want to go to the cemetery?"

"I want to go. But I don't want you to take me there. You shouldn't have gone there asking questions."

"I didn't ask questions. The woman told me."

"She just told you without you asking. Why would she do that?"

"She thought I was in a family way and I had lost my 'loved one.' She felt sorry for me."

"In a family way?"

"She thought I was pregnant and my man had been killed."

"Oh." He pondered that and then asked, "What did she say?"

"Apparently the military came in a convoy of trucks and had twenty-nine graves dug. They wouldn't tell Rose's husband who they were burying."

"Rose's husband? Do you know this woman?"

"She's colored. She lives across from the cemetery. I don't know her."

"You called her by name just now."

"She introduced herself."

"And did you introduce yourself?"

"Of course not. She did most of the talking. She told me something very interesting. Do you want to hear it?"

He nodded.

"They played taps when they buried them. And they had a gun salute."

"Then they must have been their own boys."

"No, I don't think so. Rose said that first they heard they were merchant marines and later someone said they were Germans."

"Will you tell me where the cemetery is?"

"I brought more clothes for you. If you're in clean clothes and we are together, no one will notice you."

"Like no one noticed me until your little friend came to find you?"

"If we don't go the most direct way, we should be able to stay away from places where people know me. I'll even disguise myself."

"You are 'in a family way.' How do you propose to hide that?"

"I'm not the only pregnant girl in Hampton. Look here."

"What is it?"

"My little friend gave me the idea. This is Liquid Stockings. I can rub some on my face and arms and, with my hair tucked up in this hat, no one will recognize me."

"Look, it's nice that you want to help, but I have another idea."

"Tell me."

"If you'll just tell me where the place is, I could swim there. It's on the other side of the creek, right?"

"Yes, but the creek doesn't come up to it. You'd never get from the creek to the cemetery without being spotted – all wet and very suspicious-looking."

"I might. I came a long ways here without being spotted. Is that more bread I see in your bag?"

"It is. Homemade, by Bertie's mother."

"It would help me if I had some good bread to eat before my swim."

"You may have some bread – all of it – if you'll agree to let me take you to the cemetery."

"Do you think a German can be so easily bribed?"

"Do you think you can get information out of an American?"

"Why are you so determined to get involved?"

"I inherited certain traits from my mother's side of the family. It's just the way I am."

"Do you think my family is helping an American GI hide from the Gestapo?"

"I don't know your family. What do you think?"

"I think they'd be risking a lot."

"But do you think they would?"

"I hope they wouldn't be so foolish."

"Do you think they would?"

"Yes. For a GI. For a Brit. For a Jew. It wouldn't matter."

"Did you volunteer for submarine duty?"

"All of the men in the Kriegsmarine are selected to volunteer. The pay is good. Like I told you, we're treated like heroes at home. They feed us well… until the food spoils. Admiral Donitz meets each u-boat when we return. He's very proud of his submarine fleet. Our job is to sink ships. As we sink ships, we display our successes on the conning tower."

"How many ships have you sunk?"

"It is the tonnage of the ships that we record."

"Oh. Do the passengers count as tonnage?"

"Our orders are to sink ships. We're to stop shipments of supplies to Europe."

"But." Julia continued, "How could ships defend themselves against your torpedoes?"

"The only advantage the u-boats have is surprise. If a captain can shoot off his eels before he is spotted, he can sink ships. Making a hit – listening and then hearing the target explode is a thrill. When we score a 'kill,' the crew cheers. But if we're spotted, or if the torpedoes don't find their target, we're in trouble.

"We have to dive quickly," he continued, "and pray they can't find us. Being underwater and being depth charged from above, we have lost our advantage. Now the crew is trapped while the enemy drops depth charges all around. The boat is jolted by the explosions and men are tossed about inside the boat. We cannot see the enemy. We cannot charge back at them. We can't run. All we can do is sit and pray. Pray none of the charges make a direct hit.

"Outsmarting the enemy, dodging his cans, slipping up on him without being seen... these are the responsibilities of the captain," the man concluded.

"Cans? Depth charges?"

"Same thing. They are big barrels of explosives designed to drop on submarines."

"Do you and your wife have children?"

"I'm not married," he said.

"You said your family... I assumed."

"Marriage isn't for u-boat captains. When you're on a sub, you're married to it."

"You'd rather..."

"It is not by choice. It was not my plan. When I was young, I thought I'd grow up to be a pharmacist like my father."

"Why didn't you?"

"The government had other ideas."

"What's it like being under water all the time?"

"We don't stay under water unless we have to. We can't stay down too long. But it isn't a sightseeing tour when you travel by u-boat.

"In a u-boat there's no room for error," he continued more seriously. "Every man on the boat is needed, but that doesn't mean there's any room for him. We don't have water to wash our faces and some of the guys seldom get to come up to the conning tower. The torpedoes have to be cleaned and rotated regularly and they are heavy and extremely dangerous. The boys stayed down in that shitty-smelling cylinder counting on me and their silly little lucky pieces to get them home alive.

"You aren't collecting information for your government, are you?" he asked.

"Perhaps, I am."

"Then tell them they didn't finish the job. They left one man alive who can tell what they did. And would you like me to tell you what some American pilots did?"

"I don't think so."

"Then you better go."

"With what Rose Washington told me, I believe what you said about your boat. Please don't tell me it wasn't just that once."

"People believe what they want to believe."

"You don't think Germans 'believe what they want to believe?'"

"Of course. Everyone does."

"Germans want to believe the Jewish people are not human beings," Julia said. "They want to put them all in prison camps. That's not right."

"And in America, haven't the whites done much the same thing to the Indians? Where do the people who were here first live today?"

"We didn't force them to live in ghettos."

"How is a reservation different from a ghetto? And don't you call them savages?"

"It is not the same thing," Julia said.

"Why do you think this? How do you know?" he asked.

"Many Germans do not like what is being done to the Jewish people," Eberhard explained. "We have friends who are Jewish. We are concerned about what's happening to them."

"Can't you speak up? Can't you stop the Nazis?"

"Not so long as Germany is at war."

"The Nazis are wicked. Certainly you know that."

"Your political leaders have been known to do some pretty awful things. Your government talks of equality, but it is not a reality for the American Indian, or the Negro, or many others who you might say look different. I lived here for awhile. Perhaps I noticed things I wouldn't notice in my own homeland."

"I don't want to hear what our planes did."

"Then I won't tell you... Julia Keegan, you should go home."

Julia refused to leave though the German had a know-it-all way about him that upset her.

Indians live as they want on their reservations.
Did he live with the Indians when he lived here?
I should have asked him that.
We have no racial problems in Hampton.
We have Hampton Institute for the colored students.
He thinks he knows so much about us.

"I have offended you, Julia. I'm sorry."

"I was the one who said your leaders were wicked," Julia admitted.

"Yes, you did." He paused. "And you are right. I'm not sure a man can be a leader without becoming 'wicked,' as you say. Germany suffered greatly after the other war. The depression years were horrible. People were starving. Many were homeless. That's when my family sent me here to live with my uncle."

"Didn't you like it here?"

"I missed my cousins in Germany. I have no brothers or sisters, so they are like siblings to me. In the United States I had to hide that I was German. My aunt and uncle told me I must never tell anyone my family lived in Germany. 'Americans don't like Germans,' they said. 'Tell people you're from Austria.' "

"When I returned home to Germany, things had changed. People were employed. They were dressed well. They ate well. Germany had been revived. The man you say is wicked did this for Germany. Is it so surprising that his people should love him?"

"Why has Germany invaded other European countries?"

"That, my American friend, is but a continuation of history. Czars, kings, pharaohs, emperors, sultans and sheiks... all they ever did was conquer other countries. Countries used to fight their own wars. Now, they form alliances and the whole world is divided into two great forces."

"You wanted to fight for Germany?"

"I wanted to serve my country, because that is what a man is supposed to do."

"That's an argument I'm familiar with."

Julia handed Eberhard a newspaper.

"You brought the newspaper too?"

"My landlady passes hers on to me. This is yesterday's paper. I haven't had time to read it. You had some newspapers here. How did you get them?"

"I stole them off someone's front porch. It didn't look as though they were home. Several papers had accumulated.

"Do you suppose the war has ended without our knowing it?" he asked.

"That would be news," Julia said. "What would you do if you opened the paper and the headline read: THE WAR IS ENDED?"

"The Allies won?" he asked.

"Of course," she answered smiling.

"I'd turn myself in and ask for passage home."

It's good he isn't still talking about wanting to die,
Julia thought.

"What if Germany won?" she asked. "Would you do something different?"

"I'd turn myself in and demand passage home. I'd go back to Germany and become a fisherman. I'd fight nothing worse than a stormy sea and a struggling carp. I'd pull the rascal in and take it home for the evening meal. I'd sit down with my family in the kitchen and tell them of the giant wave that about flipped the boat over and the shark that circled around the boat until I had to throw him the really big fish I'd caught. And then we'd all laugh. Well, the children and I would laugh. My wife would say, 'Eberhard Greger - you shouldn't tell such stories!"

"Your wife?"

"I wouldn't be a u-boat captain anymore. There's a special girl back home who I intend to marry if I survive this war. And I'll build a cottage in the woods for us where we can breathe fresh air and grow vegetables in our garden. We'll have a dog and a cat, some chickens – fresh eggs – and perhaps a goat."

The German stopped talking. Julia watched a smile disappear from the man's face as his vision of a home slipped away from him. There was an embarrassing silence – neither of them could think of anything to say.

Finally she asked, "You would feed your whole family with one carp?"

"It would be a big carp, of course."

"Even my father doesn't tell such fish stories as you do."

"I'd throw anything back that wasn't big enough to feed the family. Is your father a fisherman?"

"He's a story-teller who may, or may not have caught a fish. I wonder if he doesn't buy the fish from Mr. Byrd before he comes home."

"Well, the war didn't end yesterday," Eberhard said looking at the paper. "Seems the Allies want to open a second front."

Eberhard shifted the paper to read, "ATLANTIC SUB SINKINGS, 394," but another paper fell out of the first.

"Mrs. Bryan must have put two day's papers together as I wasn't home," Julia said picking it up. "This is today's paper." The larger headline about Rommel in Egypt didn't hold Julia's attention. Just below it she saw:

> 29 German U-Boat Dead
> Buried At Hampton; First
> To Reach U.S. In This War

Julia quickly skimmed the article before handing that paper to Eberhard. "Here it is. The Navy announced they sunk a u-boat."

" 'Victims of Atlantic-Patrol Destroyer Given Full Military Honors As Dusk Falls Over Peninsula National Cemetery,' " the German read aloud. "The bodies of 29 German Submarine crew members ... brought to Norfolk naval base... buried with full military honors in nearby Hampton... the date of the funeral unreleasable... reports of a mass interment... the bodies and a few life-jackets were all that remained...

"I can't read anymore." Eberhard handed the paper back to Julia.

"It says that full military honors were rendered by both the Army and the Navy and that a Catholic and a Protestant clergy participated. They fired three volleys and a Navy bugler played 'taps.' "

"If they hadn't honored them with depth charges, they wouldn't have needed to act out this 'military honors' charade."

"Apparently Rose Washington's husband wasn't the only one who called the newspaper."

"Mr. Washington called the paper?"

"Yes, but when the Washingtons looked for a story, they didn't find one. It says here the Daily Press got numerous inquiries."

The German gathered all the newspapers about them. He shoved them back into the bag Julia had brought them in. He took what was left of the bread he had and threw it into the bag. He grabbed the hat Julia had put on her head and put it in the bag. "Go, Julia Keegan. Gehen!" He shouted and thrust the bag at her.

"Why?"

"Because at this moment I would do anything to get back at America... and you are American and you are here. Get out before I do something I will regret!"

Julia reached for the cat, "May I?" she asked.

"Yes, take the cat. Go!"

Holding the bag in one hand and nestling the cat in the other arm, Julia went to the kitchen to go out the back way. "The man is upset, Snarls. We must give him time to cool down. I don't believe he would hurt either of us."

Through the pane of glass in the back door Julia saw Ricky and his friends playing on the side street next to the house. "Sh-h-h-h, Snarls, we'll have to wait."

Julia didn't want to put the cat down. He might go back to the German. She placed the bag at her feet and listened to the boys outside. They were flying airplanes over enemy territory and dropping bombs. They were having gunfights in the sky and enemy planes were going up in flames. They were radioing each other:

"Got 'em, Joe! I'm returning to base. zzzzzzzzzzz"
"Look out, Mac!
    There's a Jap on your tail.zzzzzzzzzzz"
   "I'm low on fuel. I may have
                 to bail.zzzzzzzzzzz"

Snarls wiggled out of Julia's arms and darted back towards the front of the house.

"No, Snarls. Come, kitty!"

She couldn't get him back and she could still hear the children flying their imaginary planes outside. The German would know she was there when Snarls showed himself. What could she do?

Moments later she saw Eberhard Greger standing in the next room.

"I'm leaving," she whispered. "But I can't go out there now. The boys are playing beside the house."

"Julia Keegan." That's all he said. Her name.

"What?" she asked. "What can I do? You see the boys out there. Do you want me to go..."

"No. I don't want you to go."

The captain of the sunken u-boat said no more. There were warring nations between them, but there they stood only feet apart.

Why do I feel such compassion for this man?
He speaks harshly.   He's a German.
Before our destroyer shot them down,
they were sinking our boats.
If he could somehow get back to Germany,
would he not captain another boat?

Why am I here?
Because the boys are playing in the street.
Otherwise I would be gone.

"Was die Augen nicht sehen, bekommt das Hertz nicht."

Now he speaks German.
I suppose that means I stayed too long.

"Was die Augen nicht sehen, bekommt das Hertz nicht," he repeated. "That's a German proverb my uncle in New York used to quote. In English, you would say 'What the eye does not see, the heart does not grieve for.' I never understood its meaning."

"Do you now?"

"Was he trying to say he could not worry about those he left behind in Germany? For me it is not so. Back home my girl was waiting for me. They must have told her my boat is missing. She must think I am dead.

"My home town sponsored my boat. We had the emblem of a wild boar painted on the conning tower. When Lieberose sponsored us, we added a rose in the boar's mouth. Lieberose means 'dear rose.'

"All right. You can show me the way to the cemetery," he said.

"Only you are not going to disguise yourself. We won't go together and we won't go the long way around. I'll get on the streetcar at one stop. You'll get on at the next."

"Suppose..."

"Suppose you were covered in this stuff and someone did stop you. How would you explain your disguise? Now listen. You are not to get off at the cemetery. Just give me a signal and stay seated. That will tell me all I need to know."

"But..."

"Julia Keegan. Thank you. I will never forget your kindness."

"Then what?" she asked.

"Then you go back to your apartment."

"And you?"

"I will vanish. Can you do this?"

"I can. You will put on the clean clothes?"

"Yes," he said.

Eberhard reappeared in the change of clothes. These fit better than the others she had brought him. The two of them took everything else, clothes and papers, and filled the bag Julia had brought with her. "I will take these things back to the apartment. We must wait until after the peak time when so many military ride the streetcar. Okay?"

"Yes, catch the first car that isn't crowded. I will be on it. Do not sit next to me."

"But..."

"Do not sit next to me."

"What good am I to you? How am I helping?"

"You don't have to go."

"But I have to stay on the streetcar. I can't get off with you?

"No, you can't. You must agree."

Sixteen

"Rose, the newspaper finally got around to printing the story of what was going on in the cemetery. They were German men all right, just like Reuben said."

"You don't mean it. In today's paper?"

"Front page. Everyone that came into Fuller's today was talking about it."

"What's it say?"

"It doesn't say much. They didn't give a date of the funeral."

"You sure it was that night?"

"Look here it says -
29 German U-Boat Dead
Buried at Hampton"

"Does it explain why they buried Germans over here?"

"Something here, ah here it is, they were doing like they did in the War of 1812."

"Hum. It just doesn't seem right. None of their own people at the funeral."

"They could hardly invite German families to come. We're at war with Germany, you know," Thomas said. "I just don't see a need to bury Germans in our national cemetery."

"A white girl came to the cemetery today," Rose said. "I was sitting on the porch fixing to go into town. She came up from Mallory. I noticed her because she was looking around almost like she was afraid of someone. She walked up to the gate and paused like she couldn't decide whether to go in, or not. She just kept looking about as if she thought someone was following her."

"Did you see anyone else?"

"A group of people were there already, but she didn't go near them. She meandered around reading the markers and then she stopped over where the Army buried those Germans. I thought I heard her gasp. She walked about all over that area, but seemed not to want to walk on the graves. She was crying and talking. I was sure she knew someone who was buried there."

"Curious."

"I thought so. Well, she came on out of the graveyard and went up to the streetcar stop to go into Hampton. So I walked on up there, though I knew the streetcar wasn't due to come for another five or six minutes. I asked her if she was all right. She said she was, but Thomas that child had been crying."

"It must not have had anything to do with those graves. We know now, for sure, the Army buried Germans there."

"She told me she didn't have anyone buried there. But I know that girl was grieving. And she was anticipating a child – that much, I know. The streetcar happened along just as she was about to say something,"

"Rose, she said she was all right. Don't you have enough people to worry about not to have to find strangers on the street?

"Looks like the Army is taking a group of Negro men – 40, it says," Thomas continued reading the paper.

"From around here?"

"Yes, sir-re. From Elizabeth City County. They say they expect to have a much larger number called up next month."

"I don't know why I fear Samuel being sent overseas. There are so many stories about boys crashing the planes in training exercises right here in the states. Like Mayor Snow's son who crashed in the middle of the shipyard."

"He was showing off – barnstorming they call it," Thomas answered. "Samuel says Tuskegee has a better record than other air fields. He says they are going to prove their unit can measure up to the white pilots. They can't afford to make foolish mistakes acting like stuntmen. If they do well, they are lucky son-of-a-bitches. If they mess up, they're lame-brained niggers."

"You want me to read you Samuel's letter, or do you just want to keep on with that ugly talk?" Rose asked Thomas.

"Why didn't you say we had a letter?"

> Dear Pop and Mama
>
>   Hampton seems downright friendly towards the Negro since I came to Alabama. The government has set up separate facilities for us on the far side of the airfield. The white boys probably don't even know we are here. A

couple of our unit went into Tuskegee, the town, one day. They met some white guys on the sidewalk. The whites told them they had better get off the sidewalk if they didn't want to get themselves lynched. This is the first time these colored fellows have been south of the Mason Dixon Line. They came back to the base talking about getting the law to do something about those ruffians in town. When we said that wouldn't happen anywhere in Alabama, they said it wasn't much of a town anyway. We've all decided to stay on base and on the colored side of the airfield. Don't worry, Mama, the chief keeps us plenty busy.

Chief Anderson told us the Army calls this an experiment. He says the Army doesn't want any colored fliers, but they are having him try to train us so they can prove we can't do the job. They want us to fail. They say we're cowardly and superstitious and that we can't be trusted to fight. They say we will turn and run from the enemy.

Chief says he's going to be tough with us because he knows we can do it. He says any slackers are not going to last. We're going to be held to a higher standard than the whites. But, Pop, this is a mighty fine group of men and we're going to prove the Army doesn't know what it is talking about. Some of these guys have Phds.

Chief Anderson taught himself how to fly. He said he couldn't get anyone to teach him, so he bought his own plane and learned on his own. He has flown all the way across country and he's been put in charge of the "Negro Experiment" at Tuskegee.

Some of us will be trained as mechanics, or radiomen. Chief says we have to service our own planes – the white guys aren't going to do it – so we can't all be pilots. That hit us hard. Most of us joined so we could fly. I'm hoping my training at the institute in Hampton is going to get me in the pilot's seat.

Gen. Noel Parrish, our Station Commander is a white southerner and he looks like one. When we first had to go before him, we were all sure he'd give us you-know-what. Chief says he's a good man and he'll be fair with us.

Take care of each other and don't worry about me. I've a lot of studying to do. I wrote this long letter, so you'd know what was going on. Mama, don't get all in a stew if I don't write. I'm okay. I've got to do a lot of studying.

    Your son,
    Samuel

"Maybe, the good Lord will keep Samuel's feet on the ground after all," said Rose.

"Now, Rose, he said he probably will get to pilot. Don't be wishing against him, Mama."

"I will never like those awful planes," Rose said. "Too many things can go wrong."

"Samuel is levelheaded – he's nobody's fool. He's going to learn how to handle that thing. He'll be just as safe up in the air as a foot soldier, or a man in the belly of a ship "

"I don't know how you can think so."

"You remember how Samuel watched Errol Flynn in Dawn Patrol, those war movies of the allied planes fighting the Red Baron, when he was a little fellow?"

"Young British boys going off in rickety planes to be killed?" Rose remembered too well.

"Mama, that was the First War. Aircraft has improved now."

Thomas chuckled as he recalled, "Samuel played all the time with the model planes he built. He's wanted to fly a plane ever since. He's working harder than he's ever worked because he wants this opportunity. If he succeeds, we have to be happy for him."

"You have…"

"Rose, Samuel is in the Air Corps and that's that. I hope they don't cheat him of the chance to fly. It would devastate him."

Thomas made Rose mad. She did not respond. He had another article from the paper to share with her. This would make her say something. He read:

SWEARING AS A SAFETY VALVE

"According to the newspaper, you should stop crying… and swear."

"It does not say that."

"Perhaps I need glasses, but I'd… here, you look at it."

Thomas passed the paper to her.

"Uh, uh, uh." Rose grunted as she read.

"Well, isn't that what it says?" asked Thomas.

"According to some Philadelphia doctor. He's just making up an excuse for his own behavior," Rose replied. "Swearing is sinful."

"The doctor says the apes have been swearing since the beginning of time."

"Then the doctor should limit his prescription to apes. Certainly we're not supposed to pattern our behavior after apes."

"He says here that many women are getting as good at swearing as men. Instead of getting all weepy, women are learning to release their frustrations..."

"Thomas, that's enough. The man shouldn't be a doctor if that's the kind of advice he offers."

"Here's a story you will like."

"Don't be making me mad again, Thomas."

"You will like this. It says that there soon won't be any auto thieves."

"Well, now, how do they suppose that?"

"What they're saying is, a thief can't get gas for a car he steals. If the driver of a car doesn't have the ration book issued for that car, gas stations can't sell him any gas. He won't get far without any gas," Thomas laughed.

Rose laughed with him. "I declare! There is something good about ration stamps. Can you beat that?"

****

A man called in sick. There was no one else to run his evening route. Charles Magivens would pull one shift after the other. The city had deputized the drivers. If any passengers were causing a disturbance on the streetcars, the motormen had the authority to put them off. This didn't happen on the day shift, but sometimes when men had spent too much time in the bars, they might act out.

Most often disturbances were started by soldiers having a last fling before shipping out. And, most often, a word of caution that they would be reported would quiet them down. Still the evening shift was more likely to have something happen out of the routine. This night would be no exception.

A jeep came up behind Charles. He was not going to go any faster just because the soldiers in the jeep were making a hullabaloo. "Those young whippersnappers can learn a little patience and good manners," Charles said as he kept his pace. The jeep followed closely.

The jeep pulled over beside Charles' streetcar and a streetcar coming the other direction appeared at once. They all hit their breaks and there was a terrible noise – breaks screeching, metal hitting metal, glass breaking, people screaming.

Charles stopped the car and called out, "Is anybody hurt? Speak up, if you need help," He stood facing his silent passengers. "Good. Then stay in your seats."

Charles got out to survey the damages.

Julia moved several seats back to sit beside Eberhard.

"You must get off now. Do not wait for the driver to return. The cemetery is on the other side of the bridge. Go."

Eberhard stood up and went to the door of the streetcar.

"Sit down, sir," Charles said.

"Oh, please let him go!" Julia shouted. "Please, Greg, go get my mother!"

"Oh, my goodness. Is she hurt?" The driver asked. "Go! Go, do as she asks!

"Someone, come over here and sit with the lady. I do hope that fellow hurries back with her mother.

"Now, the rest of you sit down. Don't crowd her. I'm going to hand out an accident report for each of you to fill out. The most important thing is that you give us your complete name and address – in case we need to get in touch with you. This is standard company procedure."

"Are you all right, miss?" asked the man who had moved next to her. There were no other women in the car.

"I think I'm going to be all right now. I just felt dizzy. I don't know what possessed me to come out this evening. I must get off this streetcar and go home where I belong."

"Are you sure you should stand up?"

"I'm fine. It's just a short distance to the house."

"Then I will walk with you. Driver, the lady says she's fine, but she doesn't want to stay on the streetcar. May I escort her home?"

"I'll need you both to fill out a card before you go. We can have a police car take her home."

"Really, I'm okay. I can walk."

"You may think you're okay, but you may not be. No, Ma'am, I cannot let you walk home," Charles said.

Julia filled out the card and then accepted their inescapable assistance to the police car.

A young officer got in behind the wheel. "Where to, miss?"

"It's just over on Acorn Point," she gave him her parent's address foolishly hoping he might agree to let her out. "I could easily walk."

"We couldn't take the chance you might have been injured."

"Officer. Could you let me out on the street? I mean, do you have to go to the door with me? I'm sure I've got everyone most upset as it is. If they open the door and see you... you know what I mean?"

"Sure. I'll pull up and let you out. But I won't leave until I see the door open and that they have you safely inside."

> *Whatever would Mother say if she opened the door*
> *and there I stood with a police officer?*
> *If I had stayed on the streetcar,*
> *I could have gone to the cemetery.*
> *Eberhard didn't want me near the cemetery*
> *before I caused a scene.*
> *He is gone. He will find the cemetery.*
> *I'll never know anything more of him.*

"Is this where you want out, miss?"

"Yes, thank you."

"You haven't changed your mind? You still don't want me to walk you to the door?"

"I haven't changed my mind. My parents can be overprotective. I don't need to give them more reason to be, do I?"

"I guess not. But you be careful."

"Thank you, I will."

Julia opened the door and waved to the officer. He drove away.

"Mother, it's Julia. Where are you?"

"We're out on the porch."

"Hi."

"Hi, to you. What brings you back tonight?"

"The daylight got away from me before I knew it. I was wondering if Dad could give me a ride home?"

"I could do that "

"Or you could stay here tonight and go home in the morning," suggested her mother. "I haven't even changed the linens on your bed."

"To be honest, I'm rather tired. Not having to go any further tonight sounds very nice."

"Good, let me get you something refreshing," her mother said. "You've got to take better care of yourself."

"Sit down, Julia," Mr. Walters said. "Your mother is right. You need to be taking better care of yourself. You look tired. What were you..."

"Dad, listen to the frogs. Kate and I used to sit out here and make up things they were saying. Anything with two beats. Like 'Cheer up, Sit down, Stop it, Jump on.' We'd keep it going until one of us couldn't think of another... listen."

They sat there listening to the frogs.

"Maybe your sister is sitting near a brook in the heart of England listening to frog-talk," her father said. He laughed. "I caught her kissing a frog one day when she was little."

"Ugh, why on earth?"

"She said it might be a prince." He laughed again. "I told her that was just a fairy tale. And she told me, I'll never forget, 'Daddy, my kisses are magic!'"

It was strangely dark in Julia's old neighborhood. Hampton people were good about cooperating with the dimout. Black shades blocked any indoor lighting. Streetlights, and even the lights on the bridge, were turned off. Beams of searchlights crisscrossed the sky reminding them that their darkened hometown was watching for invaders.

The quiet was interrupted by sirens.

"Whatever is going on now?" asked Mrs. Walters returning with a tray.

"If it's anything to be concerned about, they'll sound an air raid," Mr. Walters said. "Since that article in the paper about Germans caught just off the coast, everyone is imagining spies are all over. It's probably another 'possible sighting' that will turn up nothing."

"You can never be too careful," Mrs. Walters said. "Those men buried in the National Cemetery were probably sent here to blow up our military bases. We live in a very dangerous area."

"They were here to sink shipments of supplies to Europe," Julia said. "That's what I read," she added.

"Surely they have proven that is one of their intentions," answered her father. "Ships are having to take a zigzag course and travel in convoys in hopes of not being torpedoed. The u-boats attack mercilessly."

The sirens stopped.
Did they spot Eberhard?
What will happen to him if they did?

"Julia. Julia."

"Yes, Mother?"

"I asked if you'd like some crackers. I wish I had some cheese to go with them."

"I don't need cheese," Julia said. "These are good just as they are."

"I made a pitcher of tea," her mother offered.

"Oh, that does look refreshing."

"I'm so glad the sirens have stopped." Mrs. Walters said. "That is such an eerie sound. Now, let's talk."

"Julia and I were enjoying listening to the frogs and thinking of when she and Kate were little," Mr. Walters said.

> *I wish I knew what happened.*
> *Did he make it to the cemetery?*
> *I had to tell him to get off the streetcar.*
> *They were going to give him a card to fill out.*
> *He should have been able to get across the bridge*
> *before they got the streetcars going again.*
> *But what were the sirens for?*
> *I don't think Eberhard's boat was bringing spies.*
> *I don't.*

"Julia."

"What?"

"Are you upset about something?" Mrs. Walters asked.

"No, why do you ask?"

"You're here, but you don't answer us," Mr. Walters said.

"I was thinking about the baby," she lied. "You two are going to be grandparents."

"The baby's grandparents would like you to take it easy," Mrs. Walters said. "You're pushing yourself too much. What is it you do to wear yourself out so? And please don't be walking alone in the evenings. What if you ran into a German spy?"

"What..." her father started to ask...

"You're right," Julia said. "I must be more responsible. There's no excuse for me getting this tired. And I'm going to take your advice and go to bed. Goodnight"

She kissed her mother. Turning to her father, she said, "If I had a magic kiss, I might turn you into a frog."

"All my girls have magic kisses. That's what keeps me young."

Julia went to her old room. She felt like a child again. She had been up to mischief and had nearly been caught. Someone may have noticed her moving over to speak to the German on the streetcar. Someone may tell the authorities she and Eberhard Greger looked suspicious. She heard the doorbell. Had they come to question her?

Julia tiptoed quietly out to the top of the stairs.

"... lady left this in the car." Julia heard only part of what the man said.

"Yes, it is my daughter's," her father answered. "Thank you for bringing it by, officer."

"It was no trouble. I hope she's all right."

"Yes. I hope so. Did she say she was hurt?"

"Oh, no sir. She insisted she was fine. She seemed more concerned she would upset you folks."

"Well, she was acting a little strange, but she obviously didn't want us to know about the accident. I think she's okay."

"Goodnight, sir."

"Goodnight."

"How did that police officer get Julia's purse?" Julia heard her mother ask.

"Seems he... well, Julia was on a streetcar when there was a little accident. The officer drove her here."

"But she didn't say anything about...."

"He said she was worried she might upset us."

"Well, she has. I'm going straight...."

Julia rushed back to her bed.

Oh, what am I going to tell them?
That I was showing a German the way to Phoebus?
That I faked being hurt so that he could get away?
Why was I on the streetcar?
What can I say?

Julia waited breathlessly, anticipating her Mother's inquisition. But Mother didn't come.

I guess Father told her there
   must be a reason for my behavior,
   "No matter how strange," I can hear him say,
   "She'll tell us in due time."

Julia knew she must never tell them... unless the police came back and she was taken in for a real inquisition. Then, and only then, would she ever tell her parents

   What happened to Eberhard Greger?
   Will I ever see him again?
                   Will I ever know?

Seventeen

- Autumn of 1942-

Dear Julia,

    I thought it would never stop raining, but it did. It even warmed up a bit. There are still oceans of mud everywhere we go. But the clubmobile isn't so tight now that we aren't all working inside all the time. During the rainy months someone joked we didn't have enough room to change our minds – we hardly had enough room to laugh when she said this!

    Lately we've had to be our own mechanics. We've learned how the generator, distributor, fan belts and fuel lines work. I now know thirty-six points for greasing the chassis. I never thought I'd even talk about such things. I fear the day we have to change one of those enormous tires.

    Last night the nicest guy spent time talking to me. We sat on a blanket in a field with nothing but the stars for light. He talked about playing football in high school, about his grandma who raised him and his dog. He was so dear. When he got up to leave, he said, "Goodbye, I hope I'll pull through this war and see you again."

    I received a letter from Peter. He's such a kidder. He said this is one theatre where he doesn't want a front row seat, but to save him a doughnut in case he's lucky enough to be marched by this way. It would be nice to see him.

    Tell Bertie her letters are wonderful! Matthew

wants them read to him over and over again. He tells the other fellows in the ward that Bertie is his little sister. He would like her to send a picture of herself. There are several guys who don't get mail. Does Bertie have friends who want to write someone? It makes a soldier feel important just to hear his name at mail call.

With all my love,
Kate

There was also a letter for her from Peter...

Got a pass to Rennes, Brittany. They have a swell Red Cross Club. Too bad Kate isn't stationed there.

You would like the way the people dress – the women actually wear wooden shoes and little white aprons and caps – like we were always told the Dutch do.

Then there are the French girls from the big cities that wear very short skirts. I bet you'd look good like that!

Just teasing. Grandma would say those kind of girls are Jezebels.

Tonight we had a 'Jeep Show.' That's what the Army calls a traveling USO unit. They play at a different spot every day. Mickey Rooney did imitations of Lionel Barrymore, Clarke Gable, Gene Autry and Edgar G. Robinson. He was so funny. I don't think I stopped laughing once.

They had a dandy band and a lot of swell acts. Mickey is a little fellow, but he was as good as he is in pictures. Better.

Joe's correspondence, though fairly regular, seldom was more than an expression of love and a request for Julia to write him, which she did faithfully. Ostensibly to save space and speed delivery the government began photographing mail.

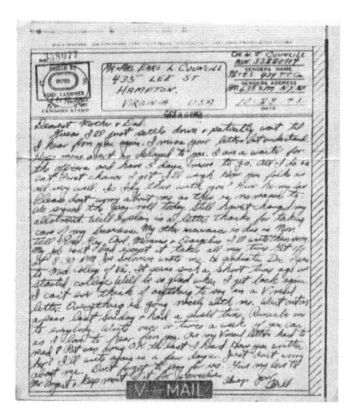

Special 8 1/2 by 11-inch stationery was designed to be photographed. The film was sent to distribution points and then printed on 4 by 5 1/2-inch postcards. Sometimes words, or whole lines, were blacked out during this "space-saving process."

Julia thought of her cousin's protests about the censors when she read in the newspaper that a little three-year-old girl drew a picture of a cow and sent it to her father who was overseas. The army censor returned it to the little girl with a note: "It is against military regulations to mail outside continental limits of the United States, drawings of public buildings."

"I have to tell myself these regulations were made for a good reason," Julia said, even though sometimes enforced without reason."

Julia asked no questions, mentioned nothing political and didn't draw pictures when she wrote. When she wrote about the baby, she couldn't help but say she wanted Joe home for the birth. Julia's letters were mostly about Bertie and Ricky and a cat named Snarls that she and the children were feeding.

The vacant house wasn't going to stay vacant what with the shortage of housing in Hampton. Julia had thought about this probability, and sure enough, one day in August she and the children discovered workers there cleaning up the house. Soon people would be living there. "The people who move in will adopt the cat," Julia told Bertie and Ricky.

"Julia!! You can't let them have Snarls," they answered. "He's our cat."

"We were only looking after him until someone came along who wanted a cat."

"Snarls won't know them. He won't like them. You can't let them have him."

"I could ask my folks if he could live at their house," Julia said. "But Mother will never agree unless we promise to take care of him."

You bet they'd take care of him! Julia left Bertie and Ricky petting Snarls with crossed fingers while she went to phone her mother.

"I wouldn't ask except the children have become so attached to the cat," Julia explained. "They will be heart-broken if they lose him."

"I'm so busy right now. I'm hardly ever home."

"That's okay. Snarls isn't used to having someone around all the time. He's really quite independent. The children and I will take care of feeding him."

"You're a streetcar-ride away. I expect you'll be calling me to feed him before long," her mother said. "I thought you'd outgrown bringing strays home. You don't even live here and you want me to take in a stray."

"When Joe comes home, we'll get a house and we can take him there. It's just for a little while," Julia said. "He'll make a perfect pet for your grandchild."

"A cat you call Snarls?"

"He's really sweet. You're going to love him. I know you will."

"I hope my boarders like cats. We can't keep him here if that's a problem."

In the afternoon Julia, the two children and Snarls rode the streetcar to the house where Julia had grown up. That evening she wrote to Joe and Kate. "Mother pretended not to like him, but Snarls has won her over. He is a most unusual cat."

On the days Bertie had piano lessons, Julia took the opportunity to go into town by herself and stop at St. John's. She talked to Lizzie of Joe and Kate and Peter, too. Of fears they wouldn't return home after the war and fears that the war would last another year. She told Lizzie of dreams she had for her baby. Of things she'd learned from her little friends, Bertie and Ricky. And each time, before Julia left, she would talk to Lizzie about Eberhard Greger. She couldn't talk to anyone else about the German u-boat captain.

He told me when his boat was trapped,
All the men of his crew counted on him
to make the right decision.
And when he told them to abandon ship,
He assured them they'd be all right-
They'd be taken prisoners, not killed.

He told me how the crew cheered
when they sank an Allied ship-
Once they heard the explosion
it was such a relief.
But then, he could only imagine the devastation
And hope the men from the sunken ship
would be rescued.
It was his job to sink ships and
they were forbidden to stay around
to rescue men in the water.

He didn't want to kill our sailors.
He didn't think our captain would kill his men.

I hope he'll return to his family when this war is over.
I wish I could know he made it.
Or at least, that he is only being held prisoner –
that he is alive.

The battle cry that justified the war, and the sending of our boys to fight, continued to be "Remember Pearl Harbor!" But the people on the East Coast didn't feel threatened by the enemy on the other side of the globe. It was the threat of German saboteurs that rallied the people of Hampton to cooperate with the blackouts. The arrests of German spies, brought to our coast by u-boats, dominated the news throughout the summer of '42.

Julia followed news stories of the teams of German spies who had landed at Amagansett, Long Island and at Ponte Vedra Beach near Jacksonville, Florida. They had been apprehended before they could carry out any of their plans to reek havoc on the United States.

Stories of the tribunal ran on the front page. A military commission of seven generals was to determine the fate of the Germans spies. Though much of the record of the case had to be kept sealed until after the war, the FBI did say the agents carried maps of vital spots to be targeted and enough explosives and incendiaries to provide for a two-year campaign of destruction of America's war plants.

A month later the headline read "FBI Warns Nation 3 Trained Saboteurs May Be Loose In U.S." The FBI distributed "wanted" circulars with mug shots of three Germans. Hoover said these men had received orders from the German High Command to come to the United States to destroy vital war industries.

And the next month the headline read, "6 NAZI SABOTEURS EXECUTED." Two of the eight, who had been caught at the first of the summer, had collaborated with the government and therefore were given a lesser sentence. Julia read every word.

Was Eberhard Greger's
boat here to bring saboteurs?
Was he a Nazi spy?
I should have reported him to officials.

On page 8 she read:

At present there is no special statute for punishing the harboring or concealing of persons who have committed sabotage or persons who have guilty knowledge of such acts but fail to inform law enforcement officers.

I don't think Captain Greger was a spy.
He told me the truth about his men... I'm sure of it.
But he is German.
I should have told officials he was here.
What if they believed he was a spy...
even if he wasn't.
They might have executed him.
I wonder if they picked him up that night.

Surely there would have been a story in the paper.
If they did, he didn't say anything about me.
He was always concerned of implicating me.
No, I believe he was just
a u-boat captain, as he said.
And until I know otherwise,
I will pray that he survives this war.

Bertie was pleased as punch the FBI was calling on the public to look out for suspicious people. She and Ricky started their own spy team and Julia would see them lurking in the shrubbery pretending to be watching enemy agents.

"Did you see the pictures of the spies?" she asked Julia.

"Yes, I did."

"Well, no wonder they were caught. They looked like spies. I could spot a spy just like that," Bertie snapped her fingers.

"I bet you could," answered Julia.

"Did you see the death house?"

"The drawing in the paper?"

"Yes," Bertie said. "It showed the death cells and the electric chair."

"Nobody'd get me to sit in no 'lectric chair," Ricky said.

"It's not like they say, 'Would you like to sit down?' The guards strap them into the chair," Bertie explained. "And then they turn up the electricity and zap them until they croak." She shook all over and then dropped limply to the ground.

"Does it hurt?" Ricky asked.

"I don't know. They're just dead. Fini. Kaput. Ready for the grim reaper."

"Ricky," Julia said, "the government says they think the person looses consciousness before he feels any pain."

"Well, I still wouldn't sit down. And I'd be mighty mad at the ones who squealed."

"Ricky, the men were caught sneaking onto our shore," Julia said. "They had to be punished."

"Yeah, stupid," Bertie said. "They had dynamite and stuff like that and they were going to blow us to smithereens."

"The newspaper says the home front – that's us – has saved enough brass for one billion, three hundred and seventy-seven million, seven hundred and sixty-six thousand rifle or machine gun cartridges," Julia read to the children.

"That's a lot!" Ricky said. "Like a trillion, trillion!"

"You see, we're making a difference here at home."

"Do the Japanese and the Germans have to do without things too?" Bertie asked.

"I'm quite sure they do."

"Then when they torpedo ships," the child answered, "they are shooting us with their old pots and pans."

"I never thought of it like that. I suppose you could be right."

In September World News told of the sinking of the British Liner, The Laconia, in the South Atlantic by a German u-boat.

In New York City the FBI announced the arrest of eighty-seven dangerous enemy aliens – Germans, Italians and Japanese. They were taken to Ellis Island for interment hearings. All totaled, 425 enemy aliens had been arrested since the first of July. Some of these people were said to have photographs, flares and even ammunition that could incriminate them. Fifteen Germans had registered with their consulate for military service in the Nazi Army.

> *Talk of German espionage is not just foolishness.*
> *Even people who used to think*
> > *the war would not come to our shores*
> > *are beginning to think differently.*
> *Will the government intern all*
> > *German Americans?*
> *I wonder about Eberhard's uncle in New York.*
> *What if the government finds out*
> > *Grandfather's real name?*
> *Will this war ever end?*

It didn't look as though the war would end before Christmas. Joe would not be home for the birth of the baby. Kate would not be home. Through the mail, Joe and Julia had agreed on 'Kathryn Marie' for a girl and 'Joseph Junior' for a boy. Julia had rearranged the apartment to make room for the baby's crib.

"But at first you'll want to use the bassinet I used with you and Kate," her mother said. "In fact your father and I want you and the baby to spend the first couple of weeks at the house with us."

"Will the baby's crying disturb your boarders?"

"I think not. It takes a while for the baby's lungs to develop to the point that their crying is that loud. No, you and I will probably be the only ones to hear him."

"Then we accept your invitation, Grandma."

"Good. Your father and I were thinking it would be a blue Christmas. The baby is going to change all of that. The Sunshine Market advertised Canadian Spruce trees. I'll send your father to get one. We'll decorate the house. I can't believe we're going to be grandparents, and we're already acting like them."

"Mother, I can't wait to hold him… still I feel that it's wrong to bring a baby into a world at war."

"Nonsense, the war won't last much longer. Your baby won't even know there's a war. We can hold him in our arms and sing carols. He won't feel the war."

"I hope you're right. Think about the children in Europe and Asia. How frightened they must be. I don't want my child to ever be so frightened."

"I know what you mean. You know, *your* baby is too young to be drafted. Too young to go to Europe in the midst of this war. You see, our babies will always be our babies. Your father and I are proud of Kate, but it scares us that she is over there. And we love Joe as a son. Let's hope this war will be the last war any of us will have to see."

"Why can't the killing stop? Why don't people just go back to their own countries and take care of their people? Why can't Joe come home?"

"Cry, my child," Evelyn Walters said pulling Julia into her embrace. "You have a right to cry."

Eighteen

- 1943 -

Elizabeth Gray, the midwife Joe had wanted Julia to have, was pleased to be called, "Most women are going to the hospital these days. I don't get many calls anymore."

"Joe said I must have you deliver his baby," Julia said. "He told me so before he left."

"I knew that boy was some stuff the first time I saw him... and I was the first to see him!" the woman laughed.

"I didn't bring him into this world to go off fighting in no war. He's supposed to be here." Elizabeth spoke her mind.

"His mama and I quite agree."

"How is his mama?" Elizabeth asked.

"She'll be here in awhile. The grandparents are all very excited."

"How about you, Missy?"

"I wish Joe was here."

"Course, you do," the midwife said.

"I kept hoping the war would end and he'd be home before I had the baby. If I thought he could be here, I'd be willing to carry this baby a while longer."

"Well, from the looks of you, it's not gonna happen that way."

"What do you mean?" Julia asked.

"I mean this baby isn't going to wait for a peace treaty. This baby is ready. You and I are going to find out what you've been hiding these last nine months. You ready, Missy?"

Julia answered with a scream as the contractions got more painful.

"I want you to breathe like I showed you, Missy... What do you think you're gonna have?"

"I don't care... just as long as it is healthy."

Julia refused to say so but deep down she wanted a girl. If she had a boy as her mother-in-law had, would she also loose her husband?

That's crazy, she told herself.
Breathe in, breathe out, breathe in, breathe out...

"Ohhhhhhh.!"

When the baby was born, Julia anxiously waited to find out. She heard Elizabeth hum – a cheerful hum that told her all was fine. As she placed the baby in the mother's arms, the midwife announced, "She's a peach! You've got yourself a beautiful baby girl, Missy."

Julia beamed with delight for she was truly relieved.

****

"Western Union," Carrie Beall answered the phone at the telegraph office.

"Yes, Miss Carrie. This is Julius Walters. I'd like to send a telegram."

"Where is it to go?"

"It's to go to my son-in-law... to tell him he has a daughter!"

"Well, congratulations! I cannot believe little Jules is a grandpa. Why I remember your mother pushing you about in a stroller. A little girl? What did they name her?"

"She's Kathryn Marie Keegan and she hasn't one hair on her head. She's beautiful. Her mother is doing just fine."

"That's the best news I've been able to send out in some time, Jules. I'm happy for all of you."

"Thank you, Miss Carrie. I suppose this year the holidays are pretty rough in your business."

"Most of the messages I get are sad news, if not the worst. People are usually afraid they'll alarm someone sending a telegram. But this isn't the first war I've dealt with. I was sending messages when all we had were Morse code machines." She added, "The new father will be expecting good news, right?"

"Right. She was two weeks late. Joe will be looking for this telegram."

"Do you want to tell him his daughter is baldheaded?"

"He's going to want all the details. This telegram is going to cost me. And then I'll have to send one to Kate in England. Her niece was named after her. Ready?"

"Give them to me, Gramps," Miss Carrie said. "I'm ready."

****

Katie's grandmother had been right, her crying disturbed no one other than the mother and grandmother. Grandmother got up to check on them each time Katie woke. Julia wondered if she was sleeping in the hallway just outside her door.

"Gracious, no." her mother answered. "Women hear babies cry. It's just the nature of us all. Now your father, he could sleep through your crying fits."

"Did I cry a lot?"

"I don't know. I guess it wasn't so much. I just didn't know what to do."

"Where was Grandmother?"

"She couldn't come and the midwife was called to another birthing almost right after you were born. I was on my own."

"You did good. Here I am. Just fine."

"And here is your precious little Katie."

"It's been so nice being here with you, Mother."

Dear Kate,

    I don't know if Mother has changed, or if it is me. Perhaps I know now, that I have a child of my own, how much a mother loves a child. It's been so wonderful being at the house with Mother. I hate to leave, but if I don't she will have both Katie and me so spoiled we won't know how to do for ourselves.

    Your namesake is very tiny. At first I couldn't believe it. Such tiny fingers and toes. Mrs. Bryan was horrified when Bertie said the baby looked like a tadpole. But it's amazing how much Katie has filled out in just a couple of weeks. She's cute as a bug in a rug. Bertie likes to call her "Poopsy-Woopsy." She sits and stares at her announcing every time she opens her eyes. She's very excited we are coming home tomorrow.

    Joe answered the telegram saying someone told him they're cheaper by the dozen. He says he's fine, but that was when he wrote. Is he still fine?

> Take good care of Katie's aunt.
> I wish you were here.

Julia read the newspaper daily searching for some sign the war would soon end, but the news was full of horror. European cities were bombed. Civilians were killed. Age-old monuments and buildings were destroyed. There were reports of killed, or missing in action. Of sinkings. Of crashes. There were pictures of local boys serving in the Philippines, in Europe, on ships, or in the Air Corps. How long before they'd be in a ward, like the boys Bertie wrote, looking down at their broken bodies?

Katie's grandmothers kept her well supplied with bonnets to cover her little baldhead. By spring she still didn't have but a little fuzz on the top of her head.

"I think your grandmothers fear someone will think you're a boy, my little bonnet baby," Julia said. "But that's all right. Your bonnets are most becoming."

Every first move the child made was not only recorded in the baby book, but a full report was sent to Daddy and Auntie.

> Katie slept through the night.
> Katie smiled when we played the music box.
> Katie is focusing on things. She loves bright colors.
> Katie rolled over.

> Katie didn't sleep last night and neither did I.

The child was a delight to Julia, her grandparents and the Bryans. Bertie wanted to help Julia mother the baby and her answer for Katie's crying was always, "I think she wants to go for a stroll, Julia."

Julia and Bertie strolled with Katie. During the winter months the cold water, the ships across the way and the sentry standing guard made the war seem too close. Julia didn't stroll the Boulevard anymore than she had to. As the temperature climbed and the breeze was more enjoyable, strolling along the Boulevard was pleasant again.

Several times a week, the girls would ride the trolley into town to go visit grandparents and Snarls. Often Ricky would go with them. Snarls accepted that he had to relinquish his reign of the household when Katie arrived. He would come down from his perch on the back of the sofa and walk about everyone's feet rubbing against their legs until someone would scoop him up.

"See, Katie. See Snarls."

When Julia and the children left the Walters, Snarls would walk along with them until Julia told him to go home. He never snarled and Julia wondered why she had let that awful name stick. The cat reminded her of the u-boat captain and his crew of men buried in the National Cemetery.

I will go back there.
They have no one to bring them roses.

But it wasn't easy for her to get to Phoebus. She had the baby. And most often, she had Bertie.

I will go back.

Occasionally Julia's mother would take care of the baby and Mr. Walters would take Julia to the movies. Hollywood was quick to join the war. As soon as the US entered the war there were thirty-eight war pictures in production. Everyone was talking about the tearjerkers like *Since You Went Away* and *So Proudly We Hail*. After just one of those with the line "Now go darling, and don't look back." Julia didn't want to see anymore of them. She accepted when her dad offered to take her to see *Meet Me In St. Louis*.

The newsreels played first. "I wish they wouldn't show us pictures of the war with a full orchestra's accompaniment," Julia said as she came out of the Langley Theatre with her father. "Like the western films when the cowboy in the white hat rides his white horse across the screen, a gallant melody goes with him."

"That's Hollywood," answered her father.

"That's okay for the movie. But Lowell Thomas presents the news of the war like a ringleader at the circus," Julia said. "Trumpets introduce the Allied forces. Pounding drums when the enemy is mentioned make the audience feel the room tremble from their heavy footsteps. Isn't it misleading to have musical background to accounts of the war?"

"What's happening is so ugly," Julia's father said. "Your mother says they do that so people can watch."

"There was an editorial recently," Julia said. "A representative from North Carolina suggested that Americans are getting a Pollyannaish view of the war. He said perhaps we are propagandized with slanted news. How can we know if what we're being told is the truth?"

"There are reporters all around the world sending us first-hand accounts of the war," Mr. Walters said. "Still the Domestic Radio Bureau limits what can be broadcast. They cannot allow news commentators to get overly dramatic and create hysteria in this country."

"Yes, they must approve what is going to be said on the air," Julia

Time Will Tell

said. "That's what the representative was saying. How do we know they aren't censoring out something we need to know? Not so long ago, we were told the Russians were evil. Now we are to believe they aren't nearly so bad. The radio is trying to sell us Russians like it tries to sell Ivory soap. We're supposed to be happy our men are fighting alongside of the Russian soldiers."

"I was reading Walter Lippmann today," Mr. Walters said. "He says a nation must do what is in it's own best interest. He says that's why we are at war. But in order to sell the war to the population the government makes people think we're in it for moral reasons."

"How is fighting alongside the Russians in our best interest?" Julia asked. "Charles Lindbergh said staying out of it was in our best interest."

"Perhaps he was thinking of his best interest," Mr. Walters said. "Lippmann says that although Russians and Americans have always had a difficult relationship, they usually find it best to support one another in critical times. He says neither country feels they would gain anything from going to war with the other."

"What will we gain going to war with the Germans and the Japanese?" Julia asked.

"We have to protect our interest in the South Pacific."

"Yes, Lindbergh said we either needed to fortify the islands adequately, or get out of them. I don't think he was thinking that would mean going to war," she added. "And why are we fighting the Germans and the Italians?"

"Our government would have us believe it's because they are doing terrible things to some of their people," Mr. Walters said.

"What country hasn't? Why did people come to America if not to escape the injustices of their governments? – all of them, including England." she said.

"But we need to fight the Axis powers so that they don't gain control in Europe. Lippmann says that the isolationists in this country were living in a fantasy world. The idea of peace diverted attention from the idea of national security when in fact a nation must do things to sustain security," Mr. Walters said. "We cannot have the respect of other nations without a strong military. Lippmann thinks we should have been in the war years ago, but for the best interest of this country – not for sentimental reasons that seem to be the only way to get the American public to respond."

"Lindbergh believes in a strong military, too," Julia said. "He thinks our men should be prepared to defend our shores, but it is not our place to control internal conditions in Europe."

"I'm surprised you've studied Lindbergh's ideas with such interest."

"I respect him for saying what he thought. I thought the President reacted like a bully. He turned the people of America against Lindbergh. Newspapers accused him of being a Nazi."

"Yes, and many people believe he is. You shouldn't go around quoting him," her father cautioned her. "What Lippmann says makes sense to me. We Americans tend to think we are morally superior to the rest of the world. If we'd just been honest in that a nation must look out for itself, we would have been prepared for war... as we should have been. It's too bad Lindbergh allowed himself to be swayed by the Nazis."

Julia's father drove her home. She went to bed with images from the black and white movie screen of scenes of the war in Europe – men and jeeps and tanks moving through mud while loud explosions are heard in the background. If she had watched closely, would she have seen Joe? Would she want to?

What if I saw Joe on the movie screen?

In the summer Julia had turned the living area couch around so she could sleep by the opened window. Though it was September it was still quite warm in the apartment. She checked on Katie and then sat on the couch by the window. She liked to talk to the moon. Tell it to tell Joe she missed him. Ask it to tell her he was safe. After her evening at the movies, she tried to block out the newsreels from her mind. She focused on the moon, but it drifted behind clouds.

Please, come from behind the clouds.

Even the searchlights seemed to disappear within the clouds. Her room was black. Julia imagined Joe marching bravely into battle while trumpets and violins played heroic music. Marching into explosions of artillery. She searched the sky for that sphere of light that could be looking down on Joe.

In the still of the night Julia could hear waves breaking along the shore. It was a soft sound that on most nights could lull her into peaceful sleep. The chirping of crickets was interrupted by a jeep passing by. A couple of dogs barked as if answering each other. And then it was quiet again. She heard the waves and the crickets. The moon was still hidden. She wanted it to reappear so she could give it a message for Joe. She finally fell asleep.

****

Time Will Tell

Bertie's knock on the door came just after Katie's first cry of the new day.

"Come on up, Bertie," Julia called as she lifted Katie from her crib.

"Mother says it may be rainy this afternoon. I think we should take Katie for her stroll this morning."

"It's so early. How about you let me get some things done before we go?" Julia asked.

"What do you need to do?"

"First I have to bathe and dress Katie. Then feed her. But before we go out I'd like to defrost the icebox. And change my bed linens."

"Can I stay and play with Katie while you work?"

"Does your mother know where you are?"

"Yes."

"Okay, I'll put her on the rug after her bath and you can keep her company."

After Julia had finished her work Bertie pushed the carriage out of the garage and up to the sidewalk, "Here it is. Is our little Poopsy-Woopsy ready?"

"You are such a help, Bertie. Thanks for getting Katie's buggy."

"I like to. Did you have fun at the movies with you father last night?"

"Yes, they had beautiful costumes and wonderful music. Judy Garland sings like a canary."

>(Julia sang) "In you Easter bonnet
>   with all the thrills upon it
> You'll be the grandest lady in
>   the Easter Parade."

"That's prissy stuff. You should have gotten him to take you to see *Der Fuehrer's Face*."

>(Bertie sang) "When the Fuehrer says
>   We is the master race,
>   We heil (sp-p-p*), heil (sp-p-p*)
>   Right in the Fuehrer's face.
>
>   Not to love the Fuehrer
>   Is a great disgrace,
>   So we heil (sp-p-p*), heil (sp-p-p*)

Right in the Fuehrer's face."

"Does your mother know you're singing that?"

"Have you seen Donald Duck sing it? He's so funny! I bet Katie would like it. Let's see."

"Oh, no you don't! You aren't going to teach her to make that awful noise before she even learns to talk."

"When is she going to talk?" Bertie asked.

"Oh, she'll surprise us one day. She recognizes you, you know. She looks for you. One day she's going to stand up and say, 'Stop calling me Poopsy-Woopsy.'"

"No, she won't. She loves me to call her that. She looks for Snarls when we go to her grandmother's house. But when she's unhappy she wants you."

As they strolled along, Julia started singing a silly song to the girls.

> Mairsey doats and dosey doats
> And little lambsey divey.

From across the water came a loud explosion. Bertie screamed. Katie cried. Julia looked about. Everyone in sight was running in different directions.

"Come Bertie, we must get home!"

"Katie is crying!"

"I know. We'll get home as fast as we can. Hold onto me. I'll push the stroller."

Mrs. Bryan met them on the front sidewalk. "Thank God, you're here! Let's get in the house."

"What is happening?"

"I'm afraid the war has come to us. There's a tremendous sheet of flames. Look!"

Across the water there were more explosions – one after another. Flames leaped hundreds of feet into the air.

"They must have blown up the whole naval base," Mrs. Bryan said.

"The Germans," Bertie said. "They have bombed the base. Now they'll come here and bust down our doors and take us prisoners."

"Sh-h-h-h, Bertie," Mrs. Bryan said. "Your daddy is here. We're going to be all right."

Mr. Bryan came running in the house, "Are you here?" he shouted.

"We're all here," said Mrs. Bryan.

"Are they getting closer?" Bertie asked. "Are they coming here, Daddy?"

"There was an accident at the naval base," he told the women. "It's not the Germans, Bertie. No one is coming to get you."

"What kind of accident could cause all of that?" his wife asked.

"Apparently they were transporting explosives and something broke loose."

"All Hell broke loose!" Mrs. Bryan said and she made no apology for her language.

****

The next day in Phoebus, Rose Washington listened anxiously to her husband. "Lord have mercy, Thomas! You're telling me we blew up our own base?"

"Well, that does seem to be what it says here. They were transporting explosives. Twenty four people are believed dead and hundreds of others injured."

"I bet that's what we've seen on Military Road going over that way," Rose said.

"What?"

"Those huge trucks we saw. I bet they were carrying explosives. Thank God they don't bring their convoys by here anymore."

"Well, Military Road isn't far enough from here to save us if it happened here."

"There isn't a place on this earth where one can feel safe anymore."

"Tell me the truth, Rose. When all the explosions went off today, weren't you glad Samuel wasn't here?"

"Don't try to twist things, Thomas. Lord knows, we all thought the Germans were bombing Norfolk and we were next."

"Several planes were destroyed, parked automobiles were wrecked, two barracks building were demolished, a storage building flattened and a big hangar was badly damaged." Thomas read from the newspaper. "The electric light system for the whole base was knocked out. What a mess!"

"I thought it was the Germans, for sure," Rose said. "But if you think that's going to make me feel one bit better about Samuel being in Alabama, you're wrong."

"You don't need to worry, they're not going to let those boys fly," Thomas said. "Makes no difference that Samuel graduated. The Army can't find a place to send them. No one wants a unit of Negro pilots. They're stuck in Alabama. Going nowhere. They might as well have flunked them all."

"It was a great accomplishment that Samuel kept in the program and graduated," Rose said. "He can be proud of that. Thank the good Lord they didn't do him like they did his friend Jesse. That would have broken his spirit."

"Samuel said they wanted to flunk them all and there were other boys who got booted out on trumped-up charges. It must have been some kind of tough trying to stay out of trouble."

"Does he have to spend the duration of the war in Alabama?" Rose asked. "Alabama isn't very friendly towards the Negro."

"Where is? They've had race riots in Indianapolis, then Detroit and now New York. We used to think the North was friendlier to the colored, but that isn't so," Thomas said. "Samuel and a lot of folks were hoping the war would help the Negro improve his position," he continued. "But I hear the Army and Navy told the Red Cross not to accept blood from Negro donors. They said white soldiers would refuse blood plasma if they knew it came from Negro veins – suppose they think it'll turn their skin dark."

"A lot of good people tried to get Odell Waller's death sentence blocked," Rose said. "Even Mrs. Roosevelt spoke up saying that the man he killed had pushed him beyond reason."

"Well, the man refused to give him what was rightfully his as a sharecropper. How was he supposed to feed his family? But you notice President Roosevelt didn't feel the same as his wife. No, he wouldn't stop the execution. A colored man is never going to be let off for killing a white man no matter what the white man's done to him."

"That boy they electrocuted in Richmond," Rose said, "He was the same age as Samuel."

"Yes, but he did kill a man."

****

Aside from the increased heart rate of residents, no injuries occurred in Hampton due to the explosions at the naval base that Friday midday. Everyone traded stories of what they were doing when they heard the first explosion. The conversations would lead to discussions of how dangerous it is for the government to be transporting explosives through this area. There were those who insisted that espionage had to be involved. And there were those who thought this was a message from God saying we (the United States) shouldn't be involved in the war.

Sunday morning congregations of all denominations met to pray for the dead and injured. Reverend Harrison at St. John's had revised his sermon to address the concerns of his congregation. Julia walked to her parent's house with them after church as had become her Sunday routine.

"Daddy, do you think these explosions were just accidents as they claim?" she asked.

"From what little I know of explosives, someone really needs to know what they are doing when they are messing with them. Yes, it's quite likely we didn't need the enemy to do the damage. We did it to ourselves."

Fishing boats   *Cheyne's*

Nineteen

In the middle of an October night there was an explosion in a building on Kecoughtan Road not far from the Bryan's neighborhood. Several businesses went up in flames before firefighters could tame the blaze. A month later there was an explosion at the Yorktown Weapons Station that lit up the skies of the Peninsula again and woke everyone at midnight. The fire caused only minor injuries, but the explosion in Yorktown cost the lives of six Negro civilian workers on the base loading explosives. For those who listened to rumors, there was plenty of evidence of enemy sabotage. There was plenty for the spy team of Bertie and Ricky.

War movies gave them a new vocabulary. Bertie and Ricky picked up lines from movies and repeated them over and again much to their parents' dismay:

"Come on suckers! Why don't you come and get us?
 Those mustard-colored monkeys.
  The little yellow bellies.
   The beast. The slimy beasts."

The children got a good scolding one afternoon when Bertie's mother found them sneaking around in the back yard camouflaged with big branches they had ripped out of her bush.

"That's how the Japs snuck up on the Allies in *Bataan*," Bertie said.

"Not with my Camellia bush, they didn't. Oh, dear," Caroline said looking at the mangled bush. "Why don't you jump rope? Or play hopscotch?"

"Can we go to the movies?"

"You may not. Those movies put ideas in your head and then you tear up my bush. You better go play something before I decide to use a branch of this bush on you."

"Come on, Bertie," Ricky said wanting to put some space between himself and the branch.

"You might as well take these broken branches with you," Caroline said. "I wouldn't want my bush to die for nothing. But if I ever catch you..."

"I know," Bertie said. "We're not to break up your bushes anymore."

"Is Julia home?" Ricky asked.

"She took the baby over to visit Joe's mom," Bertie said.

"Then, go ask your mom if you can come to my house. I'll wait out here."

****

"Julia, why don't you go into town?" Mrs. Keegan asked. "Let me keep Katie for a few hours."

"She might wake up cranky."

"So? If she does, she does."

"You don't need to..."

"Julia. I've never had her by myself. May I?"

"I hadn't meant to..."

"No, dear. I know. But it's the truth. You're always around when Katie is here. Perhaps if you're gone when she wakes up, she'll let me hold her."

"Okay. She should sleep for forty-five minutes. When do you want me back?"

"Take as long as you want. Go visit a friend. Go shopping. We'll be fine. I have nothing else I have to do today."

"She shouldn't ask for another bottle for awhile, but if..."

"If she does, I can take care of it. You go. I don't want you here when she wakes up."

"All right. I know when I'm not wanted," Julia teased.

Mrs. Keegan is so sweet.
I hope she isn't hurt
that I haven't asked her to sit with Katie.
She knows Mother has kept her.
There could be a little jealousy.
I'll have to be careful.
I hope Katie is good for her.

So what am I going to do?
It's not a good time of day to find people home.
I don't need to shop for anything.
I'll have to come back
  in town tomorrow with Joe's package
But I don't have it today.
  I'll walk over to St. John's.

Julia saw a large group of people in the churchyard and decided she could not visit with Lizzie Burcher this time. When she reached the curb, the streetcar stopped and she stepped onto it.

I said I'd go back to the National Cemetery.
That's what I'll do. For once, I'm by myself.

It had been months since Julia had been there. It was difficult to find time.

Two young women got on the streetcar at the next stop and sat right behind Julia. Their conversation distracted Julia from her own thoughts:

"We've been saving for a trip to Vermont this Christmas. Fred thinks we can make it."

"Are you taking the train?"

"Trains are so crowded with troops and servicemen wanting to get home for the holidays, civilians have to get special permission to go on the train. Fred's been accumulating our monthly gas ration so we can drive the Model A. He fastened a second tank in the car and has been slowly filling the two tanks.

"We'll take the ferry from Old Point to Baltimore which will save a lot of gas. We'll coast down hills. That will help too. It's going to take us longer with the maximum wartime speed limit of thirty-five miles per hour."

"You must really want to go."

"We do. We're hoping we don't have any car troubles along the way. It's impossible to get automobile parts."

"George went back to Wards to get a tube for our new radio. They told him he was out of luck. We probably won't be able to get a replacement tube for the duration."

"If we break down on the road, we may be stranded somewhere for the duration."

"You sure you want to go that badly?"

"I'm so homesick. I will walk if I have to."

"Then you should go. And be glad you're not going on the train. There's been a lot of train wrecks lately. The one in Philadelphia was terrible. They said the derailed cars were scattered like matchsticks. Eighty people died. The trains go at such terrific speeds. No, I think you're better off in your automobile."

"Train travel isn't what it used to be."

"Traveling any where, any way isn't like it used to be."

"Shopping isn't going to be much fun this Christmas either. The only things they have plenty of are the things I can't afford."

"Yes, me too. Perhaps we ought to postpone Christmas 'til after the war."

"Here's where we get off. Did you tell Amanda where to meet us?"

Three soldiers got on where the girls got off. Two of them took the seats the girls had been in; the other sat beside Julia.

"This isn't such a bad little place," one of the men behind her said. "I'd like to live here and own a sailboat."

"I'd like to be where you could get fresh crabmeat, but without the smell. How do people who live here stand it?"

"They get used to it, I suppose," the man seated next to Julia said. "Are you from here, miss?"

"I've lived here all my life."

"Do you get used to the smell?"

"What smell?" she teased.

"You don't smell anything?" he asked.

"Were you here in July?"

"No Ma'am."

"Then you don't smell anything either."

"Oh." He laughed. "We're going to take the ferry over to Norfolk."

"Norfolk will be easier on your noses, but ..."

"But, what?"

"You know it's been called the worst war town in America?"

"It must get pretty wild over there at times," answered one of the boys smiling.

"A sailor was stabbed to death at the Casablanca not long ago. The girls get the sailors to drink Mickey Finns, and when they're out cold, they rob them." Julia wanted to warn the soldiers that 'disease' was prevalent, but she didn't know these boys. She couldn't speak of such to them.

"Do you want to go with us?" the one beside her asked.

"No. I'm getting off on the other side of the bridge. I hope you..."

"If you went along, you could keep us out of trouble."

"I doubt that. Sounds like you're looking for excitement."

"Have you heard of China Solly? He's an ex-sailor who runs a place called The Stars and Stripes Forever."

"No."

"His place is..."

"Probably not a place a girl should go," Julia suggested.

"Maybe not. But we're shipping out soon and we want to have a good time. It's too quiet in Hampton. Nothing's happening."

"This is my stop," Julia said. "Be careful."

Julia got off the streetcar while the three soldiers protested, "It won't be fun without you."

She stepped to the ground. Another man in uniform got off the streetcar behind her.

Why did he get off here?
I hope he's not looking for female companionship.

Julia walked towards the cemetery gate. The man followed. She slowed down for him to go around her. As he did, he turned to her and said, "I hope those fellows didn't upset you, miss."

"No, I'm fine," she answered.

"That's good. Which way are you going?"

"The way I am going."

"Oh."

"I'm not looking for company, Lieutenant. Please excuse me."

"I'm sorry," he said, and he stepped away so that she could go ahead of him.

She picked up her pace and turned into the gates of the cemetery.

If I had Katie with me,
they would leave me alone.

"I beg your pardon, I thought you were someone I'd met – the Walters' daughter."

Julia turned back around. "I am and you're...?"

"Lt. O'Neill. I was one of the chosen few who had dinner at your parent's home a year or so ago."

"Yes. I mean, I'm sorry... I didn't recognize you."

"I couldn't think of your name?"

"Julia. Julia Keegan."

"And your husband works at NACA. Right?"

"Wrong, but he did. You have a good memory."

"Where is he now?"

"He's somewhere in Europe."

"How did that happen?"

"He wanted to go so badly, he made it happen. You're still at Langley?"

"Yes, I've landed a test pilot job. Sometimes I work with some of the NACA men. It's pretty fantastic how they can calculate things with paper and pencil and solve problems like how a pilot can develop a roll."

"Develop a roll?"

"Yes, when a fighter plane has the enemy on his tail, the way to loose him is to roll. The technical term is 'rolling moment.'"

"Sometimes one of the NACA men goes up with us. I've wondered if I'd met your husband in this way."

"I doubt it. He left Langley right after I saw you at my folks. He said there was talk the NACA boys were going to be locked in their jobs and he wanted to get out while he could."

"He was right about that."

"Well, it was nice seeing you again, Lieutenant."

"Thank you," He turned as if to walk away, then added, "I don't know where you're going, but if you want company... no, you already said you didn't want company."

Julia laughed. "Lt. O'Neill, that was when I thought you were flirting with me like those GIs on the streetcar."

"Then may I walk with you?"

"That would be nice."

"May I ask, what are we doing in this bone orchard?"

"No, you may not."

"You have someone buried here? 'Cause, if you do, I'm sorry about how I..."

"No, Lieutenant, I don't have anyone buried here. It's pretty, don't you think?"

"Yes, I suppose it is," he said and he let her lead the way.

Julia circled about the graveyard not wanting to go directly to the graves of the German soldiers with Lt. O'Neill there. He tried to talk with her, but soon caught on that he was supposed to be quiet.

They had circled back to the graves of the Germans though Lt. O'Neill knew nothing about it. Julia didn't say anything aloud.

Twenty-nine boys will not go home.
Does anyone in Germany know this?

Their wives, mothers, children,
girlfriends might be waiting...
Just as I wait for Joe.
Perhaps one of them has a child
he will never see.
Did Eberhard Greger make it here to say goodbye?
If he didn't, I want you to know he tried.

She fought back tears and then turned suddenly and said, "Are you ready to go?"

The puzzled lieutenant nodded and they exited the gate moments later.

"Is everything all right? You were expecting when I met you. Nothing hap..."

"The baby is fine," Julia interrupted. "I have a little girl. We call her Katie after my sister Kate."

(He sang) K- k-k-Katy, beautiful Katy .
You're the only g-g-g-girl that I adore.

When the m-m-m-moon shines
Over the cow shed
I'll be waiting at the k-k-k-kitchen door.

"You never stop singing," Julia laughed. "There were three of you from Langley at the dinner. You could start a quartet. You just need one more."

"Two more. Didn't Mattie tell you Lt. Arnold crashed his plane?"

"Mattie and I don't know each other well. She probably told Mother. I'm so sorry. Is he... dead?"

"Yes, about two months ago, it happened."

"Was he a test pilot, too?"

"No, he was in the real thing. Got shot down somewhere in Europe. A couple of his buddies saw him go down. I'd rather get it myself than watch my buddy get it. I suppose that's why I'm happy to be here. Not that we're not asked to do some dangerous stuff."

"So you think you're here to stay?"

"As long as the war lasts. Which way are you going from here?" he asked.

She didn't know. "I suppose I'll take the streetcar back downtown."

"Oh, couldn't we go to another cemetery?"

"As you wish," she answered.

The streetcar stopped for them and they traveled back across the bridge and on through the busy part of Queen Street.

"This is it," Julia said as she pulled the cord to ring the bell.

"I was kidding," Lt. O'Neill said following her to the grounds of St. John's.

"Come. I think you'll find this cemetery very interesting. Some of these graves are really old. And look at the headstones. These have footstones, too."

"Is the church open?" he asked.

"Usually it is. Would you like to go in? We can get in this side door. This was built in 1728. The people of Hampton burned this city to the ground during the Civil War."

"You burned your own city?"

St. John's   *Cheyne's*

"Not me. You see, Ft. Monroe had always been a government base. The Union troops were there. Which put Hampton in between the Union fort and our Confederate capital in Richmond. Much closer to the Union fort. Confederate General Magruder told the people of Hampton the Union planned to quarter their troops here. He sort of ordered them to burn the town before the Union could occupy it. And they did."

"But they didn't burn the church, did they?"

"Yes, they burned the church but the original walls stood against the fire. About all that was left of Hampton was the courthouse, the fire-blackened walls of this church and chimneys of a few houses.

"After the war, they restored the church But, as you'll see, the inside was done in the Victorian style. Makes for a curious building with a colonial exterior and a Victorian interior."

Julia opened the doors into the sanctuary.

"Still it is splendid," Lt. O'Neill said. "Quaint, but splendid. I was raised in a huge Catholic church, you see. I like the dark Gothic woodwork and the wonderful color. It's cozy. Relaxes me. The windows are magnificent."

"I belong to this church. There is an ongoing debate as to whether they should redo the sanctuary in the original colonial style to match the brick walls."

"I hope they leave it as it is. Do you agree?" the lieutenant asked.

"This is the only way I've seen it. I can't imagine it any other way."

"Think of all the beautiful architecture that is being bombed in Europe."

"My sister is in England," Julia said. "I'm more concerned about her."

"Why is she there?"

"She's with the Red Cross. It was my suggestion that she join the Red Cross, but I didn't think she'd have to go where it would be raining bombs."

Julia walked outside and the lieutenant followed.

"Look at the inscription on this stone," she said leading him to Lizzie Burcher's grave.

He read what it said. "Do you know her story? Do you know what she did?"

"No." Julia answered but then seemed to drift off in her own thoughts.

He stood there with her. She didn't say anything more.

Finally he broke the silence, "Mrs. Keegan."

"Yes?"

"I need to get out to the base. Duty calls. Thanks for the tour of the old church. Maybe I'll see you again sometime."

"Thanks for the company, Lieutenant. It's probably time for me to go get my daughter."

****

"Last year I thought Thanksgiving Day was going to be difficult," Evelyn Walters said to her husband. "It was such an adjustment not having all the family here. But I worked hard baking cookies and fixing packages for the ones overseas, we had Rachel and the Potters come for dinner and we managed to put the day behind us although it wasn't how we'd have liked it."

"You did a good job and you can do it again," Jules said. "We'll have little Katie sitting at the table with us this year."

"That's the only bright thing I can think about it. Knowing we're going into another holiday season with the young people still over there, doesn't put me in a thankful frame of mind."

"Evelyn, it's not like you to talk like that."

"Well, that's too bad because I can't say I'm thankful when I'm not. I'm worried sick about the bombing in England, with Kate over there, and there are explosions going off all around us. I look at that precious baby and wonder if her father will ever come home. I try to be positive, but with the holidays coming, it's depressing."

"Hopefully, after two accidents with transporting explosives, that won't happen again. Our navy seems to have chased most of the u-boats away from our coast. That's something to be thankful about."

"I'll be thankful when the war is over. When I can read the paper without fearing a notice that someone we know has lost their son in the war, or some boy is coming home a cripple. I'll be thankful when we don't have to hear that air raid sounding again and our street lights can be turned back on."

"You haven't mentioned rationing."

"I can put up with rationing. There's always something I can substitute. But there's no substitute for the ones we love and there's no substitute for peace of mind."

Jules embraced his wife. "You work so hard, Darling. You're tired. You try to take care of everyone. I know you, you'll put out a wonderful Thanksgiving feast just like you always have. I'm counting on it. It will be a tough turkey if I have to cook it."

"You in my kitchen? I can't let that happen. I'll pull myself together."

"That's my girl".

Evelyn Walter's family, minus the ones overseas, came to her Thanksgiving dinner though certainly not in a holiday mood.

"Katie is going to have her first birthday soon," Mrs. Keegan said.

"It doesn't look like Joe will be home for it," Julia answered. "General MacArthur was reported to say he needed more weapons, planes and supplies. More men. Nobody is coming home for Christmas."

"Kate writes that they plan to do everything they can to bring a little bit of home to the boys," Evelyn said. "I'd rather she just come home, but I know she and the other girls are making a difference for a lot of our boys."

Rachel Keegan commented over and over that the dinner Evelyn had prepared was the biggest meal she'd had lately, but she barely ate anything. Katie had taken to her since the day Rachel babysat. Julia was thankful of that.

"If Katie could talk," Mr. Walters said, "she'd say she's thankful that she finally has hair on her head."

"Oh, Grandpa," Julia answered, "you're going to go bald one day and you'll be sorry you teased her."

"Then today, I can be thankful I still have hair on my head."

"Jules," Evelyn said, "stop clowning around."

****

"First Lt. George G. Goldstein," Julia read, "has been awarded the distinguished flying cross for gallantry and extraordinary achievement in flight!"

"He is credited with shooting down one Nazi plane over Munster and another over Bremen," Margaret Goldstein said who had brought the article to show Julia. "I wish he had taken off the hat for the picture."

"Your brother wanted to look serious. He wouldn't even smile. The flying cross, that's terrific!"

"I'm so proud. I want everyone to see this. But then I see right here on the same page Artie Potvin's picture. He's been missing since Armistice Day – somewhere in France it says. He had received the flying cross last month. Now he's missing. It scares me. Maybe I don't want George to be such a hero. If the Germans captured Artie, weren't they supposed to notify someone?"

"Yes, but war is not played by the rules," Julia said. "You mustn't assume he's dead."

"Did you read about the American pilot in Italy? It was in today's paper. A bunch of reporters and pilots had their Thanksgiving dinner together. This one boy said he wanted to say grace."

"That was nice. Didn't they let him?"

"They told him to go ahead. So he started off like you would expect – thanking God for the food and asking blessings on their loved ones back home. Then he stunned every one."

"Why? What did he say?" Julia asked.

"He said, 'Dear God, bless all the fighting men on all the fronts around the world – on both sides because they are all fighting for what they believe is right.'"

Twenty

-1944-

"The Army is trying to calm rumors of sharks," Lt. O'Neill said to Julia. "Listen to this from 'Uncle Sam's Shark Specific' – this handy booklet of what-to-do's if a shark approaches. First they give us a cake of 'shark chaser.' It's supposed to produce some sort of chemicals that will keep sharks away.

"But in case we don't happen to have our cake of shark chaser handy, it tells us in this little booklet "tactics when confronted by a shark."

One. Stay as quiet as possible and avoid other fish.
  Two. (if the first doesn't work)
  Make a quick feint toward the shark,
      slap water and shout
    Three. Face the shark and turn abruptly
      Four. Grab his fin and play piggy-back
        Five. Hit him in the jaw
          Six. Use a knife on the underside

"Then it says there are only four – only four really dangerous varieties of sharks. Now that makes me feel better."

Julia laughed. "That's a lot to think about when you see a hammerhead."

"I think it was written by a hammerhead."

"Is this a chance meeting, Lt. O'Neill?" Julia asked.

"If I said it was, would you believe me?"

"I don't think so."

"Is it all right? My waiting to see you."
"Not if you're thinking of a boy-girl sort of thing."
"No, I know you're married and that's good with me."
"Good with you?"
"It's good. I mean, I like that you're married."
"I like that I am married."
"Good."

"Where are you going?" he asked.
"I thought I'd go to... a cemetery."
"What is it with you and cemeteries? That's what I want to know."
"Let's just say I'm a little nutty. I'm married and I'm a little nutty."
"I don't buy that."
"Lt. O'Neill, I think you're a nice guy who needs to find a nice, unmarried girl."
"I don't want to find a nice, unmarried girl."
"And why not?"
"When the war ends, I'm going to marry my girl back home."
"Do you have a picture of her?"
"Do I have a picture? Right here. She goes wherever I go."
"She's very pretty."
"So, you see, I don't want to meet anyone else. If a guy doesn't drink and he doesn't want to meet girls, what's he to do?"
"In that case, Katie and I are going to the post office to mail a package to her daddy. You may walk with us if you like."
"I would like. Thank you. You're not walking all the way to town, are you?"
"I am, but if you don't wish..."
"I'm just surprised you walk that far."
"Most everyone walks these days, Lt. O'Neill. Besides, it's good for Katie."
"So this is Katie. She's pretty like her mother."
"Tell us about your girlfriend, Lt. O'Neill."

I hope he wasn't making her up.

"Her name is Susanna. She's rather tall. Much taller than you."
"Have you known her long? Does she know you want to marry her when you get home?"
"Oh, she knows."

"How did you meet?"

"She joined the chorus. She loves to sing."

"Then, she's perfect for you."

"I wish our folks thought so."

"They'll come around, if you love each other. They'll see you do."

She must be real.

"No, they won't. But it doesn't matter."

"Do you write to Susanna?"

"Let's talk about you."

"Okay. What do you want to know?"

"The cemeteries."

"That's just an old habit of mine. Remember the grave I showed you at St. John's?"

"The one with the long inscription? Yes."

"I've gone there to talk to Lizzie since I was very young."

"Why?"

"I can say anything to Lizzie. She won't repeat it."

"Yes, I think you can trust her not to repeat anything you say. She's been dead for a long time," he added. "Are you, the prim and proper little mother, hiding some dark secret?"

"No. I decided Lizzie must have done something very unselfish and she died early because of it. I go there to keep her company. I told her when Joe took me to my first dance. I told her when I got in trouble for giggling in class. Now, I go to talk to her when I don't know what I should do."

"And she tells you what you should do?"

"I'm not crazy. I don't hear voices. It just helps me to talk things out."

"You're not Catholic, are you? That's right, you said you belong to St. John's."

"Yes, I'm Episcopalian," Julia said. "Why?"

"We Catholics have our saints. You have some of your own."

"I never thought of it like that."

"Were you looking for another saint at the National Cemetery?" he asked.

"Perhaps."

"You just led me around to see if I would follow."

"I most certainly did not. You make it sound like I was flirting with you."

"I didn't mean to. I didn't think you were flirting. Just laughing at me, sort of."

"No, Lieutenant, I wasn't laughing at you either."

"You're not going to tell me, are you?"

"Why don't your folks like Susanna? Is it because she's not Catholic?"

"That's right."

"Then your church wouldn't accept your marriage to Susanna, would it?"

"My church, my parents, her parents, Milwaukee, the country! No one!"

They walked the next block without talking. Katie had fallen asleep in her stroller. Julia looked towards Lt. O'Neill and held her finger to her lips, "Sh-h-h."

Julia thought of a newspaper story she'd read some time ago. "At the beginning of the war," she broke the silence, "I read about a couple in Washington. He was a lieutenant in the United States Army and she was the secretary of the German military attaché in Washington. When the two countries announced they were at war, she asked to be allowed to stay in the United States with him.

"The government set up a hearing as they were skeptical that she would use her marriage to an American officer for subversive purposes. When she came to the hearing she withdrew her petition saying she didn't want to embarrass the lieutenant by his having a German wife. She left America with the other Germans. They'll probably never marry and all because of this war. You think you have troubles?"

"You think, I don't?" he asked.

"Lieutenant, is your Susanna German?"

"She was born here in the United States. But her parents were born in Germany."

"And your folks don't like that she has German blood?"

"That's only part of it."

"Well, not Catholic, and German too. But after the war, perhaps they will think different."

"Mr. Reese was arrested by the FBI soon after the war started. Susanna doesn't know why and the government won't tell them. I tried to help them find where he had been taken, but I was told I could get in serious trouble if I got involved especially as I had already enlisted. Susanna heard this and she won't let me near her for fear it will make trouble for me."

"You write, don't you?"

"The whole family went away and didn't say where they were

going. When the war is over, I will find them."

"Do you think her father might be a Nazi?"

"Mr. Reese?"

"Yes. Why else would the F.B.I. arrest him?"

"Mr. Reese, no way. He was a scoutmaster. He was always helping neighbors. No. Mrs. Reese said his competition did it. To get him out of the way."

"How could they?"

"It would be very easy to suggest to the authorities that someone has Nazi connections. That's all it would take. The F.B.I. woke them in the middle of the night. They handcuffed Mr. Reese and took him away. Mrs. Reese pleaded with them to tell her what he was accused of and where they were taking him. They wouldn't answer her.

"Everyone on their street came outside as they took Mr. Reese away. By morning no one would have anything to do with Mrs. Reese. They whispered about 'Mrs. Nazi,' just loud enough to be sure she heard them. The same folks who had let her take care of their children, turned on her like she was a two legged rat."

"Is Mrs. Reese also from Germany?"

"Yes."

"But the F.B.I. didn't arrest her?"

"Susanna has a sister who was born in Germany and another sister and a brother who were born in the states. I don't know where any of them are."

"My aunt in Norfolk told us their city manager had forty Japanese aliens arrested within minutes of the Japanese attack on Pearl Harbor. We had seen where the Japanese people – whole families – were taken into custody on the West Coast. A magazine article said they will be detained for the duration of the war," Julia said. "But such a wide scale internment of the German people hasn't taken place. Why would they select certain people if they didn't have proof they were Nazis?"

"That's just the thing. They don't care about proof. Just a pointed finger."

"Don't these people have rights?" Julia asked.

"Mr. Reese had been here a long time, but he never got his citizenship papers. In times of war, the Feds apparently can lock up citizens of an enemy state who are living here."

"Is there nothing you can do?"

"My father said I'd be dishonorably discharged from the army, if I stuck my nose in. If that was all, believe me, that wouldn't stop me. But he says I could get us all labeled Nazi sympathizers – my whole family. He forbade me to do anything as long as we're at war."

> *As long as the country is at war...*
> *Isn't that what Eberhard Greger said?*
> *No one can stand up for the Jewish people in*
> *Germany as long as the country is at war.*

"Mrs. Keegan?" the lieutenant said. "I didn't mean to tell you all this. If you don't believe me, I understand. I will say no more about it."

"No, I believe you. Our country is perhaps as anti-German as Germany is anti-Semitic. It wouldn't be hard to ruin a man in this country by calling him a Nazi. Look how quickly the nation stopped loving Lindbergh when the newspapers labeled him a Nazi because he spoke out against entering the war. People were ready to hang him."

"He didn't just speak out. He launched a campaign. I heard people say he was more interested in the medal the Germans gave him than in his U.S. citizenship."

"Is that what you think?"

"I don't know," he answered. "Maybe Lindbergh was trying to sell peace to the wrong country. Maybe he should have taken his campaign to Germany though I doubt the Nazis would allow such free speech."

"You're right, of course. At least our government allowed him to speak his mind. He brought the criticism on himself, I suppose, but this country may look back some day and decide he was right. Certainly you don't believe as our newspaper when it says all Germans are warmongers?" she asked.

"The Nazis have occupied Germany just as they have other European countries. I'm sure the average person there has no say in his government."

"But the Nazis are Germans, aren't they?"

"Hitler is from Austria. The Nazis are a bad lot of human beings who have gotten too much power. The German troops have to serve their government same as a man in any country. What I couldn't understand about Lindbergh was he suggested that the United States should recognize the Nazi government as a world power. He didn't see the Nazis as a threat to us."

They turned onto Queen Street. There were too many people on the sidewalk to continue their conversation. Instead they made their way along the business street.

> *Dad told me not to talk of Lindbergh.*
> *The lieutenant doesn't seem to like him.*

He isn't going to worry about what I said.
He's got his own worries.

I wonder if Susanna's dad is a Nazi?
Maybe Lt. O'Neill will drop Katie and me
        like hot potatoes.
He's probably wondering when to make his break.
    I really do talk too much.

    Each time they parted on the sidewalk to allow others to pass, Julia and the lieutenant would exchange weak smiles and continue on towards the post office. Finally they were at the post office steps.

    "May I mail the package for you, Mrs. Keegan? So that we don't have to take the buggy inside?"

    "Yes, thank you, Lieutenant. I'm sorry I got on such a serious subject, but I did appreciate the company."

    "Won't you wait for me?" he asked. "On the way back... we'll talk about Katie."

Twenty-One

The people of Hampton, like people everywhere, grew tired of the subject of war. Dramatic war movies weren't popular anymore. People wanted to forget the war. But banners displayed in the windows of some homes indicated the people there could never forget it. A blue star meant they had someone serving. A gold star meant their someone wasn't coming back.

Samuel Washington had told his father not to hang his service flag in their window unless the Army sent him overseas to fight. When he finally sent word from Alabama that his unit was being shipped overseas, Thomas put the banner up.

"You were so sure the Army wouldn't send them over there. But I knew it," Rose said. "I told you we shouldn't let him go to aviator school."

"Rose, most of our friend's boys have been in the fighting for a year, or more. He was going to be called up one way or the other."

"I don't like airplanes. Why couldn't he stay on the ground?"

"He's been marching on the ground for months at Tuskegee. Be proud of him, Mama. And be happy for him. He's finally getting the opportunity he's wanted."

"Opportunity? You call it an opportunity. I call it something else."

"Rose, he's going to be all right. He says he knows his aircraft better than he knows himself. He says," Thomas laughed, "he could fly blindfolded."

"Lord sakes! He's not going to try flying..."

"No, no, no. That was his way of saying he feels confident."

"I don't feel confident. I should have stopped him. You should have, Thomas."

"Rose, our boy is going to come home with ribbons on his coat. And you're going to be mighty proud of him then."

Rose looked across the street. The rows of headstones naming men who had died in wars were there to make the consequences of heroism very clear to her.

"I want my boy back alive, Thomas Washington. I don't care about ribbons. I want my boy."

Rose almost got her wish sooner than either of them thought. Samuel wrote that Col. Benjamin O. Davis had been called to Washington:

Dear Mom and Pop,

I'm hoping this gets to you. It seems some mail isn't making it home these days.

The government called Col. Davis to Washington. It seems there were complaints about us. We had to keep flying missions while the colonel was gone. He came back with three more squadrons of colored men, but we'd expected they would be sending us all home disgraced. Col. Davis must have convinced somebody important we were doing a good job.

Col. Davis got his training at West Point Military Academy. He was the only colored man there, and they were not friendly towards him. But he graduated.

He's tough on us sometimes. Sometimes he seems hard as s nails. No one dares to question anything he says. He speaks. We move! But he's fair and we know he went to bat for us when he was called to Washington.

The planes we fly are called Mustangs. We painted the tails of our planes red and we're called the "Red Tails." The colonel says we're not to try to score any personal victories. We are fighter escorts. So we're still kept behind the white guys. We're here to protect them.

The men in the squadron are top notch. The Army keeps us distanced from the other men. As usual we're billeted on the far side of the base. But we're the best and we're happy not to have to put up with their arrogance.

Take care of yourselves.

Your son,
Samuel

2nd Lt. Howard L. Baugh
99th Fighter Squadron
Sicily Summer 1943
P40 Warhawk

****

Julia received a letter from Peter.

If only the war would quit interrupting, we get some good entertainment over here. Bob Hope caught up with us last month. I've seen Phil Silvers and Martha Raye. I'm sure the Andrew Sisters are looking for us. Just hope they find us before the Jerries do.

Julia was reading Peter's letter when a news bulletin broke in on the radio music program to say "Glenn Miller, who left for Paris to prepare for a show for our boys over there, never arrived in Paris. It is believed that the single-engine plane he was in went down in the English Channel."

"Will the war ever end?" Julia said as she hung an ornament on her parent's Christmas tree. "Or are we staying in it 'til the last man falls?"

"It will end soon," Lieutenant O'Neill answered. He and the boys that boarded with the Walters were now included in the family gatherings. Katie now had three adopted uncles. Mike was her favorite.

"Hitler refuses to admit defeat," Mike said.

"Is he defeated?" Julia asked.

"The Allies have bombed all of Germany's big cities," Al, one of the boarders, said.

The other boarder, Mitchell, agreed, "Hitler has called on old men and boys and – if needed old women and girls – to defend Germany."

"Do you really think the war will end soon?"

"The Allies are beating the Reich and Hitler is trying to say his "people's army" is going to change the outcome," Mitchell said. "Yes, I think the Allies will end it soon."

"I read our army is making men who have already had six months of combat stay on the frontlines," Julia said. "The men say they want replacements. They want to be rotated out. Hitler's army of old folks and children might be able to beat men who are suffering from battle fatigue."

"An untrained army of civilians against our boys," Mike said. "They won't have a chance. The worst thing about it is our boys don't want to shoot civilians, but they can't trust them. Some civilians wave white flags and snipe at the American troops at the same time.

"Well," he said stepping back to look at the tree, "Do you think the birthday girl is going to like the way we decorated this thing?"

"I think Katie is going to want to grab everything off of it. I just hope she doesn't pull the whole thing over on herself," Julia said.

"Do I hear singing?" Al asked.

"There are carolers out on the street," Mrs. Walters said hurrying to the front door. She opened the door and the group turned up the sidewalk.

Silent Night, Holy Night
... Sleep in Heavenly peace.

"Won't you join us?" one of the singers asked.

"You young people go on," Mrs. Walters said. "Mr. Walters and I are going to stay inside in the warmth. We'll be here if Katie should wake up."

Julia looked like she might protest and so her mother insisted, "There's not much we can do to make it seem like Christmas, but singing you can do. Get your coat and go out and spread a little of the Christmas

Time Will Tell

spirit."

"Come on guys," Mike said to Al and Mitchell.

"We used to carol back home," Mitchell said. "It would be kind of fun."

"I've never done this," Al said. "I don't know the words."

"Just come along," Mitchell said. "You'll know more than you think you do."

The four young people hurried to join the others and they rounded the corner singing "Jingle Bells." When they came to the verse, "A day or two ago..." most of the group just sang

                dah, dah, dah, dah,ago

Al laughed until they got back to "Jingle Bells" and then he joined once more and most enthusiastically.

Mike sang like a choirboy – his voice prompting reluctant carolers. He soon learned that he shouldn't try to get them to sing third and forth verses – they simply wouldn't know the words.

"We're all going back to the Webber's for some hot apple cider," they were told. "Please, come along."

"What do you say, Julia?" Mike asked. "Do you want to go back home?"

       Dorothy has been eyeing Mitchell.
         If I go back to Mother's and
           these three men go with me,
  I'll have all the girls angry with me.   Julia thought.

    It's good for us all – singing and having fun.

"No," she answered. "If the Webbers don't object to a few party crashers, I think it would be very nice."

There were some other men in the group, but as always, the girls outnumbered the boys.

"You know we'd be pleased to have you, Julia," Dorothy said.

The Webber's house had a beautiful wreath on the front door. No one in Hampton decorated with lights during the war years, but Mrs. Webber had decorated inside and out with fresh greens and berries.

"Your home looks so festive and lovely," Julia said. "And I have enjoyed caroling."

"As we don't have anyone in our family serving overseas, we feel a responsibility to some who do to try to put a little joy in the season," Mrs. Webber said. "Mr. Webber is getting some more logs for the fire. You all can sit by the fire and thaw out."

The fire's light caused flickering shadows about the room. There was only a minimum of other lighting. The wonderful smell of pine, cedar and apple cider filled the house. Stockings hung from the mantle labeled: Dorothy, Mildred, Lillian.

Dorothy was the oldest of the girls. Mildred and Lillian were closer to Bertie's age. Mr. Webber and the girls had gone caroling. Now the younger girls helped their mother in the kitchen and Dorothy entertained the guests.

"Would you like to hear some records?" she asked.

"Who plays the piano?" Mitchell asked.

"My sisters are taking lessons," Dorothy said. "I don't play. Julia and Kate used to play at school functions. Would you play for us, Julia?"

"I'm a little out of practice, but if the group is still in a singing mood, I'll do my best."

"Will you need more light?"

"It's not necessary. I don't read music."

"Then, let's all gather around the piano," Dorothy said. "Perhaps with some accompaniment, we can sing the carols right."

"Then we'll have to go out and show your neighbors we can do it," Mitchell said.

But the group protested, "It's too cold to go out again." and "I think we sounded pretty good."

Julia hadn't played since before the war, now fifteen people gathered around the piano. "I hope I don't disappoint you. It's been a long time."

She played a couple of scales to loosen up her fingers and then went from one carol to the next with no real trouble. The beautiful, familiar carols heightened her spirits and the voices of those around her made Julia feel ... like Christmas!

Mitchell made a date with Dorothy and Al, with a girl named Valerie. Mike stayed as close to Julia as he could.

He's using me to protect him
from the girls who are making eyes at him.
Okay, if he's going to stay at my side, he'll have to sing.

"My friend Mike O'Neill is a singer," Julia announced. "I think he ought to sing something for us."

"I'm not a singer," he tried to say, but no one would believe him and so he agreed to sing.

"Do you play 'O Holy Night?'"

Julia played an introduction. Then she marveled as the lieutenant sang the words:

> O Holy night, the stars are brightly shining...
> O night, O holy night. O night divine.

Everyone sat quietly listening to the strong tenor voice of the Irish boy from Milwaukee. And when the song was ended, Mr. Webber said, "I believe this young man has just given us a Christmas present we'll never forget. That was beautiful."

They wanted him to sing another, but he told Julia to play "Joy to the World" and told the others he would join when they started singing. "No more solos."

On the walk home, Julia was quizzed about what she knew of Dorothy and Valerie. "They are two or three years younger than I am, so I don't really know much to tell you."

"Lt. Songbird, could have gotten a date with any girl there – especially after his solo," Mitchell said.

"Do either of you guys have girls back home?" Mike asked.

"Of course, we know girls back home. But they're there and we are here."

Twenty-Two

-1945-

Herbie Goldstein answered the phone and immediately knew it was news about one of his brothers. "Yes, Miss Carrie. What's happened?"

"Your brother George's plane was shot down over France. That's all the information they have. Would you notify the rest of your family and tell them I will be here at the Western Union office watching for further updates."

"Yes. Will you phone me as soon as you hear anything."

"You can count on it. Often I get word the pilot parachuted to safety. I'm hoping George did and I can call you back with the news. Give your folks my regards."

"Yes, I will. Thank you, Miss Carrie."

"What's happened?" Daniel asked.

"George's plane was shot down over France. Miss Carrie is going to call here as soon as she gets any other information... I'm going up the street to tell Mama and Papa."

Herbie removed his apron and stepped out onto Queen Street. His parents would be at the dress shop. He would try not to alarm them. But the sight of Herbert Goldstein rushing down the street in the daytime without his apron, alerted the whole of downtown that he had received dreadful news.

People backed off the sidewalk as he passed and a good many of them followed. He went in the dress shop. The people waited for him to come out.

"What is it Herbert?" Dave Manley asked.

"Miss Carrie received word that George's plane has been shot down."

"Did he..."

"That's all we know. We'll just have to wait. Wait and pray."

"We'll all be praying for him, Herbert," Mrs. Graham said.

"Thank you," Herbie said. "Now we must get back to work as Papa says."

Julia and Katie entered the market and didn't get the usual greeting – no one came rushing to Katie with a cracker – no one exclaimed that Julia was "looking especially lovely today." Julia looked about for Herbie and Daniel. They were talking in hushed voices to other people.

Something has happened.

Julia went over to Herbert. "Are George and Gene all right?"

"George's plane was shot down. That's all we know."

"He just received the flying cross," Herbie said. Julia remembered their sister's concern.

Maybe she didn't want him to be a hero.

Herbie asked Julia for her list. "I'm fixing dinner for the Bryans tonight. This is a big order for me."

"I'll get your things," Herbie said.

"Had you heard from George recently?"

"Oh, yes. If there's one thing the Goldsteins know, it's to keep in touch with Mama."

"How is your mother taking it?"

"On the outside, she's as tough as nails. But on the inside..." He shook his head.

He filled Julia's order and turned to the person behind her.

George's plane went down, Julia thought.
It's so hard to believe.
Is he dead? Is he a prisoner?
Will he come back?

****

"I would think an Irishman from Milwaukee would have a mug of beer in both hands and one on the table," Mitchell said to Mike outside the Langley Theatre. "You don't drink?"

"Me father drank. His father drank. And I suppose all me grandfathers back to the days of leprechauns drank. I reckon I have 'nuff Irish whiskey flowing in me veins that I don't need anymore."

Downtown Hampton   *Cheyne's*

"Well, we'll tell you what you missed next time we see you. We might find a couple of dames. It's going to be a hot time in old Phoebus tonight!" Al said.

"Try an' stay out of trouble, guys. When the war ends you don't want to be in the brig."

"When the war ends there won't be a lock that can hold us," Al said.

"There won't be enough beer in all of your hometown to satisfy us either," Mitchell said. "You sure you don't want to come along?"

"And end up having to carry the two of you home 'cause you can't stand on your own feet? Thanks, but no thanks."

"Don't tell the Walters where we went." Al said. "Okay, Buddy?"

"They won't hear it from me," Mike said as the others got on the streetcar.

"Uncle Mike!" Katie shouted.

"Not another of our chance meetings, Lieutenant?" Julia teased.

"Honest, I didn't know you ladies were in town today," Mike said. "You can ask Al and Mitchell. We came downtown and caught an afternoon

Time Will Tell

flick."

"You seem to have lost them," Julia answered.

"Well, I know. I meant, you could ask them when you see them," Mike said.

"I told the Bryans I would cook tonight. Why don't you come with us and have dinner?" Julia asked.

"That's too good an offer to turn down. My mother taught me how to help in the kitchen. What would you like me to do?"

"Do you peel potatoes?"

"You ask an Irishman if he peels potatoes?"

"Then, you're hired.

"Did Al and Mitchell have duty tonight?" Julia asked.

"I don't know what they're doing. What do you hear from Joe?"

"Katie and I just mailed him a letter. Joe isn't much of a writer. He asks questions like

> How are you?
> What is Katie doing?
> What do you hear from Kate?

And then he says he misses us and hopes to be home soon. That's about it."

"Kate's a good writer?"

"She is. I have her last letter in my pocket. Would you like to hear it? She was in Paris and she loved it!"

"Well, if you'd like to read it..."

"Would I? I read her letters over and over and this one is particularly, well, you'll see what I mean.

> Dear Julia,
> There have been times I've wished I hadn't let you talk me into joining the Red Cross. But not today. Today has been wonderful!

"That's right, I remember you telling me you suggested Kate go with the Red Cross."

"Shh-h-h, I'm reading."

> I saw Paris for the first time. It's beautiful and lovely and fantastic! Never have I had such a thrill as driving a jeep down their wide avenue and everyone waving at us!
> The Allied flags were flying from every building. The French women look so colorful and chic, and the

sidewalk cafes are so gay.

To think that I've been to Paris within a week of its liberation! I never dreamed I'd really get there. I just can't get over it.

We had dinner at an army tent just off Place de la Concorde and the boys were camping out under trees with the area roped off to keep the curious Frenchmen out. We ate at the officer's table. They opened a wonderful bottle of champagne for us. But I couldn't enjoy that meal very much because of the crowd of people lining the roped off area just staring at us.

On the way home tonight I noticed a long convoy of trucks carrying food into Paris for them.

Thank goodness!

"You two must have had a lot of fun growing up," Mike said as she refolded the letter. "What was it like growing up in a small town?"

"Hampton was a wonderful place to grow up. I went fishing, crabbing, boating, swimming. I've known Joe all my life and I knew I was going to marry him back when I was a little girl. My sister and I would invite all our friends to our house. When we were in high school, we'd bring a bunch of friends home after the ball games and we'd have cocoa and marshmallows. Hampton was a great place before the war."

"You think it's changed?" he asked.

"I used to feel I knew everybody. Of course, I didn't, but I knew everyone I saw daily. It's not that way now and I wonder if it ever will be again."

"I've never lived in a small town and I've never been crabbing," Mike said.

"You must go crabbing. Tell me about Milwaukee," she said.

"Some people think it's one big brewery." He shook his head. "There are other industries. Pop works for an automotive parts factory. Of course, they've been converted for the manufacture of military vehicles."

"Do you have brothers and sisters?" Julia asked.

"Three sisters, four brothers, one dog and some cats. My three sisters are all older than I am. Two of them are married. I have an older brother in the service and two brothers after me."

"Then you're counting yourself as one of the four brothers?"

"No, my oldest brother was killed."

"He must have been young," she said.

"Too young to die. He got drunk one night in a tavern and insulted the wrong man."

"So, that's why you don't drink."

"How do you do it?" he asked.

"How do I do what?"

"I get ribbing from the guys at the base all the time because I won't have a drink with them. Yet I've never told a soul, until you, about my brother. No one else knows anything about Susanna's pa. You could get a job working for J. Edgar."

"If the F.B.I. wanted me," she answered, "it wouldn't be to hire me."

"Oh?"

"Well, you heard me go on and on about Lindbergh. Hoover probably has a file on him that would fill a room."

"I don't think you'd be put on the FBI's most wanted list for having a crush on Lindbergh."

"I never had a crush on the man."

"Every girl in America did," Mike said. "Why not you?"

"We were talking about your family," she said. "What branch of the service is your brother in?"

"He's Navy. He's been on two torpedoed ships."

"U-boats torpedoed them?" she asked.

"Yeah. The first time he spent four days on a raft before he was picked up. This last time they were rescued right away. We heard from him before we heard about his ship."

"I can't imagine being on a ship and seeing a torpedo coming at me," Julia said.

"Steve says he wishes he could be on deck so he could see it coming. He's in the engine room. He doesn't see anything. Then all of a sudden, boom!"

"Does the ship he's on have depth charges?" she asked.

"That's a strange question coming from a woman. Yes, it does. But if the u-boats spot them first, they won't have a chance to use them."

"When your brother was rescued, was he picked up by the u-boat?"

"No, u-boats don't pick up survivors."

"Do they kill them?" she asked.

"You mean once the ship is sunk?"

"Yes. Do they shoot the men in the water?"

"They didn't when Kenny's ships were sunk. Of course they didn't rescue them, or say they were sorry." (He laughed.) "There was a story in the paper about a German captain who shouted to the survivors in the water that he was sorry that he had to do it and wished them luck. That was pretty early in the war."

"Are they supposed to pick up survivors?"

"Have you ever seen a submarine?"

"Only in newsreels," she answered.

"There's not much room in a sub and the German u-boats are said to be smaller," he explained. "Most ships the u-boats sink carry more people than would fit into their boat. There was another instance of a u-boat captain who ordered the captain of the ship he'd sunk to come on board his u-boat. They kept him a few days and then released him to a neutral. He got home unharmed."

"Suppose your brother were on a sub and a German destroyer sunk the sub," Julia asked. "The men jumped into the water rather than go down in the sub. What would the destroyer do then?"

"They'd pull them out of the water. Take them as prisoners. Kenny would be so glad to get out of the sub; he probably wouldn't care. He'd go stir crazy in a submarine."

"Oh, me too. It would be terrible being in the water and having depth charges dropped above you."

"You are a mystery, Julia Keegan. You have strange interests – cemeteries, a man people say is a Nazi sympathizer and torpedoes and depth charges. Anything else?"

"Coming from a soldier from Milwaukee who won't have a beer with the guys and won't dare to smile at a single girl, you appear to be the strangest of the two of us, my friend."

"Perhaps so, but at least you know what makes me so. Have you visited the cemeteries lately?" he asked.

"Regularly."

"Both of them?"

"No. I should go back to Phoebus."

"You should? Why should? Tell me, why do you feel obliged to go there?"

"There's no time for that now. We're here and I have to fix the supper."

****

"Do you fly upside down?" Bertie asked Mike at the dinner table.

"Sometimes."

"Have you ever been shot at?"

"No, I haven't."

"Oh."

"I'm sorry to disappoint you."

"No, that's all right. It's not important. Have you ever crash-landed?"

"That's part of my job."

"Crash-landing?"

"We have to see what a plane can do. Sometimes that means we have to try things that don't work."

"What's the worst..."

"Bertie!" Mrs. Bryan said. "Please excuse her bad manners, Mike. Bertie, I want you to button your lips and eat your dinner."

"But..."

"Bertie!"

"I can't eat with my mouth buttoned." Bertie spoke with his lips barely moving.

"Oh, child!"

Julia laughed and then, Mike did.

Mr. Bryan grimaced and shook his head. "There's too much about war that children cannot possibly comprehend. They see and hear about terrible things, but they don't understand what is happening."

"Do any of us?" Julia asked.

"I have younger brothers," Mike said. "They seem to think the war is a great adventure. They want to be soldiers. I sometimes fear they're praying the war will go on long enough that they'll be of age to serve."

"When Joe left," Julia said. "I foolishly thought the war would end any day. I waited for letters from Joe expecting each one was going to say he was coming home. I brought groceries thinking of what Joe might like me to have when he got home. When I dressed Katie in little outfits I'd say, 'Your daddy will love this.' When I cut my hair, I worried he wouldn't like it short. It's not short anymore. He never saw Katie when she was bald. It seems like he has been gone forever – almost like he was never here."

"We have to believe the war is going to end soon," Mrs. Bryan said.

"That's just it. I can't believe it anymore. It's like Joe is someone I imagined. I cannot think of what it will be like to have him come home. The silver screen tells me good will triumph over evil. Well... so long as I 'BUY WAR BONDS' before I leave the theatre. So I purchase more bonds and come out with all the proper emotions. But I loose those feelings so quickly."

Julia stopped talking.

Oh, I shouldn't say these things.

Embarrassed, she looked about. "I'm sorry. A fine hostess I am!"

"It's all right. We're all tired of this war," Mrs. Bryan said. "Julia, did you know Freddie Smith when you were in high school?"

"Yes, his father was a major general at Ft. Monroe. He married an admiral's daughter. I didn't know her. Was Freddie killed?"

"No, the newspaper said he is now one of the youngest generals in the Army Air Force."

"Julia, you are a fine hostess," Mr. Bryan said. "I can't believe you found something to do with potatoes that my wife hadn't already tried. I liked this very much."

"It's the way in which a potato is peeled that makes the difference," Mike said.

"Then you may peel potatoes for us as often as you like," Mr. Bryan said with a laugh.

Katie had fallen asleep downstairs while the adults were visiting. Mike carried her up to the third floor for Julia while Julia helped clean the dishes away. Later, when she went up to the apartment, she found Mike rocking with Katie and singing

...Too Ra Loo Ra Loo Ral,
That's an Irish lullaby.

Julia took the sleeping child from him and put her into her bed. They tiptoed out of the room.

"She woke up just as we got up here," Mike explained. "She asked me to sing to her."

Julia smiled. "My daughter knows how to get spoiled and just who will do it."

"Children should be put to bed with lullabies."

"I quite agree. She will have pleasant dreams tonight, thanks to her Uncle Mike."

"Thanks for inviting me, Julia," Mike said. "Let me know the next time you need someone to peel potatoes."

"If you'd like me to put in a good word for you – tell the Army how good you are at it..."

"No."

"No?"

"No. But do you have some pull with the Army?" he asked.

"Why do you ask that?"

"The first time I met you, you said you'd speak on my behalf at my court-martial."

"I would, but whatever would they court-martial you for?"

Time Will Tell

"Not seeing a lady to her door properly."

"But you did, as I recall," Julia said. "No, I have no pull with the Army. Not me."

"Julia, what you said about believing the war will never end..."

"Oh, I know it will end. I just don't know what will be left – who will be left."

"The news from Europe is sounding much better. You have to keep faith like Mrs. Bryan said."

"I know. Please forget what I said. Just a temporary slump. Forgive me."

"I think I brought up the subject. You going to be all right?"

"Yes. Goodnight."

"Tell the little miss Uncle Mike said goodnight," he said as he descended the stairs.

"I will."

Julia walked over to her front window. The moon looked right at her, but she had nothing to say to it. She could think of nothing to have it relay to Joe. She turned away as if the moon might read her thoughts.

What am I feeling? she asked herself.
Am I miserable because the war continues...
or because it may end?
Am I afraid Joe won't come home
...or that he will?
Of course, I want him to come home!
I want him to be with Katie and me.
I want him to hold me...
But what if he's different? What if I'm different?
We fell in love as children
sipping sodas and going fishing.
I felt I'd lost him when he was classified a 4F.
Did we lose each other?
I cannot think like this.
He will come home. We will be a family.
Everything will be right again.

Julia put on her nightgown and slipped into bed. "The potatoes were good," she said.

Twenty-Three

"The world has gone mad, Thomas," Rose said when they listened to speeches by Roosevelt and Churchill. "All this freedom and victory and there will be no one left alive to enjoy it."

On April 12th the *Captain Midnight* radio program was interrupted by *ABC News*:

PRESIDENT ROOSEVELT IS DEAD.

Rose was more certain than ever the end of the world had come. "Lord, help us all!" she cried.

Everything halted. People walked about stupefied. All broadcasting ceased, except for the story of the President's death.

"What will happen now?" Rose asked. "How can men fight without a leader?"

"Rose, the Allies are winning. Samuel's last letter sounded like they've about wrapped things up over there."

Rose sat next to their old Zenith table-top radio. She tried to catch every detail of the President's funeral though the reception was muffled with static. Tears she had held back for the last several years streamed down her cheeks.

"Do you believe what you say, Thomas? Will Samuel come home? Every time I go to the door, I expect to find someone bringing me news that our boy is dead. Mercy me, the President is dead. Did you hear, Ernie Pyle has been killed. What are the chances that Samuel will survive?"

"Roosevelt died in Georgia. It wasn't the war that killed him. The Allies have won the war, Rose. The Germans have already released some of our prisoners of war."

"Ernie Pyle, that war correspondent, was killed this month. You don't think they'll send Samuel to Japan, do you? The reporter was killed by the Japs. Until I can wrap my arms around Samuel and he tells me he's home, I won't believe it. They talk about a ceasefire, but then they say there's more fighting and Japan isn't about to surrender."

"Samuel will be home soon. And you're going to be one proud mama. They'll be parades and people will cheer for our boy. He's proven that a Negro is a man."

Before the end of the month, Senator Ed Kennedy announced that the war in Europe was over. Rose changed the sheets on Samuel's bed. "I want them to be fresh!" she said.

Then the public was informed that the senator had spoken prematurely.

"See Thomas," Rose said. "It hasn't ended. Lord have mercy on us all, it hasn't ended."

"Well, you got a letter from your boy. Open it up."

Rose hadn't seen the mailman. "How did this get here, Thomas?" she asked.

"He said for me to give it to you tomorrow. Go ahead; read it,"

Dear Mama,

Happy birthday! I was hoping I'd be there to give you a birthday hug, but it didn't work out. I love you and hope you have a special day.

I don't have anything to give you, but I thought you might like to hear that the word is out over here – the Krauts are said to be giving up. This war is coming to a halt pretty soon!

The Germans have released some of our boys who were taken prisoner of war. I received a letter from my buddy, Cecil Mitchell. He had been reported missing in action.

Boy, I went crazy when I got his letter! He's free now and on his way home.

Mama, I've said a prayer for him every night since his plane went down and finally I got my answer.

It's the first time I've cried in years!

Rose's eyes were so full of tears she couldn't read anymore. She handed the letter to Thomas. He read:

It's sad to see all the destruction of the war,

Mama.

    We've had some lousy weather and everything is so dismal. But then there are places that haven't been bombed and when flying above them, they look like precious jewels of magnificent color – almost unreal.

    Yesterday I was flying over a city that hadn't been spared. Only one lone church was standing in the midst of all the bombed and burned buildings. It's steeple seemed to be reaching to Heaven for God's help.

    Actually, there are a lot of steeples left standing when all else around them has been destroyed. I suppose no one wants to anger God.

    Take care of pop for me and I'll be home soon.
    Happy birthday!
    Love,
    Samuel

****

As radio commentators heralded the latest bulletins from the war front, it seemed that victory really was close at hand:

THE ALLIES HAVE CAPTURED WARSAW.
GERMAN TROOPS ARE HASTILY RETREATING.

PATTON'S THIRD ARMY HAS TAKEN FRANKFURT.
CHAOS SPREADS IN THE REICH.

THE FOOD SITUATION IN GERMANY IS BECOMING DESPERATE.

U.S. SEVENTH ARMY HAS CAPTURED NUREMBERG.

ALLIED AIR RAIDS ARE POUNDING GERMANY FOR THE EIGHTEENTH CONSECUTIVE DAY.

THE GERMAN PRESS AND RADIO PLEADED WITH ALL GERMANS TO TAKE UP ARMS.

IN GERMANY, THE CITY OF COLOGNE IS LIFELESS.
IT'S FAMOUS CATHEDRAL STILL STANDS, BUT ALL ELSE IS RUBBLE.

The 100,000 residents of Duisberg, Germany surrendered today... to just seven GI's.

The Nazi Gestapo newspaper says complete collapse of German forces is only days or weeks away.

Berlin falls in the hands of the Russians after twelve days of street fighting.

Even the folks who had refused to listen to the broadcasts after the first year of the war, now tuned in to hear the good news.

Thomas Washington had not missed anything on the radio or in his newspaper. He never failed to keep Rose informed. On April the 20th he announced to Rose, "Today is Adolf Hitler's fifty-sixth birthday."

"I'm not going to bake him a cake," Rose said.

"I don't think anybody will, Rose. The paper says that instead of a party, his Reich is torn by civil war with gigantic peace demonstrations in Berlin and Munich. That tyrant is getting what he deserves."

Several days later Thomas told Rose, "Listen to this: 'The German Fuehrer has cried out to Mussolini, 'The struggle for our very existence has reached its climax.' The little runt is getting worried," Thomas added.

"It says here," Thomas read, "Adolf Hitler died fighting the Bolshevists in Berlin,
    "Today they say Hitler escaped to the mountains,
        "Now they report Hitler's in Berlin,
            "He's dead. Today they say Hitler is dead,
but maybe not
        "They don't know."

The tyrant with the funny mustache was no longer in command, but they could not find his body. The skeletal remains of thousands of people who had been massacred by the Nazis were discovered.

At last there were reports of Allied troops marching victoriously in the streets of European cities while swarms of people cheered.

THE WAR IN EUROPE IS OVER

"Kate's coming home!" Evelyn shouted to her husband as she waved a letter. "Listen, she says...

...some girls are going on with the troops heading for the Pacific, but I am coming home!

Those of us who aren't going to Japan will be traveling with our wonderful, victorious troops. The last town we drove through on Wednesday had been in our hands for just one week. Everyone was waving at us and cheering.

The war is over! I can't believe it!!!

"If only Joe was coming home," Evelyn said. "If I ever find out he volunteered to stay over there, I'll ring his neck."

"Evelyn, I've been thinking for sometime that Joe was recruited into some sort of special services."

"Special services?" she repeated.

"Don't say anything to Julia, but I think he's still working with sensitive stuff. She says he never writes her anything about the boys he's serving with, or even hints about where he is, or what he's doing."

"When he wrote her he wasn't coming home yet," Evelyn said, "Julia told me that was the first time he'd suggested he's been in any danger. You may be right."

****

Julia heard the Bryan's phone ringing. She went into the front hall to answer it.

"I was hoping you'd answer," Mike said. "I wanted to tell you I'm going home on leave."

"Do you have time to come by before you go?"

"I was fishing for an invitation."

"You mean now?"

"I catch a bus for Milwaukee this evening."

"Mrs. Bryan and Bertie have taken Katie out. She'll want to see you."

"I've signed for a car. How about I come over for you, we take a ride and when we get back I'll see Katie."

"Okay. How soon?"

"I'm on my way."

Julia hung up the phone in the downstairs hall. She took the steps two at a time.

I've got to change. I don't want to go out in this.

When Mike drove up, Julia was waiting in a porch chair pretending to have been there since they talked on the phone. "How did you get the car?"

"They're trying to get me to stay on at Langley. So they're granting my every wish."

"Every wish?"

"Well, not really. But I got my leave and the loan of this beautiful army sedan."

"What more could you wish for?"

"Where would you like to go?" Mike asked as he got in the car.

"You're the driver. I'm just along for the ride."

Mike turned onto LaSalle and again on Kecoughtan Road. He drove down Queen Street and across the bridge to Phoebus.

"Would you like to visit the National Cemetery?" he asked.

"Is that what you've been doing?"

"What?"

"You have purposefully brought me here, haven't you?"

"Was I wrong? Didn't you want to come here?"

"No. I mean, no, you weren't wrong."

Mike parked the car and they got out to walk. He waited for Julia to lead the way.

"Would you rather walk alone?" he asked.

"No, please come. I will tell you my secret."

"I was hoping you would, but you don't have to."

She took his hand and went directly to the rows of graves of the German sailors.

"These graves weren't marked when we were here before," Mike said. "The names on the gravestones are German. Did you know?"

"Yes."

"Did you know someone who is buried here?"

"No. Only someone who wished he was."

Julia tried to figure out how to tell Mike about Eberhard Greger. Mike waited patiently.

"Early in the war, one of our destroyers sunk a German u-boat. These are the graves of some of the men from that u-boat."

"Why are they buried here?"

"Their boat was sunk. The men were killed. Our government had them buried here – secretly."

"Secretly?"

"Yes. They tried to keep it out of the newspapers, but it got out anyway. Then people started seeing German spies all about town."

"You mean Bertie?"

"No, I mean everyone. People were saying they saw Germans on our beaches. Germans spying on our military bases. Germans practically all over the place. They said the u-boat had come to bring spies like the ones who had come ashore on Long Island and in Florida."

"Yes, I heard about it. We were darn lucky the destroyer spotted them."

"They passed this area. They were out to stop shipments of supplies to Europe. There were no spies on that boat."

"You know this? How do you know this?"

"Our destroyer sunk the u-boat and the German men jumped into the water shouting for help. But our destroyer moved into the men in the water and killed them. The ones who weren't killed by the ship's propeller, were killed with depth charges. Then they pulled these twenty-nine out of the water and brought them here. They played taps, fired a salute and left them here to be forgotten."

Julia and Mike stood silently facing the graves. Tears ran down her face. "They will not be going home," she said. "Some of them were only boys."

She turned her tear-filled eyes towards Mike. "Erich went back for his lucky number."

"What?'

"His lucky number. He never went anywhere without his lucky number."

"Julia, I don't understand where this is coming from. Did you have a séance with these men?"

"I wish I could. I tell them things, but I don't know if they hear."

"I wish you'd tell me. You said you'd tell me your secret."

"I did," she took a long breath. "Mike, I met the captain of the u-boat. A U.S. destroyer found them in shallow waters off the North Carolina coast. They were trapped. He ordered his men to abandon ship and when he went to scuttle the boat, an explosion caused the boat to dive and threw him away from his men. Then the destroyer moved in on his men and dropped depth charges."

"How did you meet this u-boat captain?"

"Quite by accident. He told me he wanted to die. He felt ashamed he had lost his boat and all his men."

"What happened to him?"

"I don't know. I was showing him the way here – to the cemetery when we were separated. I heard sirens afterwards. He may have been picked up. I don't know."

"Can you speak German? How did you talk to him?"

"In English. He went to school in New York. He said others of the crew had been to the States, or had friends and family in the States."

"And these are the men from his boat," Mike said. "None of his men survived?"

"He didn't think so. He watched as the Navy pulled the bodies onto their search boats. Most of them had on life jackets, but the defenseless men must have been killed by all the depth charges the destroyer dropped on them. The paper said there were no survivors."

"Whew! This is quite a secret you've been carrying around. Did you and the German captain have something..."

"No! Why would you ask that?"

"Because I'm an insufferable fool. Was this German young?" Mike asked.

"Not old. He was concerned about his girl friend, his parents and his cousins who were like siblings to him. I hope he can go home to them now."

"His folks may not have survived the war. There isn't much of Germany that hasn't been bombed. Certainly all the major cities got hit bad."

"He was from a small town – Lieberose."

"Lieberose. You remember that?

"It's probably best that you keep your secret."

"You don't think I should have told someone about him?"

"I don't think so, but I'm the man who was in love with a German girl."

"What are you going to do now?"

"I have to go back to Milwaukee to see if I can find any trace of Susanna."

"Then you're not coming back to Langley?" Julia asked.

"I don't know what I'll do. I wanted to see you before I went home on leave because ... because Joe will probably be here when I get back."

"Mike..."

"Let me say this," he insisted. "At this moment I don't know if I want to find Susanna, or, forgive me, if I want Joe to return."

"Mike..."

"Don't stop me. You and your precious Katie mean more to me than I can express. I've tried not to feel this way. I've tried to convince myself that I can walk away from here and forget you. I can't."

"Mike..."

"Yes, I know. We have to be who we were before the war. At least, try to be. But, I have to tell you, you are everything I could ever want. Why did they end the war? Now I have to give you up.

"But how can I give up what I never had?" Mike countered himself.

"Oh, Mike. Do you think it is only you who loves us and that we don't love you in return? Katie doesn't know her daddy. You are the one she looks for. You're the one who sings to her. You're the one who taught her your Irish blarney."

"What do you mean?"

"Yesterday, when she didn't want to take her nap, do you know what she said to me?"

"What?"

" 'Mommy, when I close my eyes, I cannot see my beautiful mommy.' "

"That's my girl."

"Mike, we couldn't forget you."

Mike pulled Julia into his arms. She stiffened.

"Mike, we haven't done anything wrong. We can't ..."

"I know we can't. Well, I know you can't... and I wouldn't want you to because you would hate yourself."

"We don't know what to expect," Julia said.

"I expect to miss you. I expect to be very jealous of..."

"Mike."

"Yes, Ma'am." He backed away. "But if you ever want me..." he winked.

She smiled. "Come on, Uncle Mike. Let's see if Katie is home."

They walked towards the car.

"This German. Was he good looking?

"I heard the u-boat men were scoundrels

"Was he a smooth talker?

"Was he wounded?

"Did you have to take care of him?

"Did he wake out of a coma

and say you were an angel?"

"Michael O'Neill, would you stop this?"

"Yes, I'm sorry. It's just I've prepared myself to loose you to your husband, but not to a German u-boat captain."

"I haven't said anything to give you that impression, have I?"

"You haven't."

"Then don't suggest I have.

"Do you think our government would let him go home now?"

"I'll try to find out," Mike said. "if there's anyway I can."

"Mike, I just got another letter from my sister."

"Is she all right?"

"She's been traveling all over Europe. And she's coming home soon. I want you to meet her."

"I'll give you a call when I get back."

Twenty-Four

Stories of the triumphant Allies being cheered by the people of Europe made the folks "back home" impatient to meet the returning troops. Shiploads of men, many of them wounded – using crutches, with their arms in slings, their heads bandaged, being carried on stretchers – were soon arriving at the C&O terminal in Newport News. But they could wear their wounds proudly for they had been victorious.

Peter wrote, rather typed, about celebrating the German surrender with a couple of French girls before going to Germany. He said he was typing on a "German liberated typewriter" which his battalion now owned. He told of the "souvenirs" he was collecting to send home – rifles and German bayonets, clips and bullets and a German helmet and belt buckle. He also had a "dandy pistol" he would keep with him. He couldn't wait to show it to Joe.

He said he and a bunch of other guys put up a few days in a house on the water living the "Life of Reilly," and riding German bicycles all over the place.

Then we were bivouacked for a night in an established camp just outside of Nancy, France. It had been constructed just a few days ago. Huge mess lines with tables to eat at. Tents with cots for sleeping. And real honest to God, showers. We could hardly recognize each other once we cleaned up. The best of it all was there were dozens of prisoners of war here. We just grabbed us a PW and made him get our chow, wash our mess kits, gas and oil our vehicles and carry our bed rolls. Just a little retaliation for a few of the discomforts they have caused us. Besides, we're lazy!

Peter hadn't said when he expected to be back home. Julia was unprepared when he came up to the Bryan's porch one afternoon not too very long after she'd received his letter. The mail took longer now that the war was over and troops were in transit.

"Peter! What? How? Oh, my goodness! You're here. Does your mother know? Thank God, you're home and you're not injured!"

"Hello, Julia."

"Hello, Julia? That's all you've got to say?" she teased.

"You look good."

"No, I don't. I wasn't expecting anybody. My curlers!" She grabbed her head. "Oh, my hair is in curlers. Why didn't you let me know you were coming?"

"I can leave."

"No!" Julia realized he was quite serious; he would leave. "You come on up and, just don't look at me."

Peter climbed up the porch steps listlessly.

"I'm afraid I don't have anything to offer you. I wasn't..."

No Julia, don't say that again.

"Would you like a glass of water? Please, come up to the apartment."

"Yes, that would be fine," he said and followed her.

"I got a letter from Kate just yesterday," Julia said to him as she fixed two glasses of water. "She wrote that she wondered if you were near where she was. I don't guess you were..."

As Julia turned around with the two glasses in her hands, Peter had started down the stairs.

He's leaving!

"Peter! Please, come up and sit down. I want you to tell me about Europe."

He returned to the table where she had placed the glasses. "Julia, there's not much to say. There's not much left of Europe."

Peter cast his eyes low. Julia wondered what to say to him.

"Tell me about you, Peter. Were you injured?"

"Not a piece of shrapnel. Damn lucky, I guess."

"When did you get back?"

"I don't know exactly."

"You've been home already to see Aunt Lucille?"

"No."

"Then you should call her right away! Mrs. Bryan will let you use their telephone."

"No, Julia, not yet."

"What's wrong, Peter? Why don't you want to call your mother? She's frantic to see you – to know you're all right."

"That's just it, Julia, I'm not all right."

"What do you mean?"

"I'm not 'all right' and I'll never be all right. I'm breathing and I have had no parts amputated, but I don't feel like celebrating. Can you understand? I don't feel like celebrating."

"Do you want to talk about it?"

"No."

"Then please go lie down and rest. Get some sleep. We can talk later, if you want to. I'll be here. Katie is asleep..."

"Your sister's here?"

"Katie's my daughter. Remember?"

"Yes. You wrote about her. I'm sorry I forgot..."

"It's okay. Don't apologize."

Peter allowed Julia to lead him to her bedroom. She left him sitting on the side of the bed, his eyes still looking down refusing to let her make contact.

"What do you hear from Joe?" he asked as she was about to close the door.

"I haven't for..."

"He hasn't been shot..."

"No, I haven't heard anything." She started to tear as she pulled the door closed behind her.

> *Peter is so unlike himself,*
> *yet somehow this feels like déjà vu.*
> *I've felt this way before...*
> *He's like he's in shock. Or is he grieving?*

Julia didn't see or hear Peter for several hours. When he appeared again, he looked apologetic. "Peter, I wanted you to rest. You needed to rest. I am cooking some vegetables and you will join Katie and me for supper."

"No, I've..."

"No, nothing. You are staying."

He looked around. "Where is your little Katie?"

"She's downstairs. Bertie Bryan, the landlady's daughter, likes to play with her. I'll call her up in a little bit."

"You don't need to feed me."

"I want you to stay. Please, stay."

"I don't want to talk about the war."

"Peter, look at me. No, look me in the eyes. I understand. We won't speak of it."

His eyes finally met hers. And then Julia and Peter embraced each other. He sobbed.

What could have happened since the war ended?
    Since that last letter
        when he was collecting souvenirs?

    Will the war have changed Joe?

****

"Mr. Magivens, this is my son, Samuel."

"Get in here," Charles said. "There'll be no charge for you gentlemen today!"

Thomas and Samuel got onto the streetcar.

"Well, now, your dad tells me you've been flying all over Europe. Your papa is some-kinda proud of you. I wondered if he was gonna think he was too good to ride my streetcar anymore."

"Nonsense, Mr. Magivens," Thomas said. "But my boy here is too good to be made to ride in the back."

"I ah, I don't know..."

"Forget it, Pop," Samuel said. "Let's just sit down like we always have." Samuel paid the fare for the two of them.

Thomas allowed his son to pull him to the back of the streetcar, but all the while he shouted to the white folks on the car, "This is my son. He just got home from Europe. He flew Mustangs over in Italy. My son is a pilot."

Other passengers kept their eyes on them until they were seated and then with condescending grimaces murmured amongst themselves.

"Poor man thinks his son is a pilot."

"The boy probably told him so and he doesn't know any better."

"One of our senators from Montana says the Allies ought to work for a negotiated peace with Japan," another passenger changed the subject.

"I don't think those little monsters can be trusted," another said. "The president says we need their unconditional surrender."

"They say our B-29's bombed Tokyo with 700,000 fire bombs.

Time Will Tell

And then forty-eight hours later, 500 B-29's gave it to them again. They may have hit the Emperor's Palace.

I would think they would be ready to talk a peaceful end to this thing."

"Japan says they're out to avenge the German defeat. Doesn't sound like peaceful negotiations are being considered by anyone. Did you hear about the POWs from Bataan?"

"No, what?"

"They say they were forced to watch while the Japs chopped off the heads of their buddies. That senator you mentioned won't get to first base with any talk of negotiating with the Japs now."

"I suppose you're right. But what's it going to take to stop an enemy who employs suicide pilots?"

"If the Japs have to resort to their Kamikaze, they are frantic. They are launching huge paper balloons with bombs from submarines off of our Pacific coast. They're counting on the wind bringing them ashore and blowing us up, I suppose. All they've done so far is start a couple of forest fires."

"My heart goes out to our boys out in the ocean seeing one of those Kamikaze with his nose down coming at his ship. How do you dodge a manned bullet?"

"So far they have been an awful nuisance. We've lost some men, but the Kamikaze haven't sunk any ships. They can't win the war that way."

"They must know this. What's the harm in offering them something short of unconditional surrender? The Japanese are a very proud people. Will we have to kill them all before we can end the war?"

"They may be proud, as you say, but they are arrogant and mean."

In the back of the streetcar Samuel tried to explain how things were to his father.

"Pop, I'm sure we did a good job – an excellent job – but things haven't changed. When we got off the ship, Pop, there was a gate for the white soldiers and a gate for the colored. These people don't know what we did because the military doesn't want to tell them. The experiment didn't turn out the way they wanted it to. We weren't supposed to be brave. Remember, we were cowards."

"You did all that for nothing?" Thomas asked. "You're just going to let..."

"Pop," Samuel interrupted. "They don't know what we did, but we do, and they can't take that away from us."

Julia pulled the bell cord to get off at the stop nearest St. John's. She wanted to say something to the pilot...

If his dad says he was a pilot,, why can't it be so?

... but she couldn't think of what to say and she got off without speaking to him.

It had been a week since Peter's visit. He had gone home for a difficult reunion. His family who loved him so, could never break the habit of criticizing him. He'd always been too loud and boisterous. Now he was rude and unsociable. Peter's war injuries were not the kind his family would understand.

They'd hoped the Army would
*   'knock some sense into him.'*
I think it did more than they bargained for.

Mother Keegan was keeping Katie for the morning, so Julia was alone. It was hot and humid. Most everyone outside had a make-do fan – a newspaper, a hat, anything to stir the air. Julia used the letter she had received from Joe.

How will I tell Mother Keegan
*   Joe isn't coming home yet.*
*   She'll be heartbroken.*
*   She'll ask me why. Did he have to stay?*
I'll say, I'm sure he did. But I don't believe he did.

"It seems like so long ago when I came here after Joe and I were married," Julia said as she approached the tombstone of the young girl from the nineteenth century. "Joe was miserable because the Army had refused him. He was miserable and he was making me miserable. When he found a way to get over there, he was happy as a child who's been told he can go out to play. I knew I had to let him go. But now Katie isn't a baby anymore. I'm not a young girl anymore. He's had his chance to serve his country. It's time he came home to his family – if he wants a family."
"Lizzie, listen to what he says...

Dearest Julia,

"Since when did he start a letter with 'dearest'?

This is not the time to desert my buddies. We have been through Hell and back and we can do it again as long as we stick together. They're saying over here that we should have the Japs where we want them in a matter of weeks.

Don't you worry. We've made it this far and we're gonna come out clean as a whistle.

"Sounds like he made the choice to stay. Like he still wants to play war games with his buddies.

"People say the Germans and the Japs are beasts. Were they beasts before this war started? Or has the war made them so? Has the war made beasts of men on both sides? Do they see so much death around them – kill so many of the enemy that they find satisfaction in the killing?

"Like that man on the streetcar was saying, why can't the Allies offer better terms of surrender to the Japanese? If we stopped it now, would we save some GI's from loosing their heads? Would we save some Japanese children from endless bombings? Why must we bomb more of their cities and kill more of their people? What will be gained?

"Why must Joe stay over there? Will Katie have a father when the shooting stops?

"Oh, Lizzie, how ridiculous of me to stand here trying to feign the part of the indignant wife. You can't be fooled. You know I'm relieved he's not coming home yet. I don't know him. To me he is my childhood playmate.

"Am I trying to think badly of him to make myself feel better? Where are my tears? How can I read that he's going to Japan without some emotion? Where are my tears?"

Julia sat on the ground beside Lizzie Burcher's tombstone.

What's the matter with me?
Has the war made a beast of me?
Do I have no loving feelings for my husband?
What has happened to me?

"Lizzie, I do love Joe. I love Joe, the little boy – crabbing, fishing, boating, building mud huts in the marsh and sand castles on the beach. Sneaking behind the school building to smoke cigarettes and maybe steal a kiss. Going to the senior prom and him ripping the seam of his pants doing the splits on the dance floor. Joe is so much a part of me... of my youth.

"But I don't know where he'll fit into my life now. When I think of him coming home, I see him in that overstuffed chair sulking because the Army wouldn't take him. I don't know him. His letters tell me nothing. Now he says he's been to Hell and back. Has he tried to protect me – to keep me from worrying – is that why he's never written anything serious in all the time he's been gone?

"I'm blaming him again. Blaming him for how I'm feeling.

"Katie and I have been fine. Will Joe want to change things? Will he be good with Katie?

"Katie thinks Mike is the greatest. She already misses him. Even if he stays at Langley, he certainly won't be coming to visit us as he has. He'll probably disappear out of our lives.

"We never did anything to be ashamed of, but Mike and I have been so close. It's hard not seeing him. He hasn't called since he got back from Milwaukee. Perhaps he found Susanna."

Julia stood up to leave. She tried to dismiss the thoughts she had.

> *Could Mike be right?*
> *Was there something going on*
> *between the German and me?*
> *Do I wish I were Eberhard's frau,*
> *going to live in a cottage in the woods?*

"No. I hardly knew him at all. Besides he said he was going to marry his German girlfriend if he survived the war. He wasn't interested in me."

Julia went out of the cemetery making a mental list of things she needed from the market. She worried people she met might be able to see what she'd been thinking. If they could see into her heart, what would they think of her?

> *My husband is overseas, but am I thinking about him?*
> *Am I longing for him to come home?*
> *No, I'm thinking of Mike O'Neill*
> *and a German u-boat captain.*
> *Will I see them,*
> *or even know what became of them, ever again?*

Sunshine Market was crowded with people. Julia met an old neighbor coming out as she was going in. "Did the government announce that rationing is over?" she asked.

"No, we still need our stamps. But they have something else to celebrate. The Goldsteins have received word that George has been in a

German prison camp. He is alive and he will be coming home."

Julia squeezed into the store. Everyone was excited over the news of George. Soon he would be home and the entire family of Goldsteins would be together.

George is alive. What wonderful news!
It seemed so unlikely. But, thank God, he is alive.

Julia tried to get to the counter to give Herbie her order, but decided to come back later – when the crowd had thinned. After making her way back outside, she started walking up Queen Street. She had gone less than a block when she heard the streetcar coming up behind her. She stepped up to the streetcar stop and waited.

She didn't have a letter written to Joe. Well, she did... before she opened his. No, she would answer his letter tomorrow. The one in her pocket, the one that said how thrilled she was he'd be coming home soon, he'd be able to hold their little girl for the first time – Julia would not post that letter. No, she'd write another. Tomorrow. Or maybe the next day.

The streetcar passed the Goldstein's dress shop where another crowd was celebrating the good news. It went on by the theatre, the furniture store, the stationery store and the post office and on across the bridge to Phoebus. Julia got off at the National Cemetery.

She didn't look about to see if anyone was around. She had been here many times. No one seemed to notice. She walked deliberately to the rows of German graves. She paused at each stone reading the name "Heller, Hahnefeodt, Horst Spoddig, Kleibrink, Roeder...

Why do they not have all of your first names?

"...Erich Degenkolb

You were the last one your captain saw alive.

"...O. Hansen, Werner Schmacher, Ganzl, Ungethum, Jan Letzig, Karl Schultes, Herbert Albig, O. Prantle, Hans Sanger, Behla...

You were about to jump without your lifejacket tied.

"...Metge, Gerhard Ammann, Heinrich Adrain...

Eberhard said something about you,

I can't remember...

He thought you were all the best.

"...Helmit Kaiser, Waschman, Herbert Carl Waack, Artur Piotrowski, Walter Kiefer, Gunter Schulz...

The ladies man.

You must have been something!...

"Schulze, Konstantin Weidman, Schoen and Friedrich Strobel.

"The others of your crew are not buried here. Their bodies may have been left in the sea. Or perhaps some of them survived. I wish I knew what happened to your captain.

"The war is over," she said. "Your war is over. It didn't turn out well for your country, but at least no one is dropping bombs on Germany anymore. People here are saying terrible things about Germans, but I know Eberhard Greger's crew wasn't like that. You were fine young men, serving your country. Some of you were only boys, not even as old as Lizzie when you died. I hope you had some happy years before the war. And I hope someday someone in your family will learn that you are here. That they may come here and look at these rows of stones amidst the rows of our GIs. That you may be remembered as the brave young men you were.

"Your sponsor city must have been very lovely – "Dear Rose" – Lieberose. I wish I had a rose for each of you, but I cannot draw such attention to you now. I ask you once more to hear me when I tell you Captain Greger wanted to be with you. Believe that he cared and rest in peace."

Julia found her tears in the cemetery. Her face was soaked as she thought of boys returning home from the war – but not these boys. These boys who had died while pleading for help will not return to their families. Will Eberhard Greger be going home? Will the Gregers be alive to welcome him home as the Goldsteins will welcome George? Will his fraulein be waiting? Will the war have changed them?"

Is Eberhard Greger alive?

****

Julia was pleased to see that it was Kate who had written the letter that was waiting when she got home.

I don't know how to answer Joe's letter.
It will be wonderful having Kate home.

Julia opened Kate's V-mail. Though Kate gave the names of places, nothing was lined out in this V-mail.

Dear Julia,
Yesterday they told us we were going to Germany to deliver donuts to our boys who are there. This was the first time I've entered Germany proper. I've been on the border several times. We went to Cologne today. It must have been a lovely city, but it has been leveled. Only the Cathedral is standing. Each successive town we passed through is much the same.

One doesn't feel sorry for the poor people whose homes are destroyed – only a curious detachment and the thought that at last the Germans know what other nations have gone through at their hands. It feels so strange not to wave to the civilians and have it returned with a cherry smile. Here we merely stare at them and visa versa.

I'll be glad to get back even to Belgium. This Germany is a morbid, gruesome place.

Julia crumpled Kate's letter in her hand as she visualized the scene her sister had described. Julia saw people standing in the midst of their ravaged homes searching the convoy of Americans passing by for some explanation of where their sons were. For Julia they were the families of the young boys whose graves she visited. And they were the pharmacist and his wife, looking for their only son to return.

Is his young woman waiting for him to return?
Or did the war twist and turn her feelings for him?
What was that quote Eberhard said?
Something about out of sight, out of mind.
He said he couldn't forget them.
But how do you hold onto someone
when both of you are changed?

****

In the first months of '45, Julia heard reports of Nazi atrocities interspersed with news of the war in the Pacific. As each concentration camp was discovered, horrendous pictures of the victims of the Nazi effort to wipe out a whole race of people were released upon the public. Thousands of people had been put in gas chambers, for God's sake. It was said that only in Germany could a man so evil as Adolf Hitler have risen to such power. It was the popular opinion that Germans and Nazis were the same.

Everyone feels as Kate does.
Everyone thinks the Germans
got what they deserved.

Are the people of Germany
responsible for what their Nazi government did?

In April, even as the war in the Pacific continued, the Allied countries who had fought and defeated the Germans worked out a plan to help keep world peace. The paper said fifty nations had organized as the United Nations. Julia sat on her parent's porch reading the paper as Katie played on a beautiful spring day. The future looked brighter – a better world for her little Katie to grow up in.

But then Julia read of the repeated air raids on Tokyo, Nagoya, Yokohama and other Japanese cities. "Our bombers are wiping out cities – people. They talk of human rights and the dignity of man, the equality of men and women, of being tolerant of others and settling differences without armed force. But they keep bombing the people of Japan. How can they talk like that and be dropping bombs on women and children at the same time?"

"The Japanese believe it's better to die for their Emperor than live in shame," her father answered. "If they won't come to the table, there is nothing we can do but keep fighting."

"Fifty nations against one and no one can get them to surrender?" Julia asked.

****

President Truman made an incredible announcement on August 6, 1945. "The world's first atomic bomb was dropped today on the city of Hiroshima, Japan by a single B-29 aircraft."

It was certain that most of the Japanese city was destroyed. This was a city of 343,000 people and most of them died in a split second. The flash of the bomb was seen for hundreds of miles.

Three days later on nationwide radio the President threatened Japan with atomic obliteration if they didn't surrender. Julia listened as the commentator told of a U.S. plane dropping a second atom bomb. The city of Nagasaki, with a population of 253,000, was the target of a larger bomb than was used on Hiroshima.

"They called it the Manhattan Project while thousands of Americans have been working to build atomic bombs," Julia said. "Most of them didn't know what they were building."

"The Secretary of State explained this was the best way to end the war," Mr. Walters said. "It would possibly cost thousands of American lives to launch an invasion of Japan. The Japanese refused to surrender. We had to end this thing. Our boys have been fighting for years. They need to come home."

"Did you read where Japan is filing a protest against the U.S. government for use of such an inhuman weapon?" Julia had only begun. "And then our government answered, the a-bomb is legal because it can be guided so as not to hit undefended areas? How can they justify dropping the bombs on populated cities and say they didn't hit undefended areas?"

"War is ugly, Sweetheart. It is cruel and unfair. But we must do everything that is necessary to protect our democracy. The war was dragging on too long. Joe will be coming home. The war is over and, horrendous as it is, we have the atom bomb to thank for ending the war."

"There is already talk of the Russians wanting us to share with them how to build such bombs. How long will it be before they make one to drop over our democracy? They aren't really such good friends. If we don't share with them, what's to stop them from figuring it out for themselves?"

"You've been reading what the scientists are saying?"

"Yes, I have, Daddy. They say there are going to be bombs made thousands of times more powerful than what was dropped in Japan. They feel it was a mistake to make such a thing. They hadn't realized radio activity and ultra rays would continue killing people long after the bombs were dropped. What if the aftereffects spread around the world? I want Katie to be able to grow up without fearing something so horrible could happen. Oh, Daddy, some people are cheering because the war has ended, but some are saying this is the beginning of the end"

Twenty-Five

Katie was enchanted by her spirited aunt who had been "on the other side of the world." Though at one moment she was exclaiming how wonderful it was to be home; the next she seemed to be sad she might never see "the boys" again. Then she'd pick Katie up and whirl her around and tell her she was the most beautiful child she had ever seen "and we have the same name!"

"Mother says I couldn't have named her better," Julia said. "She's so much like you. She's already become quite the flirt."

"With your looks and my... my coquettish ways, she'll be the most popular girl in Hampton."

"Do you think she looks like me?"

"Mother had written that she looked exactly like you. Yes, she's you all over again. I can't figure how she got an Irish brogue. It's so darling the way she talks."

"You should hear her tell a story. She loves books, but she prefers to make up her own story to go with the pictures. Her stories don't make sense, but they sound like poetry."

"Is there Irish in our ancestry?" Kate asked Julia.

> *I don't want to tell Kate*
> *how much Mike has been with Katie,*
> *She might think it was something*
> *more than it was.*

"I think there's a little bit of everything," Julia answered.

"May I have Katie for the day?" Kate asked Julia. "I want to take her to Buckroe. Take her on the carousel. Would she like that?"

"I'm sure she would and, of course, you can take her."

Julia was home alone. Mrs. Bryan and Bertie had gone to town for Bertie's school supplies. Bertie was so pleased they were going to Mr. Wornham's stationery store. "Everyone will be there."

Julia knew "everyone" meant one particular boy Bertie had a crush on. Bertie had grown up somewhere between Pearl Harbor and Nagasaki.

Julia decided to go by her folk's house to take Snarls for an outing. She put on a sweater and walked out onto the Boulevard. The leaves on the trees were aglow with splendid yellow, orange, and red. Julia knew weeks from now they would shed these leaves and their bare limbs would be left with no color.

> *Will Joe get home*
> *before all the leaves have fallen?*

Joe was coming home. He was back in the States. There were so many troops needing transportation from the West Coast, Julia didn't know when to expect him. But the war was over. General MacArthur was now the supreme commander and ruler of Japan.

Julia caught the streetcar into town and looked out the window thinking of how Hampton had changed during the war. It was different. She passed apartment houses, where there had once been only trees and streets that hadn't been there before, with rows of houses. The newer housing didn't have big front porches, or beveled glass windows. They were more like the stones at the National Cemetery – all standing in a row and very much alike.

She got off the streetcar near where she had grown up. Julia sighed as old feelings of happy childhood days came upon her. She tried to hold on to them – to feel like she was once more the girl who lived here several years ago.

> *Joe and I used to climb that old crepe myrtle tree.*
> *We crabbed from this bridge.*

We'd go to the ice plant
*   and skate on the parking lot in the winter.*
We put our handprints in the wet concrete
*   in front of Mrs. Long's house.*
We knew the milkman, the ice man,
*   the mailman, the vegetable man -*
*   When the vegetable man came, we'd listen to him singing,*
*   "FFFFFFrrrrrrrresh veg'tables, git your*

> *frrrrrrrresh veg'tables.*
> *Grrrrrrrreen beans. Tomaaaaaatoes.*
> *Potaaaaaatoes."*
> He sold squash, too.
> But he never sang about it.

Hard as she tried, Julia couldn't feel emotional about these childhood memories. That was all they were – memories of a little boy and a little girl – not unlike Bertie and Ricky.

> *Bertie isn't interested in playing spy games*
> *with Ricky anymore.*

Julia's mother was helping at the dealership. Soon Detroit would be producing cars for the public once again. Jules had Caroline taking phone calls from people anxious to get their names on a waiting list for the new cars. So Snarls had been left alone.

Snarls bounded out of the door as soon as Julia opened it. "Did you hear me coming?" she asked the cat. "Would you like to go for a walk?"

He rubbed up against her legs as if to say, "I'll go anywhere you go."

"I've never known a cat who would follow along as you do. Perhaps you are part puppy dog?"

Julia and Snarls went across the footbridge that carried them up beside the Sunshine Market and on across the street to St. John's.

> *I hope there's not a rule*
> *against bringing pets here,* she thought.

"Come, Snarls. While no one is here."

She led the cat to Lizzie's grave and, when she sat down, he snuggled up to her.

"Lizzie, this is Snarls. He's a most unusual cat."

Julia sat stroking the cat thinking how pretty the red highlights in his black fur looked when the sun flickered through the shade of the trees. And the little ring of white around his neck, "You are an unusual cat... and fat!" she laughed.

"Lizzie, now the war is over," Julia said. "Even in the Pacific. Joe's coming home. We can pick up where we left off before the war. We'll get our own house with a stairway to the second floor and Snarls can live with us. Soon they won't be rationing anything and we can buy all the sugar and eggs we want. Dad will have cars to sell. We won't have to go through another winter with those long, black nights with no streetlights.

"The newspaper won't carry lists of casualties, or missing in action. Joe can boast of his years of service. Katie will forget what an air raid sounded like. We'll have nothing to stop us from living the American dream.

"Nothing, but fear. Before the war, I was naïve. I never thought of the ghastly things men could do to their fellow human beings. Can we purge the world of all the Hitlers and Mussolinis? Or hasn't the war hardened the population of the world? We drop atomic bombs on cities of people and all we say is, 'Well, that stopped them.'

"I wish I could put things back the way they were before the war. I wish Joe had never gone away. I wish Hampton was still a quaint little place with nothing much going on. I wish I'd never heard of a B-29, or a torpedo. I wish Peter was clowning around like he did before the war. Some people didn't appreciate his wise-cracking, but he never meant to offend anyone.

"Daddy thinks I should be glad the war is over. Why can't I just be happy like most people are? Is it because I talk to you that I get these ideas?

"I just don't think there's much to cheer about when we know someone in a single airplane can kill a city-full of people in a matter of a split second."

A shadow fell over Lizzie's gravestone. Julia looked up to see Mike standing there. "When I couldn't find you anywhere else," he said, "I decided to try the bone orchards."

"Mike. We haven't seen you since you got back. Have you been so busy you couldn't come by?"

"I felt sort of awkward. I'm real sorry I spoke to you like I did before I went home. I had no right. I just..." he stopped mid-sentence. "Anyway, I'm going back to Wisconsin. I'll be leaving Langley as soon as I can get my discharge papers."

"Have you found Susanna?"

"No. Her whole family has disappeared. Mr. Reese's store has a new name. Someone else is living in their house. And I'm the only one who has even asked about them. What little I know I learned from children in their neighborhood when I was in Milwaukee. Their parents are all certain the Reeses were Nazi spies and don't want to talk with me about them."

"It could have been someone posing as the F.B.I. that took Mr. Reese away. What do you think?"

"Possibly, but I think it was the F.B.I. An old friend of mine said he spent several years with the Army in Texas guarding an internment camp. There were families of Japanese on one side of the camp and Germans on the other. I tried to get him to tell me more about it, but he told me he could get in a lot of trouble for just telling me that."

"What are you going to do?"

"I may have to go to Texas. Susanna could be there, I suppose."

"What were you and Lizzie talking about?" Mike asked.

"Just stuff."

"Stuff?"

"I like to think Lizzie understands me."

"About what?"

"I don't like what war has done to my world. I want it back the way it was."

"Isn't Joe coming home soon?" Mike asked.

"He's on the West Coast trying to get transportation across country."

"He's probably very excited to return to his family."

"Mike, I don't know that he is, but I have to be here, if he is."

"Yes, I know. Will you tell Katie I had to go?"

"Do you? Won't you come tell her goodbye?"

Mike turned away from Julia. "Tell Katie Uncle Mike had to leave. I can't do it. It is tough enough telling you goodbye."

Snarls rubbed up against Mike's leg. Mike picked up the cat. "Tell me, why did you name this sweet, docile cat, Snarls?"

"The German named him that."

"Snarls was part of the crew of the u-boat?"

"No. Snarls was a stray. He and Eberhard found each other in the old house."

"I wish I had something to give you, that you would never be able to forget me," Mike handed Snarls to Julia. "I should have gotten a dog and named him something preposterous. Would you remember me if I gave you a big, burly, howling dog and called him 'Whispers'"?

"Mike, I'll never forget you. I don't need a dog, a horse or a kangaroo to remind me of you."

"Perhaps a monkey?" he suggested.

"Quit it, Mike. You must know I could never forget you. Whenever I sing a lullaby to Katie, or peel a potato, I'll think of you."

Mike smiled and took Julia's hand in his. "Listen to me," he said. "Don't ask questions about the Reeses, or your friend, the u-boat captain."

"Why?"

"Because that part of the war may not be over. I'm going to look for the Reeses, but I know already it won't be easy to find them. I'll be in touch."

He let go of her hand.

"Mike...will you be in touch? I have a feeling I'll never see you again."

"To quote Sir John Mahaffy," he said. " 'In Ireland the inevitable never happens and the unexpected constantly occurs.' Until we meet again, Julia Keegan..." He threw her a kiss while backing away. Then turned and went out the churchyard gate.

Julia watched Mike as he stepped onto a streetcar and gave her one last wave. She waved back and then sat on the ground beside the tombstone, her eyes burning with tears.

"The war is over, Lizzie. Now we must rejoice in the victory that is ours."

Author's Notes

The wreckage of the U-85 lies in approximately one hundred feet of water off Cape Hatteras, North Carolina. (35.55N, 75.13W)

Eberhard Greger (born in 1915 and assumed dead in 1942) was the captain of the U-85. His body was never found. He was the only son of the pharmacist in Lieberose, a small town southeast of Berlin. He planned to get engaged to his girlfriend when he returned to Germany. The rose in the mouth of the wild boar insignia on the boat, was painted on when Lieberose chose to sponsor the U-85. Eberhard was well liked and known to have great pride in his crew. I created the uncle in New York for my story. Eberhard was not educated in the States.

Many of my characters are composites allowing me to tell of true experiences of the war. Julia and her family were such; as were the Washingtons. The forty-six crew members of the U-85 were real people. Charles Flax (1904 – 1980) and his Crusaders (still an active group), the Goldsteins, the Darlings, the telegraph lady, the midwife, the man on the board and old Charlie did live in Hampton during the Second World War.

Eddie Drummond and Artie Potvin were both from Hampton and served in the war. Artie Potvin, first reported as missing in action, had died in November of '43.

His Nazi captors did not give George Goldstein proper medical attention while he was imprisoned. After his return to the States, he recovered in the Veteran's Hospital. He now lives in Richmond, Virginia.

In 1958, the National Advisory Committee for Aeronautics (NACA) became the National Aeronautics and Space Administration (NASA). The Sputnik crisis brought new respect for the scientists and engineers of the nation's space program and Hampton residents took new pride in the eminent scholars at Langley.

Also in 1958, the Hampton Redevelopment and Housing Authority made some radical changes in the city in the name of progress. Downtown received a face-lift and in the process many of the old buildings were torn down and streets renamed. The Darling mansion succumbed to the bulldozer in 1976. The pile of oyster shells, once a landmark, is no longer and the smell of the seafood industry is not nearly so strong as it was.

Hampton Institute, as of 1984 Hampton University, has a student body of more than five thousand undergraduates. Students come from throughout the United States and from many countries. It is one of the nation's top-ranked private universities.

Many of our black soldiers of World War II never received the recognition they deserved. They served in combat and service units in Europe and in the Pacific Theatre, but the military was reluctant to give medals to colored heroes.

The United States selectively interned more than 10,000 German Americans during World War II. Many were arrested and given no right to counsel, could not contest the proceedings or question their accusers. No internee was ever convicted of a war-related crime against this country. The last were released from internment in August of 1948.

Each year on German National Mourning Day, the third Sunday in November, there is a special memorial service at the Hampton National Cemetery on County Street. Colonel Josef E. Schuler, Senior German Liaison Officer to Headquarters TRADOC spoke on November 17, 2002: "We are all called upon to think about guilt, not in the sense of participation in those crimes, but in the sense of being responsible to learn lessons from history."

In 2004, sixty-two years after the burials, new tombstones replaced the ones on the German graves. Thanks to the efforts of Eberhard's cousin who was like a brother to him, Dr. Hansjurgen Fresenius, the markers are now properly engraved for the twenty-nine who are buried in Hampton's National Cemetery.

The story of the Thanksgiving blessing by the American pilot in Italy was as it appeared in the newspaper at the time:

"Bless all the fighting men on all the fronts around the world – on both sides because they are all fighting for what they believe is right."

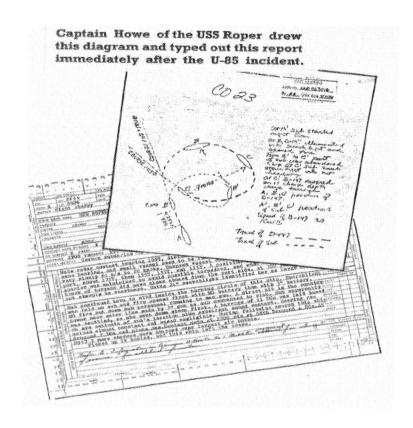

From the National Archives

Further reading:

Gunther Buchheim's ***U-Boot***
Available on video
(in English and German)

Homer Hickam's ***Torpedo Junction***
(Chaper 12) "The Night of the Roper"

Arthur Jacob's ***The Prison Called Hohenasperg***
An American boy Betrayed by his
Government during World War II

Arnold Krammer's ***Undue Process***
The Untold Story of American
German Alien Internees

Paul Fussell's ***Wartime***
Understanding and Behavior
In the Second World War

Adolph Newton's ***Better Than Good***
A Black Sailor's War

Carl Clauswitz' ***On War***
Military Strategy

Scott Berg's ***Charles Lindberg***
Lindberg the Hero
Lindberg the Man

About the Author

Ann Davis is telling the story of her hometown and how it was transformed from a fishing community to a booming war town during World War II. Ann researched her topic thoroughly. She used archive and newspaper accounts, letters, journals and personal interviews to recreate the era. Ann, born during the war, admits she was looking for a story of patriotism and romance, but found a story of the tremendous price we paid for the war - not just in casualties, but in the hearts of the survivors.

Printed in the United States
38082LVS00007B/127-192